DESTINY

Vietnamese Refugees and their
Struggle for Freedom

Thomas Nguyen

Order this book online at www.trafford.com
or email orders@trafford.com

Most Trafford titles are also available at major online book retailers.

Printed in Victoria, BC, Canada.

ISBN: 978-1-4269-2623-5 (sc)

ISBN: 978-1-4269-2624-2 (hc)

Library of Congress Control Number: 2010900985

Our mission is to efficiently provide the world's finest, most comprehensive book publishing service, enabling every author to experience success. To find out how to publish your book, your way, and have it available worldwide, visit us online at www.trafford.com

Trafford rev. 3/23/2010

 www.trafford.com

North America & international
toll-free: 1 888 232 4444 (USA & Canada)
phone: 250 383 6864 ♦ fax: 812 355 4082

PART 1

The monotone sound from the small engine below deck almost put everybody to sleep. Then, in a sudden, it puffed out the black smoke and slowly put a halt to the small fishing boat loaded with refugees. Without moving, the tidal waves began bouncing the boat side to side, and the uneasy feelings from the rocking boat quickly panicked the people on board. First, the children burst out crying for their parents, and then some of the older people began to worry about the condition of the troubling engine, demanding the boat owner to fix it.

"Mr. Van, you have to fix the engine fast before we will sink to the bottom of the ocean. We don't want to die here. I know this boat is bad luck. Oh! Buddha, please save us." The older man kneeled down, screaming, and he threw his arms upward as he prayed. "Oh! God... Buddha... please help us! We're going to die...we're going to die!"

The boat owner tried his best to explain the engine would be okay; after it cooled off, everything would be fine. "Everybody calm down, please. Just a little over-heated, that's all."

Right about the time he finished his sentence; the sound of the engine began weakening, and then choked off. The boat owner quickly got back to the lower deck to check on the condition of the dying engine, realizing if the engine didn't get fixed, more chaos would follow.

Van, the boat's owner, and his assistant worked hurriedly to fix the engine. The small fishing boat moved forward a few yards, and then came to a full stop; remaining now in a standstill position. The fear of being stranded in the middle of the ocean now escalated and was showing in peoples' faces. The women held the children tightly in their arms to comfort them. The north wind, picking up a little more strongly, rocked the fishing boat harder; again, from side to side. The small boat was leaning more deeply to one side, allowing the water to fill in, quickly.

People on board now realized that the boat was about to sink and grabbed anything they could to scoop the water out. Just when everyone was going to give up hope, the familiar sound of the engine revved up, starting weakly but it gave a sign of survival. People were relieved to hear the sound again.

The gusty wind, miraculously, shifting to another direction, took away most of the peoples' fear. Then, within minutes, the fishing boat slowly thrusted forward and carried along the sound of the applause which echoed through the silent part of the Gulf of Siam.

To preserve the possible endurance of the small, aging engine, the boat owner ran it slower than before, hoping they may reach Thailand. Now the fishing boat entered the calmer part of the gulf, and the water's surface appeared more tranquil, soothing peoples' minds.

Stressed out from the last incident, Mai Lan leaned her back against the side of the boat with her arms braced. The only company she had was her youngest brother, and both were sharing the warmth and comfort of one another. Mai Lan, watched the huge, bright orange ball, halfway down the bluish horizon, painting its million rays on the blue sky. It brought back the precious memory from a week earlier; those last days she spent with her boyfriend. They were walking, silently, on the white sand beach, and together they were indulging in the beautiful sunset. Mai Lan remembered Le's sad eyes; somehow, she had the feeling they would never see each other again. For the safety of the group, Mai Lan didn't have the liberty to tell him about her coming departure, and she felt as if she betrayed him.

At the end of September, the fall weather generated cooler air in the evening; the couple was getting closer to one other, and the body chemistry sparked. The two love birds had known one another since high school and were madly in love after their first date. Since Le's father held a high position in the Communist party, and Mai Lan's father was a failing businessman who had lost most of his property to the new Communist regime; the two families became enemies instead.

Mai Lan had had the urge to see him before her one way trip, not just to say goodbye, but to be with him for the last time. As night fell, millions of sparkling stars began to light up the vast dark sky. The full moon was bright, and yet appeared so close that the two lovers wanted to reach to it and stay there together, forever. The couple found a small cave far away from the population; they sat down closely to one other, enjoying the beautifully romantic scene of the beach at dawn.

Sitting close to her man in the white sand beach, Mai Lan felt so much love for him; the desire deep inside her was just now waking up excitingly. As her longtime love, Le, ran his hand from her neck down to her back, Mai Lan felt what seemed like lightning shock, numbing her whole body. Mai Lan let out a low moan of ecstasy and she shook vigorously when he pulled her tighter into his arms, and then pressed his lips to hers.

This was her first time, too. Deliberately, she began responding to her deep sexual desire which had always been defended by the family's code of honor. To Le, the closest he had ever been around Mai Lan was when they walked back from school. They would always look to see if anyone was around, and then he gave her a quick kiss on her rosy cheek. Their puppy love grew with a promising future.

Now alone with one another in a romantic atmosphere, Le let his true desire loose on his only long-time love. Mai Lan was trembling every time he kissed or touched the virginity of her body parts and she had no strength to resist… and her tears silently rolled down her cheeks. She closed her eyes and tried to forget the embarrassing moments which made her feel ashamed for abandoning her family's code of honor.

Close to noon, the tropical sun was rising high, spreading its soaring heat with the intention of dehydrating all living beings above sea level. Due to the very limited amount of drinking water, the people on board were only allowed a small portion of the supply. Starting with the rapidly rising temperatures of the younger children, who demanded more water, it soon traumatized the already troubled boat. Mai Lan placed her hand on her brother's forehead to monitor his body temperature and she began to worry about his condition as she recognized the building heat of his skin. She took a meager portion of water and then dropped a few drops into his mouth, just enough to keep it from drying. The unusual slowness of the boat caused people to doubt they were getting somewhere, and made them wonder how long the engine could run. The hardship, embedded with the constant fear, wore their spirits thin quickly. The family members sadly looked at one another while the hot rays from the sun, silently but deadly, evaporated everyone's will to live. Mai Lan ran her hand on top of her little brother's face and saw he had opened his pure and innocent eyes of a fawn to look at her and slightly smile. Mai Lan placed a kiss on his forehead and then turned her face away to hide the tears.

Spotting their prey on the horizon, the Thai pirates sailed for their newest victims. The formidable predators were led by a ruthless criminal who terrified the Vietnamese refugees in the Gulf of Siam. The pirates' leader, Sami S., an escaped convict from a hardcore prison in Bangkok, gathered his outlaw men to form a gang of pirates who dominated the gulf region. The people on the fishing boat were trying to stay cool, and they didn't pay much attention to the small dot growing bigger and bigger on the horizon. No one on the boat realized the imminent threat on its way; people paid more attention to the monotone sound of the weakening engine and prayed for its duration.

The flimsy fishing boat, with a heavy load of human beings on board, an over-heated motor and poor navigation, slowed down again drastically. The silhouette of the pirate's boat was more visible once it approached close to the troubled fishing boat. A child screamed, spotting the bigger fishing boat headed their way; pointing his finger in that direction.

"Look! Look, a big boat! Mama, a big boat is coming our way."

Now, everyone turned their heads to look at the approach of the much bigger boat, yelling and some waving their hands to draw more attention. Van, the boat owner, at first didn't know what to do, but more people called to him to stop and wait for the big boat. Van hesitated for a few moments and then shut down the motor, hoping they may get help. Once the pirate boat began closing in and the crew appeared less than friendly, it was too little late to avoid them. With a bad feeling in his gut, Van, the boat owner, attempted to restart his boat, but the crew from the big vessel had already hooked his boat to theirs with a steel cable.

The next thing they knew, the crew ordered the people to disembark the smaller vessel and board their boat immediately. Those on board were unprepared for this rude treatment; some hesitant to leave their belongings behind, while others feared the bad things which could happen to them. While confusion reigned, the first volley of firing tore the calmness of the ocean; the second warning would be deadly. The thundering sounds delivered from the automatic rifles also woke up the children, and between their crying and the confusion from the adults, the scene soon turned into chaos.

In the midst of the mass confusion, one older man came to the front of the boat and waved his hands, refusing to board, and not realizing the approaching imminent danger. Sure enough, just when his hands raised the second time, another volley from the automated rifle ripped through the thin chest of the resistor. The old man staggered for a moment, looking down to his chest to find his blood starting to trickle down, and then his eyes rolled up showing the intense pain that was taking his life away. The old man's shivering body slumbered down into the water while his family watched in shock.

After the execution of one of their shipmates, the people knew the pirates meant what they ordered and started to line up to board the pirate's boat. The refugees were divided into two groups: the women in one, men and children in the second.

At first, Mai Lan didn't want to separate from her brother, and held him tightly in her arms to keep him from being taken away. One pirate came and yanked her little brother out of her hands despite the child's screams of terror. He had never been taken away from his sister in such a violent manner. Mai Lan also felt horrible when the thug yanked her brother away. She screamed in a desperate voice for her little brother, who now also screamed with tears. A brave man who couldn't stand the pirate's cruelty plunged toward the pirate and tried to take the boy back.

The ear-splitting sound of a pistol was heard just before the man reached the pirate. He staggered for a moment, and then still tried to grab the boy before he plummeted to the deck; the blood oozing out of his mouth as he lost the fight. People stood speechless, their mouths wide with horror watching the cold, bloody execution. It numbed their ability to react; two people killed, one after another in less than ten minutes. The new widow, who couldn't believe that her husband's life had been terminated without any warning, slithered down on her knees and wept for his short life.

After the pirates grouped the people, they ordered them to undress so they could check for hidden personal belongings; primarily gold and jewelry. Yet again, these already frightened people had to face another impossible order from the blood-thirsty pirates. A few people slowly undressed, embarrassed to be naked in front of others complying mainly to avoid being killed. A couple of older women refused to follow the order; vowing they would rather die than be dishonored in front of their children. Two thugs noticed the rebellion of the women. They raced toward them and quickly pulled them out to the front of the crowd. Despite their resistance, one thug held tightly the arms of the woman and let another one rip her clothes off. They used the woman as an example for the rest. When they were done tearing the woman's clothes off, they threw her naked body to the floor and grabbed her clothes, searching for gold.

One found a gold necklace which was carefully hidden in the seam of her satin top, especially tailored for hiding jewelry. The thug yelled out, triumphantly, while dangling the sparkling necklace in front of the terrified people. The woman, so upset at her little fortune being taken away, was no longer afraid of the danger that lay ahead. She jumped up and scratched the eye of the thug with one hand, grabbing the necklace with the other. She did this so suddenly that the thug had no time to react. A moment after the woman got hold of her gold necklace, the other thug realized what was going on. He plunged toward the woman and tried to grab her arms in a lock down position. The woman, on the other hand, striving for her survival, dodged the wrath of the thugs, and ran quickly toward the other end of the boat knowing that she was running toward the end of her life.

By the time she reached the other side of the boat, she heard the ear-piercing sounds from the automated rifle. The sound of ricochet bullets surrounded her, and for the last moment of her life, she stopped and closed her eyes to wait for the death to take her away. When she opened her eyes again, she saw the blue ocean open up to her like the gate to forever freedom. She screamed with her last will to her family, and dived into the blue ocean before the thugs got to her. Her husband felt helpless; unable to save his wife. He screamed loudly in tears while holding down his son and daughter.

Witnessing the brave death of the woman, everyone looked at the pirates with hatred; still they were fearful for their lives. The pirates were going through the clothing in front of the miserable eyes of the captive. They yelled loudly in a mocking act whenever they found jewelries in the seam line of the old and torn off clothing. The heartbroken people were forced to witness their small fortunes being stripped away. All the women wept in pain when the thugs found their hidden precious gems.

Another group of pirates embarked on the refugee boat and began to search for more gold, and one more time, there were more worries for the already miserable people. The thugs' constant yelling filled peoples' ears as they found the well-hidden fortunes; adding to the crying and weeping.

Mai Lan, kneeling down on the floor, tried to cover up her shivering body with her small slender arms. She also looked for her little brother on the other side of the boat. When their eyes met, Mai Lan couldn't help the tears which poured down; she felt she might never see him again. The horrible image of the look in his eyes mixed with the sight of his naked little body were carved deeply in Mai Lan's memory, and all she could do was to console him with her vision, which conveyed most of her wish for a better future.

Now that the pirates had thoroughly searched everything in the big pile of clothing, they let people redress. Most of the women were upset because they had nothing left. Then the men and children were ordered to return to their boat, leaving the women in the corner with more guards. Now that everyone realized their separation, the crying from the husband to the wife and from the children to the mother or vice versa quickly created a sad scenario.

Mai Lan's little brother held both of his arms out for her, screaming for his sister but he was quickly pushed into the crowd. He only had long enough to turn around to look at her for the last time. Mai Lan collapsed on the floor, weeping, and called her brother's name in tears.

After the men and children were forced to return to their boat without their loved ones, the women still heard the sounds of their babies, calling out for them, creating unimaginable pain for these women. Most were devastated by the sudden tragedy, collapsing on the floor, crying for their children, and cursing the inhuman acts of the pirates. The pirate's boat roared its engine and then backed away from the refugee's boat. Mai Lan and other women waved to their loved ones for the last time. They slumped to the floor, weeping.

The pirate boat moved quite a distance, and then lowered an iron plate to the front of the boat as a shield. They pointed the boat straight at the stranded refugee boat. Sami, the pirate's leader, gave a signal and the giant boat headed toward the refugee's boat, sitting now idle. Those on the boat sat speechless from the horrible separation, sadness covering the faces of the children taken from their mothers. Mai Lan's little brother sat on the front of the boat, still watching for his sister, then he suddenly pointed his finger toward the approaching devil, screaming out loud…

"Look! The boat is returning, my sister is coming back."

Now, everyone stood up to look as the pirate's boat accelerated in their direction. They began asking themselves if their loved ones were returning back to them. At first, the small children were jumping in joy, calling for their mothers, and they waved joyfully to the upcoming boat.

The boat captain tried to crank the engine up; he was very sad to witness the women being taken away. He felt so helpless in front of those guns; vowing revenge one day and to bring the thugs to justice. When he looked up, the giant pirate's boat kept speeding toward his small, flimsy fishing boat. He asked himself what the pirates going to do next. But then, he finally realized their intention and he ran to the front of the boat, screaming for everyone to jump off immediately.

Most people didn't understand what the captain was trying to tell them, but when all eyes were on the imminent danger; they understood. People were screaming and yelling for their relatives to abandon the boat and jump into the water, but there were some who couldn't swim, mostly the children. The initial contact from the pirate's boat cracked the small refugee's boat into half, throwing most of the people off board instantly. A big wave created by the propeller draped peoples' heads. Some were drowning instantly; others tried to emerge from the water to breathe. Everyone gathered to hold on to one another, struggling to survive. The survivors hadn't yet regained their senses when they saw the huge silhouette was again approaching. They screamed in terror as they realized the pirate ship wood soon bury everyone in the blue water. When the pirate ship returned for the third time, there were no survivors; they were making sure no one lived to tell.

Sami checked around the area with binoculars to make sure no one escaped the refugee boat; as always, his business was to kill and leave no evidence. Sami S, robbed and murdered a whole fisherman's family and then took their boat and armed it to be the fearsome pirate boat in the gulf of Siam. His policy was to leave no survivors, so the Thai government had no idea who and what was behind all the crimes. He kept a low profile, not even keeping his mother aware of his whereabouts.

Sami watched the surface for a while to make sure there were no survivors. When he was sure only broken pieces of wood and some clothing material floated on the surface, he gave the order to head out to their hideout on a small deserted island situated between Thailand and Cambodia. There, they kept their stolen goods and raped the girls repeatedly, eventually selling them to a nasty whorehouse in Bangkok. Relatives never heard another word about these girls, presuming them lost at sea.

The women, who were now in captivity, clung together to protect themselves from the pack of wolves waiting to tear them apart. First was Sami, who as the leader, chose the best girl for himself; next came the second in command and so on among the next high ranking thugs. He came up to Mai Lan and picked her up, then placing her on his shoulder despite her resistance. Mai Lan was terribly frightened for her life, but she reached to help another woman who also soon being snatched by a pirate. All the women were screaming in terror as soon the pirates began raping them. Sami carried Mai Lan to his cabin and threw her on his bed; grabbed a bottle of wine, locked his cabin and returned to the deck. After the pirate left the cabin, Mai Lan knelt and prayed for her little brother. She cried hard as she remembered her brother's eyes so filled with fear. After all the terrible things that had happened, her body gave up its strength, and Mai Lan collapsed in the corner of the cabin.

When Sami returned to his private cabin, he saw Mai Lan still wept. He approached and tried to touch her long silky hair, but Mai Lan jerked away from him, scared that he was going to harm her. That made him even more aroused and desiring to conquer her body. He reached again to try to grab her arm but she still did her best to stay away from him. Sami was a little bit too drunk to get a hold on her; he staggered while chasing her around. Mai Lan was so frightened every time she met his blood red eyes, she screamed for help.

A young man, whose nickname "little mute" had been given him by the pirates, had been listening to what was going on inside, wanted to come in to rescue the poor girl but he knew the captain would punish him severely. Outside and listening to all the cries for help, he quickly planned something he could do to help her; at least for the moment.

As thoughts came to his mind, he raced quickly toward the upper deck and started up a small fire in the corner of the deck, screaming "fire." Then he raced back to the captain's cabin and knocked on his door. Inside, Sami still played "cat and mouse" with the poor girl; he heard the knocking and screaming from outside. He temporarily left her alone and went outside to find out what was happening to his boat. The young man reported there was a big fire on the upper deck. When the captain got to the deck, the fire had already spread to a larger area. More pirates came to put out the fire. They shouted, asking how the fire was started. By the time Sami returned to his cabin, he was too tired to mess around with Mai Lan; he left her alone and threw himself on his bed, soon snoozing away. Mai Lan felt release for now since he bothered her no longer, and so exhausted, she felt sleep while seated in the corner of the cabin.

When the first rays of the sun sheared through the dark horizon, the ship arrived at a small, deserted island where the pirates temporarily held all their female captives. They locked them up in a bamboo hut that was guarded by an old pirate. Mai Lan was among the girls. There was a piglet and a couple of chickens the pirates left for the girls for food, but they didn't allow anyone to leave the hut, except when guarded.

There were still a few girls from the previous boat raid who still remained on the island. They were desperately waiting for someone to come to rescue them. They were so happy to see the newcomer; they started asking a lot of questions about what were going on. Perhaps, Mai Lan was the lucky one because the pirates hadn't touched her yet. Once everyone finished telling their story, they planned on how to escape this small island; first to eliminate the old guard and then started a fire for any passing ships to see and know their presence on the island. They predicted when the pirates returned to the island, something would happen to their lives.

For now, they asked permission from the guard to prepare a decent meal because they hadn't had one for a long time. The girls killed two chickens and prepared a small feast with an offering prayer to those who perished at sea; Mai Lan kneeled down and prayed for her little brother's soul to be soon reunited with hers in heaven. All the girls were crying as they prayed for the members of their families who lost their lives. After the prayer, they silently ate their meal, but everyone pursued their own thoughts regarding what would happen next.

*****

Nguyen Tam, with a bottle of cheap rice wine in his hand, sat at the corner of a small restaurant, getting drunk. He hadn't eaten all day, begging for money from passing pedestrians. After the war, Nguyen Tam lost everything, from his family to his underwater special op unit. His wife and two children were killed by the northern army's rockets. When the battalion commander dismissed his unit, he returned home just to find out that his family had perished from the enemy rockets. He had nothing left, using heavy liquor to bury his memory and to live the life of a beggar. As usual, he sat in the same corner, motionless and staring at the empty space, hoping to find his loved ones. But today was his lucky day; someone had recognized him even though he was dirty and reeked with stench from the same set clothing he had worn for days.

Le Son, a Vietnamese immigrant who resided in St Louis, returned to Viet Nam on official business. Le Son was a former soldier under Nguyen Tam who was then a senior sergeant. Le Son was lucky to get away when Saigon fell to the communist regime. He later became a U.S. citizen, and now represented a foreign company to negotiate with the Vietnamese government to open a factory in Ho Chi Minh City. Le Son yelled when he recognized Nguyen Tam, his former senior sergeant who had saved his life once.

"Hey, Sergeant Nguyen, is that you? What happened to you, man? Do you remember me? It's me, Son, you saved my life before, remember?"

Nguyen Tam was still dazed; nobody had spoken to him for a long time. He finally recognized Le Son, the soldier from his old unit; but he looked so different now under his nice suit and tie, he clapped his hand and shouted.

"Is that you? Son, you looked so different, man, I hardly recognized you. How are you nowadays?"

Son pulled him up and said, "Let's go clean you up, get something to eat; we have a lot to talk about."

Le Son brought Nguyen Tam to his hotel, let him clean himself up and then gave him some of his own clothes. After Tam shaved and dressed, he was a different man.

Le Son showed Tam his reflection in the mirror and said, "Look at you now, man. You look like a new man. Come on, let's go get something to eat, I have something I need to discuss with you."

Le Son took Tam to a high-class restaurant which mainly served foreign customers only.

Nguyen Tam still thought he was in the other world, an imaginary world that he never dreamed he would live in. Seeing that Nguyen Tam was still not certain about himself, Le Son patted lightly on his shoulder, "Come on, man, you're with me now. You'll be all right. I'm going to help you get out of here."

The waitress serving Le Son kept peeking at Nguyen Tam; she thought she has seen this man somewhere else before. She pointed her finger at Nguyen Tam and asked, "Excuse me, are you the drunken man who sat in front of the Rendezvous Restaurant every day?"

Le Son gestured to the waitress, indicating *don't worry about it* and then spoke for Nguyen Tam, "No, you must be mistaken; this is my friend, just returned from America. Now, give us something good to eat because we are starving."

The waitress, still doubtful, went off to bring the food.

Le Son sipped some Tiger beer and told Tam, "Sure, I'm glad to see you. I have something to tell you, but this is a secret between you and me only."

Le Son stopped the conversation and looked around to see if anyone was listening or watching him, "Look, this is your chance to get out of here and start a new life somewhere else, I mean, to be just like me."

Nguyen Tam didn't exactly understand what he meant, "How is that possible? By the way, how did you manage to become like this now? Did you make it to America when our unit was falling out?"

Le Son inhaled a long stroke of a "555"cigarette, then let it out slowly, and with dazzling eyes toward the ceiling, tried to revive the last moment when he tried to run away from the enemy. "Yeah man, after our battalion fell out, on the way home, I found a boat about to take off. I jumped in and took a chance. Luckily, we made it to an American Navy ship and here I am, an American.

"Look, I want you to organize an escape route and I will finance all the cost. I still have a sister who needs to get out. So do me and yourself a favor."

Nguyen Tam hesitated for a moment, considering that it could be a trap. *But so what*, he thought, *I have nothing to lose but go to jail. If I make it, I have a chance to start my life all over.*

Nguyen Tam drank some more beer, felt tingling on his tongue, and looking straight at Le Son's eyes, nodded his head, "Okay. I will do it, when do we start?"

"Soon as possible, I have a connection being set up. He will contact you when he is ready. All you need to do is gather all the people and bring them to the "rendezvous point." You have to watch out for the border patrol, they're real tight down there, and once you make it to the boat, you are pretty much free. When you get to Thailand, I will personally pull you out of the camp. Trust me, my sister's life is in your hands."

When they finished eating, Le Son shook Nguyen Tam's hand and promised, "I will contact you soon. By the way, you need to change back to old clothes to avoid any suspicions. Gather all your belonging, bring as little as possible. Here is some money; you take it and spend it on whatever you like. When you are done taking care of your business, come to this hotel and meet me. By the way, you can stay here if you want, I welcome you anytime."

Nguyen Tam changed back to his old stinking cloth, and it felt like he had returned to his old world. But this time, there was some hope sparkling in his dark tunnel of life.

With the money, Nguyen Tam fixed up his wife's and child's graves. He often sat beside her grave for hours with the bottle wine; he felt like he wanted to live in the other world with his family. Sometime, he fell asleep and dreamed about his family.

One week passed and Le Son met Nguyen Tam again and told him the connection was set and ready to go. Nguyen Tam had to lead the group to a secret area, there; they had to lay low for a while, waiting for the pickup. Nguyen Tam moved into the hotel with Le

Son, stayed low, and waited for the departure. Le Son introduced his sister to Nguyen Tam; she was a nice lady and the two liked one another's company a lot. They got to know each other better because they were going to be together for a long time yet. He took her to his family's burial site, told her everything about his life and how he saved her brother's life. "You know after that day, your brother and I became good friends and somehow, he managed to escape to America. Now, it's our turn."

"I have been waiting for this moment long time, my brother promised to get me to America but I'm afraid that we might get caught at the border."

"Yeah, I know, but don't be worried, your brother probably arranged the border patrol so they will take easy on us."

Then she looked at him curiously and asked, "Will we be together when we come to America?"

Nguyen Tam looked at her beautiful eyes, responded, "I guess I have to escort you and hand you over to your brother, right."

Thuy shook her head, with the love hiding in her shyness, whispered to Tam, "No, what I mean is, are we are going to be together for a long time?"

"Oh you are young and pretty, there are so many men in America who will fall in love with you, and you will eventually forget about me."

"No, I won't. I promise"

Tam embraced her small body in his arms, slowly tightened up and placed a small kiss on top of her cute little nose.

The big red sun, slowly sinking down, painted the horizon with its colorful clouds, creating an incredibly beautiful painting. Thuy, stood silently, leaned her head on Tam's shoulder, looked toward the West and tried to picture what happened beyond the horizon. It was getting dark, Nguyen Tam had to leave the grave site, didn't know when he would return here again. He felt sadness inside his heart although he paid for someone to take good care of the graves while he's gone. They finally left the grave site; he felt like he was abandoning his family once again. The word was out; they would be leaving the next night together with five other families. Nguyen Tam would be the leading man; he would set up the route and make sure the plan was executed smoothly. The designated area would be the old bus station, the group would use passwords to identify each other. After the group shows up, they will board a different bus to a small hut which is located deep in the swamp area where nobody even thinks of living there.

The important day came. Tam and Thuy were the first ones to arrive at the bus station and waited for the others. Five minutes later, a family walked by, recognized Tam's posture by his height and weight. The husband approached Nguyen Tam, but looked at a different direction, pretending nothing was going on. Once he was passed by, he whispered the password to Nguyen Tam, "The ocean is blue."

Nguyen Tam responded, "The road is difficult."

The man answered back, "The road isn't but man does."

He gave the right password, so Nguyen Tam nodded his head, and signaled him to go to the last bus. Three more families showed up and also went to wait for the departure. Now, Tam only needed one more family to show up, and that was it. This took a long time and Nguyen Tam was a little worried about them; perhaps something had happened. The bus driver's helper yelled to warn people it was almost time for departure; the bus would leave in five minutes. While Nguyen Tam made up his mind about either leaving this family or staying to wait for them, a taxi suddenly appeared in the corner of the bus station. Hurrying to get out of the cab, the family looked around for the leading man; the man spotted Nguyen Tam and came to him to explain. Nguyen Tam challenged the password then told them to go to the bus. Nguyen Tam stayed there for a while longer to observe if anyone was following, or if there was any suspicion from the security police. When he didn't see any one pay attention to them, Nguyen Tam slowly walked to the bus and boarded.

The road to the coast was poorly built by the local people, it offered a long uncomfortable trip for everyone, but it didn't bother the freedom seekers because they were thinking of their brighter future. Despite the bumping of the road, Nguyen Tam tried to close his eyes to rest for a while, because the long trip had worn him out. Thuy sat next to him, pretending to be his wife during the trip. Somehow she felt safer whenever she got close to Tam. The love for him has been blooming since she met Tam the first time; the more she was close to him the more she felt like being a part of him. Thuy nervously thought about this dangerous trip which could end up with unpredictable consequences, perhaps death or imprisonment.

Same as Nguyen Tam, the bumpiness soon turned into a rhythm that put Thuy to a tiresome sleep. When they awoke, they learned the bus had stopped at a local station to unload the people. There was a check point not too far from the bus but nobody was inside; perhaps the guards were wandering around. After unloading, the bus just about started to roll off the station when the border patrol suddenly appeared to give the order to stop the bus for a random check. Everybody had to get off the bus, and lined up along the side of the vehicle to have their I.D checked. To legally travel, you must have a local housing document which was approved by the local authority, and a travel certificate issued from the higher level of the Communist party.

Thuy stood close to Nguyen Tam; she worried that somehow, the patrol might detect their attempt to escape. Feeling intense, Thuy grabbed hard on Nguyen Tam's arm, and she didn't let go. Alarmed and not wanting to draw suspicion, Nguyen Tam whispered in her ear, "Now, let go of my arm before you draw blood and quit shaking. I'm telling you, everything is going to be all right, all you need is to hand them your papers, and act normal."

Thuy, still worried, but listened to Nguyen Tam, and calmed herself down. When the border patrol checked her papers, he looked at her pale face for a moment, and then asked, "What is wrong with you, are you sick or something?"

Nguyen Tam, worried that she might give a wrong answer, so he responded to the guard, "Oh sir, this is my wife. She is three months pregnant; I guess she has the morning sickness."

The guard took a good look at Thuy for a moment, and then told everybody to get back to the bus. Soon, the bus slowly rolled back to the bumpy road. Now, they traveled to the deep South where people expected all the bad things from bugs to poisonous snakes, especially mosquitoes which would make life so miserable. Once everybody got off the bus, they had to travel by foot across the swamp miles away, and the scary thing was, all the travels had to be made at night. Most of these people were from the city, and they had never been around the countryside that much, so the new frightening environment of wild nature slowed them down. They had to swim across a small pond and then often found themselves covered with leeches, which terrorized Thuy the most. At night, under the clear sky which was illuminated by a million stars and the rhythm of the croaking sound from a thousand frogs orchestrated with all sort of insects' noises. The exile caravan imagined they were in of some kind of festival performed by Mother Nature. A loud scream suddenly tore through the calmness of the night; Thuy had slid off from the bank of the paddy down the deep water hole, and tried to get out of it.

Nguyen Tam tried to pull her out, but in the meantime covered her mouth up so she didn't make too much noise. When she managed to get out of the water, her whole body was soaking wet, but the wetness didn't really bother her more than the leeches that clinched to her body. Nguyen Tam had to light a cigarette and burn off the leeches; a trick he had learned from the war.

Everyone took a little break while waiting for Thuy to change out of her wet clothes. In the meantime; they listened for any strange noise from a border patrol unit. Even with dryer clothes, Thuy still trembled from the cold mist of the night. Nguyen Tam felt sorry for her and worried that she might get sick from the cold. He embraced her tiny body in his arms so he could use his body heat to warm her up. At first, Thuy felt very embarrassed, and resisted to be so close to Nguyen Tam; but soon, she let her body lean on him.

They silently stood there in the middle of the swamp, the rhythm of their heartbeats racing while exchanging their body heat. This was the first time Thuy had been so close to a man; the cold, strange feeling of body contact created a sensational warming inside, but chilling outside. Thuy leaned hard against Nguyen Tam's body heat, and felt like a small bird hiding under a big tree. Since they had started out the venture, she felt so dependent on Nguyen Tam who is the only person that she could trust.

After a while longer, Thuy's body began reaching normal temperature and allowed her to continue traveling. Nguyen Tam rubbed on her long wet hair, joking, "Be careful, next time I won't able to pull you out of the water because your long hair will get shorter!"

Thuy asked Nguyen Tam why that was. "How is my hair getting shorter?"

Nguyen Tam smiled, and responded, "If you made a lot of noise, the border patrols get hold of us. We'll have no hair at all, because they shave it all off." Thuy, with a scary gesture, promised to be more careful.

The group of people finally arrived at their destination; a small hut in the middle of the swamp. They had to wait here for a few days so when the boat arrived they could embark. Five families had to cram in a small hut and they weren't very comfortable, but for the time being, everybody had to live in close confines with each other. Mosquitoes were their most terrified foes; people had to seal every possible crack in the hut to keep the mosquitoes out. They could easily get malaria in this region. Once you got the disease it was not easy to get rid of.

From where they were, they had to follow a small canal to get to the open channel and then board the bigger fishing boat. Hopefully it would be there when they arrived. Everyone was exhausted. As soon as they were situated in their temporary position, loud snoring began. Thuy lay next to Nguyen Tam, and while they both could feel their heartbeats raging in their chest, they pretended like nothing was going on. Besides, being so closely packed with so many people, the position didn't permit any romantic thoughts; so they soon fell as sleep as well.

When morning came, Nguyen Tam was the first to wake and walked around the area to check it out. *This is truly no man's land*, Nguyen Tam thought to himself, they could have really bad luck or someone might snitch to the border patrol; otherwise, no one would expect this hideout.

Others were rising when Nguyen Tam returned to the hut. They seemed happy to see Nguyen Tam. An older lady offered him some sweet rice and meat; another also gave him fruit juice. It was hard for him to refuse the food, and he felt the passion of the people's caring.

In the evening, when the sun began fading, Nguyen Tam allowed a few people at a time, to go outside to have some fresh air; promising to carefully conceal themselves. People seemed to be in a better mood when they could breathe some fresh air. Their minds were set for a future of freedom and this would enable them to tolerate all the upcoming hardships.

Nguyen Tam and Thuy found a heavy cover and enjoyed the calmness of the end of the day. They watched the big orange bowl spread out in multi-brilliant colors which reflected on the silver clouds. Embedded in the ever green marsh land zigzagged with multi water ways, it created a beautiful nature silk painting. Thuy slightly leaned on Nguyen Tam's shoulder looked toward the direction of the sunset, asking, "Tam, if we follow this direction, we should be at America, wouldn't we?"

Nguyen Tam placed his arm around her shoulder, and as his hand caressed her long black silky hair, he also set his eyes toward the beautiful scene to the west. "Yes, but it isn't easy to get there; so many people have perished just about halfway."

Thuy let out a small sigh, stuck her tongue out, and said, "Yes! If not for you to pull me out of the water last night, I'd probably already be dead. Thanks for saving me; I'm never going to forget that."

Nguyen Tam gently held her hand, told her, "Hey, don't worry. I can't let anything happen to you, I promised your brother. Anyway, let us hope nothing is going to happen again. Okay!"

It was getting dark, and when they began to hear the buzz of mosquitoes, they got up to return to the hut.

Inside, the stale air of a large group of people produced a foul odor; everyone was hoping for a quick departure. At midnight, two small size fishing boats arrived and hurriedly loaded people before quickly disappearing in the dark of the night.

They silently traveled throughout the night and reached the open channel to the ocean in the early morning. As the sun began shining they found the bigger-sized fishing boat docked along the rocky bank, waiting for them. Everybody felt relief when they saw the boat, knowing the connection was truly happening. Often, there was no boat at all. Nguyen Tam observed the situation. Everything seemed fine, except for the silence of the boat; as if no one was aboard. Before Nguyen Tam could say anything, two loud tats of a firearm suddenly tore the silence of the morning. Through the mist, Nguyen Tam recognized the greenish uniforms of the border patrol unit as they approached in their boats. "This is the border patrol unit, everybody stay where you are. Anybody attempting to run away will be shot."

Before the border patrol agents reached them, Thanh, the boat's owner, quietly submerged beneath the water and disappeared. Nguyen Tam knew it was too late to escape; anyway, he had to stick around to protect Thuy and others. Thuy was so scared and disappointed; she covered her face with her hands and cried. Other families, as they saw the patrol agents with guns, began crying, creating a chaotic scenario.

Nguyen Tam has been in worse situations than this, but he sat still and waited for the order from the border patrol. This is a bad time to resist; they would all wind up dead.

The two fishing boats slowly disembarked and unloaded the people. With their hands held above their heads, they lined up on the beach waiting for the next order. The border patrol had the peoples' hands tightly bound to each other. They formed them in a single line so no one could run away from the group. Desperate and worried for their lives, the new captives only could pray now for their life and follow the order from the patrol unit.

They walked at least ten miles from the beach front to the border patrol guard house. The sun had slowly roasted their exposed flesh by the time they arrived at the camp. The guards made everybody sit outside in the courtyard like the first initial punishment for those who tried to escape.

The children would be the first to die under this cruel treatment. Two young children got heat exhaustion. Already unconscious, they lay in front of their parents who screamed for help. The guard slowly took a bucket of cold water and splashed the little bodies; then turned around and walked away without remorse. So they remained throughout the burning day; one young child already dead. The guards sloshed water upon a few other children, keeping them barely alive.

The older people were suffering from the heat as well. Some lay on the ground, already unconscious. Luckily, the wind picked up, gathering some huge black clouds, and soon enough, a small rain began falling on those burning bodies. Everyone looked up, stuck their tongues out to taste the precious life-saving liquid. When night came, two trucks from the higher government level came to transport all the new prisoners to a different location. Everyone was so exhausted they didn't care where they were going. They just prayed to God to bless them for the rest of their unlucky destinies.

Nguyen Tam tried to find the easiest way to escape, but still hadn't come up with any. Besides, he was still held responsible for

Thuy and the others. He felt so helpless in this situation. Even with his soldier skill, he had his hands tied before these ruthless guards.

PART 2

Since it was dark, no one knew which direction they were heading; they noticed that the truck was slowing down. They could smell the fresh ocean air, and soon they heard the sound of the tide. The trucks came to a stop close to the beach front. Two uniformed soldiers with their faces covered ordered everybody to get off the truck, and left them there alone. Soon the trucks left and Thanh, the boat's owner, appeared again and hurried to reload all the people back on the boat. They then motored out to the big boat that sat in wait.

Nguyen Tam recognized the fishing boat's owner who had disappeared earlier this morning. He was the same one who bribed the higher local authority to free all the prisoners. He saved everybody who was to be imprisoned because of their escape attempt. Once everyone boarded the fishing boat, they found more people from another team already there. The fishing boat's owner started up the engine, and slowly moved toward the Thai's waters. Nguyen Tam first looked at the small engine which pushed the heavily loaded boat; he doubted that the engine would last long enough to take them where they want to go. The cold fresh ocean air fanned his face and kept him from falling sleep. He watched a million stars glimmering in the dark sky. He tried to memorize one star's cluster, so one day, perhaps he could remember it from the other side of the earth. While gazing on the starry sky, somebody tapped lightly on his shoulder. He turned around and found the boat owner behind him, offering him a cigarette. Accepting the offer, Nguyen Tam lit it up and took in a long drag. He hasn't had a cigarette for a long time, at least since being arrested. He invited the boat owner to sit down next to him, and started up a conversation.

"Thanks for the cigarette, I needed it. What you did back there was pretty smooth; we all appreciate what you've done for us. By the way, how did you manage to get the county police to release us?"

Nguyen Tam took another drag of his cigarette, and Thanh, smiled, "This is my last trip, then I plan to go with you all. Things are getting hairy back there. I gave my house up in exchange for you people. I guess I can start again when I settle in some other country."

Nguyen Tam, with all respect, bowed his head and promised, "We will never forget what you have done for us. Someday, if I'm still alive... I will repay you."

The boat owner smiled, and replied, "Oh no, don't you worry about that. The least I could do was to save you all. I do hope the engine will last long enough to take us to Thailand, otherwise we'll be stranded in the middle of nowhere, pirates are everywhere in this area.

Nguyen Tam, surprised at the term "pirates," asked Thanh more about it, "What pirates? You mean real pirates from long time ago, they still exist?"

"No!"replied Thanh, "Thai pirates. They are cruel and the most formidable pirates in the gulf of Siam. They never leave any evidence. They rape all the females no matter how old they are, and kill them afterward."

Thuy, sleeping next to them, overheard the conversation, got up and questioned Thanh again, "Are you certain about the pirates, they kill and rape all the women?"

Nguyen Tam gave Thanh a quick signal that he shouldn't tell her the true story, which might worry her to death. Thanh changed the subject to another story, "Yes, the pirates used to appear once in a while, but lately the Thailand authority got rid of all of them so don't you worry about that."

Pointing his finger at Nguyen Tam, Thanh continued, "This soldier will protect you against the pirates anyway. Well, I have to go check the engine, go back to sleep."

When the boat owner walked away, Thuy tried to question Nguyen Tam again, "Tam, it's true what he said? I'm scared. If they attack us, what is going to happen to me?"

Nguyen Tam turned around and put his arm on her shoulder and pulled her closer to him, trying to calm her down, "Oh come on, did you not hear what he said? The Thai police already arrested them and put them in prison, beside, I will protect you anyway I can. Let's pray to God to protect us all the way. Go back to sleep, tomorrow things will be better."

Soon, both were falling into a deep sleep to the monotone sound of the small engine. Thanh sat next to the engine so he could monitor it. Everybody, but Thanh was sleeping. They weren't aware that the boat's condition was getting worse. Thanh kept trying to fix a little bit here, and a little bit there, but the small engine choked out more puffing smoke. Finally, he came to wake Nguyen Tam up for some advice, "Hey, wake up! There is trouble with the engine. I hate to wake you up but I couldn't fix it. Do you know anything about a boat engine?"

Nguyen Tam only heard a few words come from Thanh and already knew right away the small boat engine was having problems. Nguyen Tam knew a little bit about the small engine, he also knew that the engine was overworked. To push a full fishing boat overloaded with people, it required a much bigger engine with more power. After Nguyen Tam worked on the engine for a while, they both decided to shut it down and let it cool off for awhile. They could only hope that the engine would start back up again

Unfortunately, the wind began to shift and the waves started to grow. The waves began rocking the boat and woke everybody up. No one had any experience at sea, thus panic broke out on board. Once the panicked passengers found out that the engine wasn't running, some of them cried out loud about their bad luck. The big waves began rolling the boat from side to side. Nguyen Tam tried many times to restart the engine. Luckily, the last time he tried, the engine ignited but it was still ill running. Both Nguyen Tam and Thanh agreed that it was better to steer the boat toward the bank and wait for fairer weather. They could then fix the engine as well. The boat slowly moved to the coast line through the storm. Water was filling inside the boat and people tried to scoop it out with cups, cans, or anything they could find. They finally reached the bank safely.

Even though they didn't know where they were, one thing was for sure, they weren't in Viet Nam anymore. By their calculation, they were somewhere in Cambodia.

The group found a cave on shore to use as a temporary shelter during the storm. People leaned on each others' backs to find comfort because there was not enough room to lie down. Scared and hungry, no one said a word, but in their mind they were frantic. Thuy leaned on Nguyen Tam's back. Exhausted, she closed her eyes but she still couldn't get any rest. These hardships made her long for all the comforts of home, from a warm bed to a piping hot bowl of wonton soup. As the lightning ignited the dark sky, she acknowledged the power of a raging mother nature. Thuy thanked God for allowing her to live. Getting tired of feeling sorry for herself, she hoped that they would make it through this, and get to America to start a new life. This thought somehow offered comfort to her troubled mind. The thought of the new life slowly helped her drift to a more promising sweet dream.

When the sun light first pierced into the cave, Nguyen Tam and Thanh both got up and went outside to fix the boat. Later, two other men in the group also joined in to help. Inside the boat there was still a lot of water. The men took the carburetor apart and cleaned out all the water. Meanwhile, the two men tried to clear out the water in the boat. Soon everybody in the cave came out to help. The women scooped the water with their bare hands. With all of the passengers helping it didn't take long to dry the inside the boat. While the men tried to fix the engine, the women gathered some dehydrated food and prepared a small breakfast for everybody. They started a small fire to make some rice soup to eat with dry fish. Without warning a group of renegade Khmer Rouge soldiers approached.

The Khmer Rouge soldiers patrolled their territory more often because the Cambodia National force, which was backed by the Vietnamese government, had waged war against the Khmer Rouge. The point man in the patrol group spotted the thin white smoke of the fire. He gave the signal to his group leader to alert him that there are people within their territory. The leader gave him the order to go check the situation and report back to him. The point man promptly acknowledged the order and disappeared into the thick bush. About ten minutes later, the Khmer Rouge soldier returned and reported what he saw to his leader. Then the soldiers quickly advanced to capture the group of trespassers.

Everybody was so busy cleaning the boat, they didn't notice the Khmer Rouge soldiers. After observing the situation and determining that the people were not armed, the leader gave the order to seize the entire stranded group.

The first man, who saw the approaching Khmer Rouge soldiers, screamed out in terror and tried to evade them. He only could run a few yards before the soldiers saw him. One soldier aimed his Kalashnikov rifle at the running man while the leader yelled out, "Stop!" The man kept running to a ravine but didn't make it. The sound of the automated rifle destroyed the calmness of the beautiful morning. The bullets pierced through the man's back and the impact pushed him to the ground. Even though he was hit he still tried to crawl to the bush. With his last breathe he heard the screaming voice of his wife. He stopped and turned his head around trying to locate where the voice came from but only heard the sound of the automatic rifle. Everything began blurring and he no longer felt pain. Everyone knelt down and bowed their heads to pray for the dead companion, as his wife wept for her husband. The Khmer Rouge leader waived to the people to form a single line. Once more, these people became captives. This time, their lives are not guaranteed to last.

Nguyen Tam knew of the savageness of the Khmer Rouge during the war. They would murder anybody in their way. He remained silent and followed their orders. The exiled people were like the walking dead. The dreadful situation horrified everybody beyond hope. The thought of being a captive once again, turned them into stone. Thuy wondered if her life would last another day.

The Khmer Rouge soldiers lead them to an abandoned town

which was now their headquarters. They locked the captives into an old slaughter house which The Khmer Rouge had converted into jail house. They chained the prisoners together with leg irons and locked them with a long steel bar. Sitting was very uncomfortable because the steel bar restricted their movement.

The Khmer Rouge used this place to torture prisoners. Dried blood stains remained on the walls. The people discovered evidence of human bodies imprinted onto the jail walls. If it was not bad enough that the smell of decayed bodies made everyone nauseous; the thought of being kept in the same room with the dead bodies made the cell worse than any hell. The fright of being tortured or executed was haunting everybody's mind. The younger children became so sick that they didn't even know what was happening. The people's spirit today was completely opposite than that of a few days earlier. When they were imprisoned in their own country they still felt safer than here.

The big steel door suddenly opened and startled everyone. Realizing their fear once again; each person had a different expectation of what type of punishment lay in store for them. Three soldiers stormed in and pointed their already cocked their rifle at the captives. The screaming and pointing made the children so frightening that they all cried in terror. They unlocked the men and ordered them to follow them outside. Thuy and other women in the group thought that the soldiers were going to execute the men. They fell to their knees, crying and begging the soldiers to release the men, thinking that they would never see them again alive.

The soldiers brought the group of men to the far side of the jail house. Then they gave them shovels and ordered them to dig. Nguyen Tam had the feeling that they were digging their own graves; he was looking for any opportunity to get him and others free. He gave an eye signal to the other guys to slow down the digging to buy sometime. If they had to, they would attack the guards. They had the feeling that sooner or later the Khmer Rouge would kill them. He had heard that the Khmer Rouge liked to behead their captives and bury them in their own grave. While Nguyen Tam planned the attack, he heard the rumbling noise from approaching helicopters. The guards also tried to listen to where the helicopters were coming from. A few seconds later they spotted the helicopters position. At the same time the Vietnamese choppers fired rockets into two guard towers armed with machine guns. Realizing that they were under attack, the Khmer Rouge soldiers turned their eyes back to the prisoners, but it was too late. Nguyen Tam and three other men already jumped out of the hole, and swung their shovels across the soldiers head killing them instantly. Nguyen Tam found the keys in one of the soldier's pocket and then grabbed his rifle. He raced back to the jail house as all hell broke loose.

The fire fight was becoming more intense. The Vietnamese gunship was busy cutting down the Khmer Rouge force, still some distance from the jail house. Luckily, the Khmer Rouge soldiers were too busy defending themselves that they didn't pay any attention to Nguyen Tam's group. Nguyen Tam unlocked the jail house then freed everyone. Together they raced toward the thick tree line and quickly disappeared into the woods. They kept running without turning their heads. Nguyen Tam then stopped and gave the signal for everyone to stop, "Okay this is far enough everybody, we've got to stop to determine what direction our boat is. I think we're pretty safe here. We can take a break here for a moment."

Nguyen Tam took a stick to the ground to observe the direction of the sun, and then he determined the general direction to the coast line. After discussing his suggestion to Thanh, they both agreed that the direction they're heading should bring them back to the boat. Nguyen Tam felt more confident now that he had a weapon, all they needed now is to get back to the boat before someone found it.

As they traveled through the thick jungle, thorns shredded their skin like paper. No one thought about their pain, they just wanted to get out this jungle. A loud scream of terror suddenly echoed through the trees. Everybody stopped and looked around to find out where it was coming from. They found a huge Burmese python wrapped around a member in their group. The snake quickly squeezed his body to suffocate the prey and tried to break all his bones so it could swallow him up. Nguyen Tam aimed his rifle at the snake's head, and squeezed the trigger. The bullet precisely torn the snake's head into pieces killing it instantly. The huge reptile might be dead but its strength was still a threat to the victim who almost fainted from the lack of oxygen. Everyone gathered around the man; massaging his body to try and get the blood circulating throughout. After a while, the man slowly regained consciousness. He was still weak, his body bruised from the snake constriction. Two men had to carry the injured man. This will take more time than they planned, but they couldn't leave the man behind.

After a few hours, they were lucky enough to find the same trail that lead them to the Khmer Rouge's headquarters. Now everybody felt relieved because now they could find their boat. With their spirits higher they began to walk faster, as if hope powered up their fatigued bodies. When they started to smell the fresh ocean air, some forgot about their aching bodies and sore feet, and they started racing toward the beach. When they saw the sandy beach with the blue water, they kneeled down to thank God for sparing their lives. They threw themselves into the water. It felt so good to soak their aching body in the salt water, which also helped to heal all the cuts and bruises. After a quick clean up, they went back to the boat and prepared for the departure. The Khmer Rouge soldiers put a few bullet holes in the boat but Thanh repaired them with a patching kit. Nguyen Tam still heard the echoes from the gun fire and exploding rockets. He tried to finish fixing the engine fast so they could leave before the soldiers returned.

Nguyen Tam finally finished reassembling the engine. The small fishing boat though fragile and old, was the only means for their freedom. Nguyen Tam nervously pulled the rope to crank up the engine. After a few times of puffing out black smoke, the engine began to run smoother. Everyone in the boat screamed aloud with joy. They applauded to Nguyen Tam as their hero. Before they took off, the men went out to pick up some fresh coconuts for an emergency beverage, and the women gathered up some wild mangoes.

The old fishing boat was slowly carried the people off the beach, the sun slowly sunk into the West. This was also the same direction that the boat needed to follow. The surface of the ocean was so calm, it reflected a million golden sun rays that mixed with the silver tide and created a truly peaceful portrait of nature. The setting generated a serene feeling amongst the people who were trying to find a life of peace for themselves.

Nguyen Tam sat next to Thuy, with an arm around her shoulder; he smoked a cigarette and let himself become absorbed into the beautiful sunset. No matter what had happened to him, just being next to the beautiful girl he loved was enough comfort; he thanked God for saving his and her life.

It was Nguyen Tam's turn to guide the boat; he looked at the vast horizon in front of him and tried to determine his course. They lost the compass while running away and now all they could do was guess the general direction and pray that they were on the right path. The boat slowly moved all night, the cold ocean breeze blew on Nguyen Tam's face keeping him from falling asleep. He lit up another cigarette and held the warm smoke in his lungs before he let it out.

Nguyen Tam kept hoping that their little boat could make it to the horizon; otherwise they might end up in the hands of the pirates or Khmer Rouge. He heard stories about pirates robbing and murdering innocent people at sea, he didn't know what to believe but prayed that they wouldn't have to confront them. Not too far from his feet, Thuy slept like a little kitten, she was so attached to Nguyen Tam. Life is so precious and also so fragile; you risk your life in exchange for freedom. Nguyen Tam asked himself, *was it really worth what they both were trading for?*

It seemed like nothing good would ever happen, he just hoped that Thuy would be alright. Being caught twice Nguyen Tam began to have doubt his luck. But then he thought, they made it this far, so the Promised Land must be waiting on the other side of the horizon. Too busy day dreaming, Nguyen Tam didn't see Thanh standing next to him. He was waiting for the shift change. Thanh, silently stood there and watched him. He finally broke up Nguyen Tam's thoughts by waving his hands in front of his face, then he said while smiling, "Hey! What are you thinking about? Don't you want to go to sleep? I take over."

Nguyen Tam rubbed his eyes, yarning, "Wow, how long have you been standing there? Sorry, I'm kind of dreaming about the new life which we're willing to trade with our death. I don't really know if it's worth it, but it really scared the crap out of me. I have the feeling that it is not over yet, what do you think?"

Thanh lit up a cigarette, joked with Nguyen Tam, "Old soldiers like you are... tough enough. I don't think you will be scared. Let's pray to God to help us through this trip. I'm getting too old for this, and I don't know if I can do anything when I get there." He shook his head meaning, *que sera sera*, then sat down and took over the tiller.

Now that the first sun ray started rising from beneath the dark blue horizon, Nguyen Tam didn't feel sleepy so he sat down next to Thanh and said, "Boy, now that you're here I don't feel sleepy anymore. Anyway, it's a beautiful morning. It would be a waste if I go to sleep now."

Thanh smiled, agreed with Nguyen Tam, "Yes! You're right, it's nice and calm. I hope the weather will be like this all the time, we should be in Thailand by tomorrow. Hopefully we will be rescued by the Thai Coast guard. Then we will settle into the refugee camp and wait for the interview for either America or some other country.

Nguyen Tam, staring at the dark blue surface of the ocean that looked like a mirror; reflecting the bright orange sun rays that penetrated through the bright silver grayish clouds, formed perfectly into the shape of silver scales of a giant fish.

At the other side of the same horizon; pirates gathered at their ship to prepare for their departure. Spending all their money on booze and whores they needed to go back out to steal more money. Once they were out of Thailand waters, they didn't have to worry about the Thai coast guard. Today, the pirates considered it their lucky day. They spotted their prey miles away. Sitting high up in the observer tower, the lookout used long range the spotter screamed out from the tower, "I see a boat; it's approaching from the West!"

"From the West, are you sure?" asked Sami, the boat's captain.

"Yeah I'm sure, except this one is moving pretty slowly, it doesn't look like a civilian boat."

Sami yelled back to him, he was so anxious to find out what kind of boat it is; "Can you see what kind of boat it is? Is it the Thai coast guard?"

Once the approaching boat appeared clearly, the lookout screamed out loud, "Yeah! It is the Thai's coast guard, what do we do?"

Sami yelled, "Get down from up there now!" Then he gave order to his crew to get rid all their weapons. "Okay! Listen up! Hide all the weapons away and bring out the fishing net. We must pretend that we're getting ready to fish. Remember, everybody stay cool." Sami shook his head in disgust, not content with the situation, "This is not my lucky day."

Actually, their fire power is much heavier compared to the Coast guard armament; still he tried to evade the law as much as possible.

The Thai Coast guard also spotted the fishing vessel which was just about to enter into international waters. The Thai Coast guard commander, with the vessel in his view, gave the order to approach. The Thai Royal Navy ordered that all suspected boats that tried to cross into international waters would be checked for drug trafficking and piracy. It appeared that the fishing boat tried to veer away from the Coast guard, so the commander gave the order to speed up and to stop them

Sami peering through his binoculars saw that the Coast Guard chasing them. Knowing they could not outrun the Guard boat, Sami gave the order to slow down pretending that they were on a fishing course. The Coast Guard speed boat was catching up with the pirate ship and closely followed the suspected fishing boat. The Coast Guard then circled twice around the big fishing boat and the commander gave the order to check out the fishing vessel.

The pirate's boat was still idling; they waited for the Coast guard agents to embark from their ship. Sami silently gave an order to get ready for the attack. Just about the time the Coast guard commander gave the order to board the fishing boat; a rocket fired from one of the pirates hit starboard side of the coast guard speed boat causing a big explosion. A fire broke loose in the commander's control cabin while another explosion resulted from another rocket fired by the pirates. About this time the Coast Guard ship began to sink. All the surviving coast guard agents dove into the water to avoid the fire. The pirates applauded triumphantly while watching the coast guard boat slowly disappear under the water. The surviving coast guards tried to swim away but then they became live target practice for the pirates. Riddling their bodies with bullets, the ocean went from blue to red, dyed by the soldiers' blood.

Killing became a routine exercise for the pirates. They were transformed into bloodthirsty evil men that no law enforcement agency could stop. They were a threat for anybody who traveled alone at sea. The pirates possessed much heavier and sophisticated weapons which allowed them to easily defeat their opponents. After successfully destroying the Coast guard speed boat, the pirates hurriedly moved out of the area to avoid another confrontation with the Thai Royal Navy which would be looking for the whereabouts of the sunken Coast guard speed boat.

The Thai Royal Navy headquarters received the last message from the Coast guard unit announcing the chase of a suspected fishing vessel. The communications unit, combined with the radar unit, tried to locate the coordinates of the Coast guard boat. Headquarters sent out a helicopter for an immediate search mission because the nature of the last message received. They calculated the position of the Coast Guard ship based on their last known position and time of the received communication. It took an hour for the chopper to reach the designated area. The pilot reported that he found a lot of debris and oil residue on top the water. He then flew further out to look for the fishing vessel, but found nothing. The pilot reported back to headquarters about the missing ship but was forced to return to the base because of low fuel supply.

After eliminating all the members of the Coast Guard, the pirate boat raced toward Cambodian waters to evade the Thai Government. Once they reached Cambodian waters they began the hunt for more refugee boats.

After chatting for a while, Nguyen Tam felt like taking a nap, so he went to lie down, and joked to Thanh, "If you fall sleep, don't you steer us to the pirates. Okay!"

"Oh no, I'll wake you up first!" he said laughing.

Thanh looked far away to the horizon, hoping not to see a pirate ship. He thought to himself, *I have nothing to worry, I have no gold, nor jewelry, and sold of most of my properties to buy this boat and to bribe the authority to save the bunch from prison.* Now all he needed was to stay alive and start a new life somewhere else. His eyes were glued toward the clear blue horizon, looking for anything to appear. Just about when he took his eyes off the clear blue line, the corner of his eyes spotted a small dot. He thought he saw some kind of fish and rubbed his eyes to try and clear his vision.

Thanh called Nguyen Tam over for a second opinion, "Hey Sarge! Wake up, check this out!" Nguyen Tam, got up in the hurry, yawning and rubbing his eyes he looked toward the direction where

Thanh was pointing. Still he couldn't make out the object, "Well, it looked like a ship or a small island... it's too far away, I can't see that far. What do you think we should do?"

"Well! Let us keep the same course, if they approach us hopefully we will recognize who they are. I hope they are not who we think they are."

"Yeah, I agree, but let's go a little closer to the bank. If something happens, we will land quickly and get away."

Nguyen Tam went to grab the rifles which they took from the Khmer Rouge soldiers. He gave one to Thanh in case of a pirate attack. Thanh refused, "Oh no, Sarge! I have never touched a gun before. I wouldn't know how to use it. I would rather let you do that... would you old soldier?"

"Okay that's fine. But you have to let me know right away. I have to get some sleep, wake me up right away."

After Nguyen Tam went back to sleep, Thanh kept looking at the growing black dot, it seemed to be getting closer and closer. He tried to veer the boat closer to the bank trying to avoid the attention of the strange ship. Everybody overheard the conversation between Nguyen Tam and Thanh. They all looked at the direction of the small dot, and wondered what it could be.

One lady pointed her finger at the dot, and showed her husband, "Look! Does it look like a ship to you? We must be close to Thailand. It must be a Thai's fishing boat, or may be another boat like us?"

The man took a good look at it, "I don't know! But it seems like it's approaching us. Let's hope that it isn't the bad guys."

Thuy was among the most curious people in the boat, she saw the dot too. She kept asking Nguyen Tam what all the questions were. "Tam, what is the dot over there? Is it a ship? Would it save us? Or maybe a Navy ship... what should we do? I'm worried!"

Nguyen Tam shook his head, smiled at her, "Hey, hey! Calm down, will you! Everything will be all right. Just a regular ship, there are a lot of ships in the ocean. Okay now go and get something to eat, and let me take a little nap."

Thuy temporarily left him alone, but she's still starring at the black dot on the horizon, that is now growing bigger. Somehow, the term "pirate" and all the horrible things kept haunting her mind, her sixth sense was telling her something wasn't right about the ship.

Thanh now recognized it was a strange ship, but still too far away to know whether it was friend or foe. He knew one thing though; it was rare to have any big American ships in this area after the Vietnam war, mostly local fishermen, or pirates.

The lookout on the pirate ship announced to the captain there was a boat east of them. He was sure that it was a refugee boat on their way to Thailand. Using the binoculars, the pirate captain analyzed the activities on the boat. He counted how many people were on the ship before he launched the attack. It was a small boat, but plenty of people. The pirate boat captain also noticed that the boat tried to elude them. He then gave the order to pursue the small vessel. After defeating the Coast guard, they were thirsty for more blood. The captain ordered more speed since the refugee boat tried to get away.

Thanh sped up his battered fishing boat, but the engine began to overheat. He had to slow down, and he knew that the other ship was definitely following them. Then someone on the boat suggested, "Slow the boat down, or you may burn up the engine. It looks like a normal fishing vessel trying to help us."

Now the pirate ship was within visible distance. Outfitted like an innocent fishing vessel; inside it was packed with a deadly force.

Someone from the fishing boat yelled out loud, "It is a fishing boat, don't worry."

By now, Nguyen Tam woke up because of all the noise. He took a long look at the ship and determined that the ship looked unarmed. He felt relieved and lay back down.

It looked normal to Thanh also; he began slowing down but cautiously watched the oncoming ship. It looked like a local fishing vessel, but why were they trying to catch them with such noticeable speed. *Shall I stop to ask for help,* Thanh thought to himself, *or should I try to get away.*

The fishing vessel tried to cut in front of the small boat. Forcing the refugee boat to slow down, possibly will meet the vessel head on. It seemed a little strange to Thanh that the ship approached that way but he thought, maybe they want to tell us something.

The pirate ship was getting closer, Thanh started seeing faces on the boat and they didn't look real friendly. Now, everybody on the refugee boat was watching the fishing vessel. Thuy looked at the men on the fishing boat and noticed that their faces weren't very friendly, not like the ordinary fishermen. She remarked to Nguyen Tam, "Tam, Look at the fishermen! They look so mean; you think Thai fishermen look like them? I don't have a good feeling about these people."

Nguyen Tam took a real good look at the fishermen again, agreeing with Thuy. There wasn't much they could do about it now. Nguyen Tam cautiously reached for his rifle and got ready for anything. He tried to calm Thuy, "You see this rifle, if anything happens I will fire the gun. Don't you worry; let's see what happens next. I think they want to tell us something."

Sami gave the order for the pirates to act normal until the refugee boat stopped. The more time they spent chasing the boat the more likely they are to run into another Coast Guard boat. The pirate vessel was getting closer and almost blocked the refugee boat from advancing. One of the pirates signaled for the boat to stop.

Once the refugee boat came to a halt, the pirate's vessel closed in and exposed the heavy caliber machine gun. The pirates, in the mean time, pointed their rifles at the frightened refugees. There was no sign of a revolt from the refugee boat, but the pirate leader fired a volley of shots to warn the people not to do anything foolish. There were screams from the refugee boat, mostly from frightening women and children. After all the chaos and confusion of, a young voice from the pirates boat spoke with a broken Vietnamese dialect, - "People, don't be afraid! There will be no killings if you listen to us. Be calm! We want you people to leave everything in your boat, and get into our boat quickly and quietly!"

Then they threw down a hanging ladder for people to climb up. Everybody reluctantly responded to the order and boarded the pirate's boat. The people began to climb up, first children and women. Facing a desperate situation, Thuy held on to Nguyen Tam for the last time, wept on his shoulder and said good-bye. Thanh looked at Nguyen Tam, questioning if they should take action. With the machinegun pointed straight at them, there wasn't much he could do.

Nguyen Tam gave a hand signal, meaning to be calm and to obey their orders for now, "Go ahead! Go up, either way, we are going to lose, so don't make them have to kill us all."

Thanh sadly waved his hand to say good bye and followed the rest.

Nguyen Tam, a former frogman from the Southern Army, armed with the knife he took from the Khmer Rouge, quietly slid into the water, then dove underneath the pirate ship, and resurfaced on the other side. The pirates were so busy checking on the people from the refugee boat, that they didn't pay attention to the other side of their own ship. Nguyen Tam, using the knife as the grip, climbed onto one of the small ledges on the side of the pirate vessel. Using it as leverage he then jumped up and grabbed the wooden overhang on the side boat, and quickly climbed into the vessel. Once he got inside the boat safely and without anyone spotting him, he crawled and hid underneath a big pile of old tarps where he laid motionless, waiting.

Once everybody got onto the vessel, the pirates divided the people into two groups, male and female. Then they ordered them to strip off all their clothes so they could be searched. The group of people stood there motionless and confused. A woman broke the silence, telling the group, "They want us to take off our clothes so they can find our gold! I rather die than live shamefully!"

Another man began taking off his clothes saying, "If we don't do what they want…they will kill us all, anyway we have nothing to take, soon they finish checking us they will let us go."

Thuy, didn't know what to do. Fear for her life and feeling ashamed to be naked in front of all the strange men. Thuy knelt down crying, it seemed like it they were being constantly tested. Each time they nearly lost their lives. This time the chance of survival is getting thin. Thuy wondered if she took her clothes off whether or not they would they leave her alone.

A sudden sharp scream broke out; two pirates pulled one woman out the group, then ripped all her clothes off. The woman desperately fought back scratching the face of one of the pirates drawing blood. The pirate withdrew for a moment, wiped the blood still trickling from the cut and tasted his own savage blood. He then grabbed a bottle of rice wine from his mate and took a big gulp out of it. The wine turned the pirate into a wild animal. He stared with his blood shot eyes and smiled with his yellow crooked teeth which protruded out of his mouth. Now he had a big scar on his left cheek. All this ugliness put together created a monster from hell. The pirate approached the woman who was now trembling, grabbed her hair and pulled her toward him. The desperate woman screamed in terror as he locked her head in his muscular arm and began to choke her. With the other hand reached down and torn off her black silk trouser, then raped her while she gasped for air. The poor woman desperately tried to unlock his arm and somehow she wiggled her head out and loosened the choke hold. She caught a quick breath of air and then bit the pirates forearm and didn't let go. The blood started to trickle out of her mouth. The pirate screamed in great pain and then he tightened his head lock and snapped her neck killing her instantly.

The pirate, still raging, dragged her body to the side of the vessel and threw it into the water. Thanh ran toward the pirate who was still standing by the side of the boat; then dropped kick him right off of the boat, Another pirate fired a few rounds at Thanh, but missed. Before they could fire another round, Thanh dove into the water and grabbed the nearly drowned pirate and took him down with him. The pirates ran to the side of the vessel to rescue their shipmate but all they could see were air bubbles from the two bodies sinking into the depths. Their surprise turned into rage as the pirates turned on the remaining men with the wooden stocks of their rifles. One man fought back, but not for long. Sami, the pirate leader, pulled out his pistol and shot him in the chest then shot another man one who stood next to the dying man killing them both. The women and children, who were terrified, got on their knees and begged for mercy then some of them began to undress. Thuy, horrified, began to take off her clothes. Suddenly, a scream came from the observation tower alarming the pirates to an oncoming aircraft, "Hey, boss! I heard a sound of a chopper approaching to our position."

Sami told the crew to get rid the two bodies and to gather everybody up. Then they locked them up in the bottom of the vessel. After a quick search of the refugee's boat for valuables; Sami gave the order to push off and to destroy the refugee boat to hide the evidence. Then they set out to their hide-out island.

Nguyen Tam, was still hiding behind the junk pile waiting for the right time to strike. When he heard the gun shots, he peeked out through a small hole in the tarp to find out what was going on. He saw the fight between Thanh and the pirate and he silently prayed that his friend's soul would soon get to heaven. Nguyen Tam quickly analyzed the situation and knew that if he had rushed out from his hiding place, he would have been shot by the pirates. He still felt guilty because he was hiding instead of helping the group but knew his effort would have been in vain. The main purpose was to save Thuy no matter what it took. Nguyen Tam knew that once he blew his cover, both of them would die.

Nguyen Tam knew that Thuy was still alive, not well but still alive. Now being the only one still loose, he had to come up with the plan to free everybody. It would be hard to fight the bloodthirsty pirates himself, but he has no choice.

The pirate vessel sped back to their hide out island, Sami, was raging about because of all the bad luck. First, they had to engage in a battle with the coast guard, next they robbed an empty boat, and one of his best men was killed by a refugee. He hoped the government called off the search, otherwise, sooner or later they would be found. He knew that if caught, the death penalty would be his.

Now, he was thinking when and how to get rid all his captives.

Now, he felt that his luck was beginning to run out. Facing the law is not in his best interest. He knew that somehow the killing of the coast guard soldiers would return to haunt him.

Inside the bottom floor where the pirates kept their food and supplies; they were now using to temporary lock up the refugees.

Thuy, one of the biggest worriers among the women, kept asking questions that nobody could answer, "What happened to our boat? Did anyone see Tam? Thanh, was he dead? He was very brave, wasn't he?"

One little girl about nine-years-old was weeping on her mother's shoulder, "Mom, I'm scared! What is going to happen to all of us? How come bad things always happen to us? They're going to kill us all like they killed dad and Thanh?"

Her mom yelled at her not to say such bad things, "Don't you talk like that, God will help us again, and he will help us now."

Now they have no country, no government that can save them. Most of the strong men in the group either died or disappeared. While everybody prayed, a young man, who spoke the broken Vietnamese language, brought them some bread and water, then said "Hurry up and eat, if they find out that I give this to you people, I get in lot troubles."

There was only enough food for some of them, so the adult let the smaller children eat all the food even though everybody was starving. They looked at the young pirate with a great appreciation, some of them busting out crying. The young man promised to the people, "Hey! Don't cry, I try to bring you more food if I can."

Nguyen Tam, still hiding, tried to look around to see what was going on. He wanted to get inside and check on everyone, especially Thuy. The good thing is the vessel was moving fast and the pirates were so busy with their duties, nobody had detected Nguyen Tam's presence yet. For Nguyen Tam to get inside the vessel to check on everyone would be a great risk. He would rather wait for it to get little darker, then sneak inside, and he might not be as easily detected.

Nguyen Tam had to come up with the plan, quick, otherwise everybody will be killed. He remembered the M-60 Machinegun mounted in the front of the boat, if somehow he could get hold of the machinegun, he thought, he might have a chance to turn the situation around. How to get hold of the machinegun, first of all, he has to make sure nobody detects him before he could get there. Even then he still has to lock and load the ammunition before he could start firing. As Nguyen Tam laid there quietly planning his strategy he suddenly heard voices approaching his hiding place; quietly drew his knife, waiting.

Two thugs went looking for some dry goods, and were unable to find them, so they started to dig everything up. Unfortunately, Nguyen Tam's hiding place was among the junk piles, if the pirates couldn't find what they were looking for, soon they were going to expose him. Once they did that, Nguyen Tam didn't have a choice but to kill them both. His heart was beating fast, the sweat trickled down on his face, and he held tight on his knife. Suddenly, one of the pirates yelled out, meaning that he found the dry goods, so the search stopped. Watching two pirates carried the goods away, Nguyen Tam let out a big sigh of relief; at least he was safe for now.

It was getting dark, except for the navigator and the lookout everybody else was inside. Nguyen Tam thought, It's time for action. He decided to check out the machinegun first. So he stuck his head out to observe the situation, and then low crawled along the side of the ship without being detected by the lookout. All of a sudden the vessel slowed down, and then Nguyen Tam heard the screaming voice of the lookout yelling something. A few minutes later more pirates poured out onto the deck. Nguyen Tam quickly scurried back underneath the tarp to evade detection.

Nguyen Tam didn't know what exactly was going on. The vessel was slowing down to the point that it was going to stop. He had to look through a small crack in the tarp, mainly not to expose himself, so it was hard to know when to act. The boat was still moving, but slowly. The sunlight was all but gone and by now all the pirates were out on the deck. The pirate's vessel approached their hide-out island. They were ready to dock in the small cove which has natural cover providing a good camouflage from aerial surveillance. Once the pirate vessel finished docking, they brought all their captives up on deck then separated them into two group's men and women. This time they watched the men closer than before, and wouldn't hesitate to kill them.

They used their weapons to beat on the men who didn't understand what they wanted them to do, or slightly opposed to their orders. These refugee men knew that they had no chance to win over the savage pirates so they didn't fight back.

The men stripped off their clothing, Sami, the leader, ordered the men to line up against the side of the vessel and shot every one of them in the back. The loud screams of pain mixed with the screams of terror from the men's families created a monstrous atmosphere. The wife of the executed man ran toward the side of the boat to look at him for the last time. She pointed her finger at Sami and cursed him. The wolf pack leader turned his gun at her, and coldly shot her in the head. Now the remaining refugees were only women and children. Terrified, they knew sooner or later, they were going to be raped and killed. They couldn't fight back against these well armed pirates, the sense of being helpless and the terror of being slaughtered had turned these people numb, especially Thuy.

Being stranded without Nguyen Tam, she felt scared and alone. The women already stripped their clothes off, all shivering because of the chilling breeze of the evening. All of them embarrassed because of being naked in front of the nastiest human beings on earth. Thuy used her small arms to cover her naked body; this was the first time that she had exposed her body in front of complete strangers. Fearful that the blood thirsty pirates were going to tear her body apart, she silently wept inside.

The pirates went through their usual tasks, harassing and searching peoples clothing for gold and jewelry. Today wasn't their day; they didn't find anything through the torn clothes from the refugees. The pirates didn't know that these people had been through hell and back and didn't care. Sami, the leader, cursed while walking up to the bunch of women and picked the best girl for himself. He saw Thuy covering her face crying, she was skinny but she was the best looking one in the bunch. He approached her then grabbed her naked tiny body and placed her on his shoulder, and walked to his cabin while others fought each other for the remaining spoils. Then one pirate pointed his finger toward the direction on the top of the hill, yelling, "Fire, big fire!"

Sami heard the warning from the pirate and dropped Thuy on the deck, and raced toward where the pirate stood. He saw that the big fire came from up on the hill where the girls were held; he ordered everybody off the boat to put out the fire. Only one pirate stood guard over the captives and the vessel. When all the pirates left, the guard ordered the women to stay together in one group so he could easily control them. He chambered a round to show all the women as a warning that he would not hesitate to pull the trigger.

Then he suddenly felt a sharp pain on his back, and everything was blurring and he collapsed.

****

One of the girls from up on the hill looked out for passing ships. She spotted the pirate vessel from far away; however she wasn't for sure what kind of ship it was. She woke Mai Lan up to go check it out, "Lan, wake up, there is a ship approaching the island, looks like the pirate ship, but I'm not for sure that we should start the fire, you want to go look?"

Mai Lan gave her a signal to be quiet, then she scrawled out through a small corner, racing to look at the passing ship. From far away, it looked like a small fishing boat, a moment later it appeared to be the same vessel that had taken away everything from her. With a sense of worry and hopelessness about the future, she watched the image of the vessel growing larger. She and the girls have to make a decision for their life so she quickly returned to the hut to ask their opinion. When she returned, the old pirate was drunk and didn't even know the pirate ship was approaching the island. Mai Lan gathered the group in the corner, silently discussed their decision about the surviving future. Mai Lan started out with a sad voice, and she tried not to cry, "Sisters, that is the pirate ship, I know for sure. What are we going to do? We can stay here and wait for them to abuse us like animals and maybe kill us, or we can start the fire and hide on the other side of the island. Maybe some other ship saw the fire and will come to rescue us. We have to make a quick decision before the pirate ship gets here!"

Everybody silenced for a moment then they sadly agreed to start the fire. No one wanted the pirates to abuse their bodies again. After they made up their minds, to start the fire, they tied up the old drunk pirate whom with a rope and gagged his mouth. Mai Lan told the girls to run to another side of the island quickly and find a place to hide. Then she and one girl stayed and started the fire.

When the pirate vessel was docking, Mai Lan watched in horror the execution of these peoples. She fainted for a moment then raced to the wood pile and started the fire; hoping that the pirates would stop the execution to put out the fire. Since the wood was stacked neatly and the because of the dry weather, the fire started quickly and it soon began to spread across the hill. Mai Lan and the other girl then ran to the other side of the island.

Nguyen Tam felt the vessel stop, and heard some gunshots but didn't know what was going on. When he peeked out to find out what was happening and heard Thuy's screaming voice. He saw the pirate carrying Thuy's completely naked body. Nguyen Tam wanted to jump out to kill the pirate to save her. He had to hold himself back, thinking they both might get kill. Instead, he would follow the pirate inside and terminate him.

"Is that you, Tam, where have you been? I thought you were dead. Oh God! Did you know what was happening to all of us?" Thuy said. Then she got up and embraced him in tears. Nguyen Tam saw the big fire on the island. He now knew why the pirates were racing off the boat, to put out the fire. Nguyen Tam told everybody to get dressed and go find a weapon to fight the pirates. Then he went to get the M-60 machinegun ready; this time they were going to fight a real war, for themselves and for those who had been slaughtered.

Nguyen Tam loaded up the ammunition then set aside the extra ammo box for a quick reload. He knew that he might die but he was going to take as many of them with him as he could. Thuy and the women returned with some knives. Thuy showed a wooden stick to Nguyen Tam and bragged, "You see this Tam, I am going to whip the pirates with this stick; I'm not afraid of them."

Nguyen Tam looked at the wooden stick, about to laugh, he simply told her, "Yeah, I know you are brave. Now, I want you and the rest of the women and children to get off this boat and find somewhere far away to hide. I will find you my love, may God bless you all."

Thuy shook her head and said, "No, I want to stay here to fight with you. I'm worried for you being by yourself here. At least I can do something."

Nguyen Tam embraced her tightly and slightly kissed her on the forehead and said, "No, you got to go, you really can't help me here. The pirates are dangerous and well arm, and a stray bullet may hit you."

Thuy wiped the tears from her sad eyes, held on tight to Nguyen Tam's hand and said, "You've got to protect yourself. Okay?" Then Thuy, the children and all the women left the vessel.

When the pirates got to the hut where they held their captives, they found the old pirate and untied him as they sweated from the intense heat of the fire. The old pirate swore that he was going to kill the girls when he caught up with them. Sami slapped him, and told him that he was stupid to let the girls get away. He divided his mates into two groups; one group to put out the fire. The other group went to search for the girls. Sami had to deliver these girls as soon as possible; otherwise he will be in a lot of trouble with the Thai Mafia. The fire quickly spread out into the grassy area, pillars of huge stacks of black smoke rose into the clear blue sky.

Mai Lan and Xuan, after they started the fire up, ran to the other side of the island to team up with other girls. They couldn't find the girls so they went to look for a small cave so they could hide. They knew that the pirates, soon or later, will come and look for them. Mai Lan went out to the reef, hoping they will find a hiding place. After a while, Mai Lan found a small crevice in the rock. To get inside the crevice, they had to dive into the water to get to it. After they determined how to get inside the rock, Mai Lan turned around and called her team mate; "Xuan! Come here, I found the entrance to a cave, but we have to dive to it."

Xuan, hesitated for a moment, asked, "Oh no, I don't know how to swim, how deep is it? I'm scared."

Mai Lan took a look in the water, and shook her head, "No, it's not too deep, you just hold your breath and hold onto me. I will guide you to the other side, don't panic once we get in the water, no matter what happens, don't breath in the water. Okay can you handle it? We have to hurry; the pirates will be here soon. "Finally, Xuan agreed to dive into the water. Mai Lan took a deep breath then jumped into the water, stayed under for a moment, then she reemerged out of the water and told her friend, "Come on, it's not too bad, you just hold your breath and follow me. The opening is right on the other side of the rock, you can open your eyes under the water. Come in, we don't have much time.

The girl took a deep breath, held on her nose and jumped in the water. Once she was in the water, Mai Lan got a hold of her hand and guided her to the other side of the rock. When they both got out of the water, they found themselves within a large cave that was above the water. The cave was well lit by a small hole in the top of the cave. The temperature in the cave was quite cool, so Mai Lan and the girl had to take their clothes off to dry out, - "It seems to be safe in here. How long are we going to stay here? It's getting cold in here, our clothes are not going to dry."

Mai Lan, slightly pat her on her shoulder, and tried to comfort her with a story, "That's okay, at least we are free from the pirates. You know, a long time ago, when I was younger I always played "hide and seek" with my friends in caves like this one. We stayed in them for hours. At first, it felt a little cool, but later you begin to feel warmer."

Xuan still was skeptical about her future, "How long are we going to stay here? I'm scared; we are going to die here."Her eyes turned red, then tears started rolling down her cheeks, "Hu! Hu! I don't want to die here!"

Mai Lan really wasn't certain about what was going to happen, her teammate was right, how would they get water and food or how long would they have to stay in the cave. The price for freedom was too high, and she was paying for it with her brother's life and now her own.

Nguyen Tam demounted the M-60 machinegun, carried it off along with two boxes of ammunition and an M-16 rifle. It should be enough fire power to eliminate all of the pirates. Nguyen Tam found a concealed rock pile where he placed the machinegun which pointed toward the vessels direction. He was planning to ambush the pirates when they returned to the vessel. One good thing for Nguyen Tam was that he has been trained to operate these types of weapons during the war. He was carefully checking the proper function of the machinegun; he couldn't afford a misfire once he committed to firing. After a while, Nguyen Tam felt that the heat from the fire was less intense. He figured that the pirates had put it out; pretty soon they will return to the vessel. Checking the automated weapon once again, made sure that every part was functioning. He was betting his life on it so he had to make sure the weapons were well prepared. He has to kill most of them so the group might have a chance to survive.

The pirates put out part of the fire but the wind was shifting the flame to another side of the island. Unable to stop the fire, Sami ordered his men try to keep the fire from spreading to the hut where they hide their stolen goods. Sami told them to forget about the fire and to move the goods to the vessel. Sami then went to look for the missing girls. A total of eight pirates began to carry loads of stolen goods out to the boat. One after another they placed a sack on their shoulder and headed back to the vessel.

Nguyen Tam, who was sitting on top of the hill, looked around for anybody to return. He spotted the group of pirates from far away, so he hurried back to the machinegun position and silently waited. Just a few minutes later, the first pirate appeared on the trail, Nguyen Tam pulled the cocking handle, then aimed the gun at the pirate, and took a deep breath. When the last one appears in the firing line, Nguyen Tam would then squeeze the trigger. From what he could tell the entire group of pirates had walked right into Nguyen Tam's trap. The first volley of the M-60 machinegun mowed the pirates down like weeds. Since they carried heavy load on their shoulders, the pirates had no chance to hide or to get away. The sound of the M-60 echoed throughout the entire island like a clap of thunder. Nguyen Tam stopped firing to look for any survivors. He suspected more pirates will come so he remained hiding in his cover. As a senior sergeant with plenty of experiences, he would wait for the enemy to expose themselves. After a moment, he didn't see any survivors. He covered up the gun with branches and leaves, then grabbed the M-16 rifle which he took from the dead pirate on the vessel, and quickly disappeared into the woods to go on a manhunt.

Thuy and the group of women and children kept on running away from the vessel as far as possible. When they heard the sounds of the gunfire, Thuy stopped to listen for a moment, then said, "You all go ahead and get away from here, I will go back to help Tam."

Another woman suggested, "We should do what he told us, I think he can manage without us. Come on, let's get away from here and find a good place to hide before somebody find's us."

Thuy thought for a moment and agreed to continue the run with the group. She knew that they would kill her if she got caught. But she felt bad that she couldn't help Tam, at least stayed side by side with him, something happened to him she's never going to see him again. Sorry that she left Nguyen Tam, Thuy stopped and told the group that she had to go back to help him, "Go! Don't worry! I'll be all right, I have got to go back and help him, I'll be careful."

The older lady waved back to her, "Go! Don't do anything stupid, they kill you."

Thuy, wiping off the sweat on her face raced back to the vessel.

The group of pirates went to searching for the runaway women. They checked all the caves and hill tops. They suddenly heard the M-60 machinegun thundering throughout the island. Should they return to the ship, or continue the search? The senior guy in the group decided to abort the search and to return to the vessel.

Sami joined the search until he heard the thundering sounds from the heavy caliber machine gun. He also turned around and ran back to the vessel, he knew that something really bad happened because they never used the M-60.

Nguyen Tam climbed up the highest hill to observe the whole situation. Exactly as he expected, the group of pirates started to show up out of the thick woods. Nguyen Tam aimed at the last one and squeezed the trigger then low crawled to another position, and then he aimed at the next one and fired. Two shots and two pirates were knocked down causing a lot of confusion among the rest of them. They returned fire back into the general area without any certainty of their opponent's position. They went to check on their buddy's condition, and found they were dead. The pirates cursed and vowed to avenge their shipmates. The remaining pirates divided into two groups. One group would stay and stand guard. The other group would withdraw back to their vessel.

Seeing what was going on, Nguyen Tam quickly climbed back down the hill and had to double time it to the M-60 so he could get ready for the group that was heading back. This is a tactic that Nguyen Tam had learned during the war, create chaos then hit them hard on their retreat. Sami was on his way back to his vessel and suddenly heard two gunshots. He and the rest of the pirates had no idea who or where about all the gunshots were coming from. The island was always deserted and nobody came here, not even the Thai government. His instincts told him to head toward the direction of the gun shots. He needed to find out who fired the shots. This time, Sami cautiously moved through the woods because he knew there was an intruder on the island.

Nguyen Tam beat the group of pirates back to his ambush point. He quickly locked and loaded the ammunition then bowed his head to pray that God would give him strength and courage to fight these evil killers.

A moment later six pirates ran out of the woods. The lead man of the group noticed the dead bodies which laid on the trail, and gave a sign for the rest of the group to halt. The group leaders hand balled into a fist as he franticly scanned the area for an ambush. Then suddenly Nguyen Tam took a deep breath and squeezed the trigger of the M-60, unleashing hot lead into the group of pirates cutting them in half. Nguyen Tam released the trigger and peered into the woods trying to catch a glimpse of the pirates through the cloud of gunpowder's white smoke. He could see the bodies of the pirates lay still after being shredded to pieces by the heavy machine gun. Nguyen Tam smiled and let out a small laugh as he thought about the ironic twist of fate. The pirates, who joyfully killed innocent people, now have met their own demise by the same instrument of death they once used.

Now, Nguyen Tam has eliminated almost the entire crew. The captain who is nowhere to be found is probably still his most formidable enemy. After kill the whole group of pirates, Nguyen Tam slowly got up and bowed his head, said to the soul of his friend Thanh, "Now you can rest in peace, my friend, I enacted your revenge."

Sami heard more gun shots. It more sounded like the M-60 machinegun. Now, it was really throwing him off, maybe the Thai navy found the island and fought with his troops. Now Sami had to take extra caution because he didn't know what or who he was dealing with. Sami carefully advanced from bush to bush for concealment, and he couldn't afford to get caught by the law.

When Sami got down the hill, he saw the bodies of his men, and only one man who stood there alone checking those bodies. He couldn't believe this one man killed all of his people. In a rage of fury

Sami pulled out his pistol and charged toward Nguyen Tam who was still unaware of his presence. Sami aimlessly fired at Nguyen Tam, the first and second shot missed Nguyen Tam, but the third one hit him right on left shoulder. The impact of the bullet knocked Nguyen Tam to the ground. Luckily for Nguyen Tam, the bullet missed the bone and went through his flesh, exited his body. Screaming in pain, Nguyen Tam tried to hold onto his wound to stop the bleeding. Despite his painful wound, he tried to reach for his rifle which lay at his feet. Nguyen Tam got a hold of his rifle and with one hand, he returned fire.

Sami saw his enemy hit the ground. Instead of waiting to see if he was down for good; Sami kept running toward Nguyen Tam who was waiting to finish him off. Nguyen Tam fired a shot and hit Sami in the leg. The bullet struck Sami below his kneecap. The bullet didn't hit the bone but tore the flesh causing Sami a great deal of pain that made him let out an outraged curse. Sami hit the ground from the pain. Sami leaned up to look for Nguyen Tam who now lay unconscious on the ground only a short distance away.

Sami got up and slowly limped toward Nguyen Tam to finish him off. His open wound started to bleed excessively due to his movement. Sami clinched his teeth together and hit the ground once again due to the shearing pain. Sami tore his shirt off to try and make a temporary tourniquet above his wound to stop bleeding. Even through the pain, Sami kept a close eye on the unconscious Nguyen Tam.

Thuy was on her way to return to the vessel when she heard numerous gun shots from the general area of the vessel. She knew that Nguyen Tam was fighting by himself and she wished that she had never left him alone in the first place. When she exited the thick woods, she recognized the pirate leader, Sami. When she saw the pirate leader, her anger sudden escalated, she wanted to run down and kill him. Thuy stopped for a moment and thought to herself, *I really can't win over this evil man just with the stick*, so she silently approached him to try and catch him by surprise.

Sami tightened up his bandage and managed to stop the bleeding and tried to get back up on his feet. The wind shifted spreading the fire toward the boat dock. Sami could feel the heat of the fire getting closer. He knew that without the boat he would be trapped on the island; so he decided to get back to his vessel and to sail away before the fire could get to it. As he approached the boat, Sami called out loud for his men to see if anybody was still alive, but he heard no response.

Nguyen Tam lay still on the ground. The loud voice of the pirate woke him. Nguyen Tam slowly tried to reach for his rifle. Wincing from the pain he cautiously grabbed a hold of the rifle, took a deep breath, and quickly rolled to shield himself behind a rock pile. Just as he dug in behind the rocks, gunshots commenced and bullets ricocheted all around him. Luckily none of the bullet hit him.

Sami lost his balance while firing and took cover this time because he was aware of his opponent was once again armed and dangerous. This temporary setback gave Nguyen Tam more time to prepare for the next attack. Nguyen Tam was losing a lot of blood so he torn part of his shirt, rolled it to a ball, and pressed hard on his wound to stop bleeding. Nguyen Tam removed ammo magazine with the other hand to see how many rounds he had left. Nguyen Tam thought to himself, *only two left in the magazine, he must make them count otherwise he is finished.*

Thuy, who was hiding behind a rock, saw the pirate make his way to the boat. Just as she made up her mind to go to Nguyen Tam, the pirate had already reached the boat and started firing back at Nguyen Tam. Thuy stopped, afraid that might get caught in the cross fire. She had noticed that the pirate was hurt. *Maybe he wasn't as dangerous*, she thought, if she could get close to him, maybe then she could beat him down with the stick. Thuy silently crawled to Sami's position. The love for Nguyen Tam gave Thuy more courage than ever.

Sami reloaded his pistol, thinking the way to destroy his target, he knew the longer he waited the greater risk is going to be; plus he has to get back to his boat, fast. He rechecked on his tourniquet, made sure that it was still tight even though he began to feel numb below his wound, and he knew that he might lose his leg if he waited any longer. He found a stick to assist him to stand up; chances are, he thought, he could charge down there fast before his opponent regained his strength back. The injured leg restricted him from a fast attack, but the urge of revenge has boosted up his might. Sami, with the stick, humped fast to Nguyen Tam's position, and he determined to destroy his target. This time, it was either kill or be killed.

Nguyen Tam, heard the noise, got up and swung his M-16 at the charging pirate, squeezed the trigger. But the dry sound clicked back the chamber without the round; it jammed. It's too late to do anything about that now, severe pain was tearing into half of his body, Nguyen Tam bowed his head low, sweat and tears rolling down on his face, he said a silent prayer, and closed his eyes, waiting.

Sami was using all his strength to achieve a faster pace. His leg was hurting too, even with the tourniquet. Seeing that his opponent's weapon didn't fire, he stopped to take another deep breath, then knelt down to take a good aim at Nguyen Tam, and squeezed the trigger. Suddenly something struck him on the neck and made him jerk the gun to a different direction, and he missed his target. This surprise blow to his neck made him quiet dizzy for a moment, then another strike hit him right on his arm which made him drop his gun, then another whip came right on his open wound, Sami screamed out loud in agony. It was Thuy!

Thuy screamed out for Nguyen Tam's to find out whether he was still alive. About that time, all the women showed up and helped Thuy attack the pirate.

All his life Sami abused women, now it was their turn to abuse him. He was like the wounded beast that got stumped by a bunch of lambs full of vengeance. Half of the women wanted revenge and another half were afraid that he would try to hurt them again, so they kept on beating him until he couldn't move anymore. Thuy saw that the injured pirate couldn't move again, so she halted everybody, "Okay! That's enough, I don't think he's able to hurt us anymore, let's go see how Tam is doing."

Now, Sami was about half dead, all his arms were broken, and his injured leg was turning pale blue because lack of blood flow. He was paying his big debt for all the crimes that he committed.

When Thuy and the group of women found Nguyen Tam who still lay on the ground with his hand pressed on his wound. Thuy ran to him with tears in her eyes, knelt down next to him, and caressed his face which was caked with dirt and sweat, "Tam, are you all right? Are you hurt badly? Your open wound is still bleeding. I have to move you away from here. Can you move at all? The fire is coming soon. I have to go to the boat to find some kind of bandage to wrap your wound; otherwise you will be bled to death. Ladies! Help me to stand him up."

Nguyen Tam opened his tiresome eyes, and looked surprisingly at Thuy; he couldn't believe his eyes, he rubbed it a few times then asked her, "Thuy, is that you? You're Okay! Where is the pirate?"

Thuy slightly pat his shoulder. She gave him a kiss on his forehead and calmed him down, "Don't worry, my love… He can't harm us anymore. You try to stand up; we have to get out of here quick."

With the help of Thuy and another woman, Nguyen Tam tried to get up slowly. He leaned his body toward Thuy and slowly walked.

The fire now engulfed a large part of the shore, and it was getting close to the dock area. Thuy screamed out loud,

"We have to get to the boat before the fire blocks us!"

Nguyen Tam, turned his face to look at Thuy and said, "Thuy, you have to let me down and go to the boat before it's too late, I'm O.K!"

Thuy shook her head, "No! I would never let you stay here all by yourself. We have to get away from the fire."

Nguyen Tam, amazed by the decision that Thuy just made, couldn't believe that Thuy has changed so much. The hardship of their struggle for survival turned Thuy from a soft innocent girl into woman made of steel. Nguyen Tam swallowed his pain, and tried to speed up with the women.

The fire burned up all the trees around the dock. A big tree fell on the wooden dock that leads to the vessel. It blocked the only way to get to it. They had to detour to the other side of the hill to evade the fire; they were asking themselves, if the vessel burns up how they will get away from this island. They prayed that the fire won't destroy it otherwise they will be stuck on this island for a long, long time.

Another group of the girls had been hiding on top of the hill and heard the gunshots, they asked, - "Hey, it sounds like a war is going on down there, may be the government fought with the pirates, what should we do?"

Another girl said, "We have to go down there to see what is going on, we must find Lan and Xuan. Otherwise nobody knows that we're here. You'll stay here; I will go down there to find out what is happening. Don't go anywhere until I get back. Pirates may still be around here." Then she dashed out their hiding place, and went down the hill toward the boat dock.

Mai Lan and her friend still sat inside the cave, the damp air in the cave began infiltrated their respiratory system and caused them some uneasy coughs. Xuan, her teammate, whined again, "Oh my God! I can't breathe, I'm going to die in here. We have to do something, I'm scared. Let's go back outside to see what's going on."

Mai Lan didn't know what to do, she hesitated for a moment and said, "Well, if we go back outside, our clothes will be wet again, and the pirate might still be looking for us. If they catch us, they're going to kill us. I tell you what, you stay in here let me go back outside to check, if everything is Okay I will come back to get you. Okay?"

The girl wiped the tears on her face; she didn't have much choice but to agree. Mai Lan jumped back in the water and swam outside the cave. Once she was out of the water, she heard some loud gunshots from the other side of the island. She thought to herself, *it must be the battle between the government and the pirates.* Mai Lan climbed up the hill to observe the surrounding area, she looked around and saw the fire in the boat dock area but saw no sign of the pirates. She felt it was safe enough to get the girl of the cave. Mai Lan went back inside the cave to get the girl out, she hoped the government won the battle, and then they will be free.

****

The fire was spreading even faster now that it reached the tall grass in the area, plus the south wind was getting stronger. Nguyen Tam and the girls hurried to get out the area, even though the pain was nearly killing him. Thuy said, "We have to get out of here quick. Tam! We will have to carry you from here on."

It wasn't a simple thing to carry Nguyen Tam because of his weight and the wound, if he wasn't stable, he would bleed. One of the woman suggested, "Let take two branches and then get the shirts from the dead bodies. We will button the shirts up within the branches and use it as a handle, so we can carry him easier."

The women hated to mess with the dead bodies, but right now, they had no other choice but do it. So they ran down to the dead pirates and stripped off their shirts. They made a temporary stretcher to carry Nguyen Tam who was almost faint again. They laid Nguyen Tam on the stretcher and carried him out the area.

****

Trinh, a girl from the other group, approached the boat dock area, found Thuy and the group of women who were transporting an injured man. She never saw them before, but she had no doubt that they were probably refugees. *At least they weren't pirates*, she thought. Trinh, asked Thuy, "Hi! I'm so happy to see you all. What is going on? Where are the pirates? Who was fighting with them?"

Thuy, who was surprised, didn't think that there was anybody else on the island. She relaxed when she saw someone who might know their way around, - "Hi, where did you come from? Are you Vietnamese? I think all the pirates are dead." Then Thuy pointed her finger at Nguyen Tam, and proudly said, - "This man killed all the pirates by himself."

Trinh, couldn't believe what she just heard, "Really. Wow! All the pirates are dead. Oh, thank God. A lot of people were killed by these devils. Come on follow me, we need to get out of here quick… let me help you."

Trinh helped Thuy to carry Nguyen Tam to the other side of the island which fire had not yet reached, and they talked along the way; everybody seemed happier since the pirate threat was gone. The main thing now is staying away from the fire, and finding a way to get off the island. Trinh was worried about their future, "I don't know how we're going to get off this island, at least the pirates are dead, but you're sure they all dead? What about the pirate's vessel?"

Thuy couldn't believe that there was another one just as skeptical as her. She wanted to laugh because she used to annoy people asking questions one after another. Thuy tried to answer the best that she could, "Well! I think all the pirates were killed, I hope. Are there more people on this island?"

"Yeah! There are more girls hiding on the other side of the island, we were the ones who started the fire." Trinh replied with pride. "We saved you from being abused by the pirates, the best way we could think of."

Thuy, with her thankful eyes, burst into tears, "You did save me from that mean pirate, one of the ladies was killed right before the fire started, and if not for the fire more of us could have ended up dead."

Sami still lay on the ground motionless. He couldn't move

because his arms and legs were broken. The fire approached him within yards, and he felt the deadly heat to begin blanket his body. He screamed out loud for help but nobody was there to help.

The fierce fire engulfed the Sami and his lungs were drained of air and began to burn, he began to hallucinate because of lack of air to his brain; he was seeing a vision of hell, in which all of his men were waiting to drag him in with them.

****

The rescue choppers from the Thai Royal Navy dispatched on another search mission, this time they searched a wider pattern. It has been two days since the last report from the Thai Coast Guard ship. The Navy department had tried their best to search for the lost boat. They had to cover the large part of the Gulf of Siam, still couldn't find the where about of the vessel. The department however, was aware of the pirate problem that had infested the area. They had no evidence of any lethal contact between the government and the outlaws. The search crew will report any suspected ship, and will attack any ship which refused the search order.

The rescue helicopters flew high to widen their view; this was the last mission for search and rescue. The pilot spotted black smoke rising from the blue horizon, and reported back to the headquarters for orders, "Big bird! This is Dragonfly, over!"

"This is Big Bird! Go ahead Dragonfly, over!" Headquarters responded.

"We found a huge black smoke at South East Gulf of Siam, request permission to investigate the cause of the smoke, over!"

Few minutes later, the Thai Royal Navy granted the permission, "Dragonfly! This is Big Bird. Permission granted, be aware of hostile fire from bandits. How is your fuel level? Don't get caught short over!"

The pilot veered his chopper eastward, "This is Dragonfly...our fuel is fine thanks for the advice. Roger out!"

****

Mai Lan returned to the cave, and when she got back she found the girl was lying on the ground shivering. The girl body's temperature had dramatically dropped and hypothermia was setting in fast. She took her clothes off, and held the little girl tight to her body and used her body heat to warm the girl up. She massaged Xuan's whole body, and tried to circulate the blood flow through her cold body. After a while, Xuan began to regain consciousness. She opened her eyes, and tears were flowing down her cheeks. Mai Lan felt so sorry for the girl, embraced her, and tried to comfort her. "Are you alright? You scared me. Soon you will feel better and I will take you back outside. It's getting too cold in here."

The little girl nodded her head and gave Mai Lan a thankful hug, "Thank you for save my life, after you left, I felt cold all over. I didn't know what to do. I'm scared!"

Mai Lan caressed her cheeks and calmed her down, "Soon you feel better and we can get you back outside, I promise. You know, I had a little brother too.

Xuan opened her eyes big with surprise, "Oh, I didn't know you have a brother, where is he?"

Mai Lan, with a sad voice, looked at the thin streak of light piercing into the top of the cave, with tears rolling down her cheeks, she pictured the figure of her brother, "He was killed when the pirates sunk our boat, and I couldn't even look at his face when he died."

Mai Lan wiped the tears off her face, and then checked the girl's body temperature one more time before entering the cold water, "Okay Are you ready to jump in the water now? You will feel better as soon as you get some sunlight. All right, let's go!"

The young girl, still felt weak and was afraid of the cold water, anxious to leave the cave, she got ready to jump in the water, and "I'm ready to get out of here!"

Mai Lan, held the girl's hand, made sure that she's was ready, "Well! You seem okay we will do it like the last time, don't panic and don't breathe in. Now take a deep breath and jump in."

When they both were out of the water, Xuan was choking on salt water and she looked so miserable. Mai Lan prayed that no pirate would find them here naked like this. They both would be in a lot of trouble. She let the girl down on the beach, and then climbed up the hill to observe any incoming pirates. There was no sign of an intrusion but she noticed the fire was spreading quickly engulfing the small island.

The group of women carried Nguyen Tam to the other side of the island which was temporarily out of the fires range. They put him down under a shady tree, then Thuy went to look for some clean water. Nguyen Tam's wound seemed to have stopped bleeding, he felt so tired and helpless, wondering, when he was going to get out of this miserable situation.

Thuy found a spring of water nearby the area, screaming with joy, she threw herself in the water and indulged her thirst. After quenching her thirst with the cold water, Thuy called out for others to come. She found a big leaf and made a bow out of it, then carried some water back to Nguyen Tam. The girls were all happy when they heard a voice, "That's Thuy's letting us know that she found water. My God, I'm almost dying of thirst, let's go get some water."

Everybody was worried about getting away from the fire. Forgetting their throats were burning because the heat and smoke, now they had the urge for water. The girls ran toward the direction where Thuy called out, they all dove in the spring and drank as fast as they could. After they took care of their thirst, they all laid on the green grass watching a silver cloud slowly floating in the clear blue sky, and felt the fresh breeze softly caress their faces. This is the first time that they were able to enjoy the natural beauty of the island without the fear of anything. After a short moment of resting, they suddenly heard the sound of a helicopter rotor from some distance. One of the girls got up, and pointed her finger toward the direction that the sound was come from and shouted, "It's the sound of a helicopter, the Thai Government must be coming to rescue us!"

Other girls also heard the sound of an approaching aircraft. They all got up and listened for it.

Thuy gave the water to Nguyen Tam little by little; she gently wiped the blood and mud off his face. They both also heard the helicopter's sound. Nguyen Tam turned his head toward the direction of the incoming aircraft. After determining that it was the sound of a helicopter; Nguyen Tam turned his head, told Thuy to signal the helicopter. "Thuy, you have to go to the beach and do anything to show the pilot that we're still on the island. If they don't see us they will leave us here, it's important that you get them to see that somebody is here. Now, go! Leave me here, I'm Okay!"

Thuy gave him some more water and then got up to run to beach. On the way to the beach Thuy stopped and shouted at the other women, "Hey, sisters! We have to go to the beach so the helicopter can see us. That's the Thai government's helicopter. Come on, quick!"

The girls, just like waking up out of the dream, took off running to the beach.

****

The pilot, from the rescue helicopter, hovered around the dock area which was now engulfed by the fire. He saw the pirate vessel but no one on it. A little later, he found: dead bodies lying around so he called to headquarters to report the scenario, "Big bird! This is Dragonfly! Over.

A static response through the intercom from Headquarters came through, "Dragonfly, this is Big Bird, go ahead, Over!"

The pilot lowered his craft in order to observe more details and reported back, "This is Dragonfly, I see a lot of dead bodies. It looks like as if a war was going on. There's also a big vessel with a weird flag, what I should do?"

A moment later, the response came back from headquarters, "Dragonfly…this is Big Bird…be aware of the hostile fire, it's possibly a pirate ship. Wait for back up which is on the way. Good luck… over and out!" The pilot gave a positive response then veered off to another direction to look for anymore possible survivors.

****

When Thuy and the girls got to the beach, they found Xuan, the girl from the previous group, was buried with just her head showing in the white sand. They came to her to find out what was going on. Thuy shook the young girl's shoulder and asked, "Hey! Are you Okay? What is happening to you? Are there more of you around?"

The young girl slowly opened her exhausted eyes, showing her gladness to see her native people. Thuy just realized that she asked too many questions to the sick girl so she wiped the sand off of her face. About that time, Mai Lan got back to the girl, she screamed out in joy, "Hi, how are you? I'm glad to see you here." Then she pointed her finger at Xuan, explaining, "She is hypothermic, I buried her in the hot sand to help her to regain her body heat. What happened down there, I heard a lot of gun shots, are any pirate still alive?"

Thuy shook her heady yes and answered, "Yes, we disabled the pirate leader, he was tough. We are glad that he can't hurt anyone anymore." Mai Lan, with her eyes opened wide, half surprised and with disbelief broken down crying, "My little brother was killed by this evil man, now that he is dead, may his soul rest in peace."

The sound of the helicopter approached the beach. The girls were so happy and hopeful. Thuy knelt down on the sand, bowed her head and silently prayed to God for the good things to come. The rest of the girls also knelt down and joined Mai Lan in prayer. Everyone had a lost member of their family sometime during the raid. In the mean time, the helicopter approached and hovered above their heads. The girls immediately got up and waved their arms to the helicopter. The pilot recognized that there were people on the beach. He then made a wide circle and then lowered down to almost eye level to observe the whole situation below. The pilot saw the sick girl lying on the sand motionless. The pilot realized that the girl needed medical attention right away. He landed the craft, and two Thai rescue medics raced toward the sick girl.

The pilot reported back to the headquarters the overall situation, "Big bird... this is Dragonfly, over."

"Dragonfly…this is big Bird, go ahead!" headquarters responded, "There are women on this island, one is seriously injured, no hostiles are present. I sent the medics to help the sick girl. It seems like the hostiles are all dead. Haven't seen the good guys yet, stand by… over!"

"Dragonfly…this is Big Bird, your back up will arrive in approximately ten minutes…over and out!"

The two medics rushed to Xuan and they wrapped her body with a thermal blanket. When finished with her treatment, Thuy begged the two of them to go treat for Nguyen Tam. Thuy had a problem communicating with the medics who only understood Thai, and she finally figured out the way to convey her meaning by pointing at the sick girl and then pointed her finger at the woods. She knelt down to beg them to go help Nguyen Tam. One of the medics finally understood that there was another sick or injured person who might need help. He turned his short wave radio on to clear with the crew chief, "Dragonfly, this is Doc! I might have another injured person somewhere in the woods, request permission to go in for first-aid over!"

Then a static voice responded from the crew chief, "Doc, one of you goes check for an injured person. If it's not safe, return and wait for back up. Be careful over and out!"

Doc responded, "Roger out."

The medic told the other medic to stay with the girl until he got back, then turned to Thuy and told her to take him there.

Thuy was so happy, after she respectfully bowed her head to say thank to the medic she then rushed him to Nguyen Tam's position. Thuy was happy, screaming with joy to Nguyen Tam, "Tam! I got someone who can help you, hang on. You're O.K now. The Government is here to help us."

Nguyen Tam, raising his head up to look at the upcoming person, saw Thuy and the medic so he lay back down and gave Thuy a thankful look. The medic went to work on his wound right away; he cleaned it up and applied a temporary bandage. He gave him an antibiotic shot and a shot of morphine to help ease the pain. Then he told Thuy, by using his hand gesture, to move Nguyen Tam to the beach front. Thuy bowed her head again to show her appreciation for helping Nguyen Tam, then she went back to get some help to move Nguyen Tam.

Xuan, the young sick girl, was gaining some of her strength back; the thermal blanket did help a lot. Mai Lan gave her a little bit more water; the other medic gave her a piece of chocolate. It had been a whole day since both of the girls had anything to eat. Xuan was so hungry, she ate the chocolate to fast and almost choked. Mai Lan told her, "Hey girl, slow down, otherwise you're going to choke to death. That's Okay now, you're going to have a lot of food when the Thai Government gets here."

Just about the time Mai Lan finished her sentence, another helicopter hovered above their heads trying to find a place to land. She pointed her finger at the aircraft, smiling, "See! What did I tell you, hang on, we will get you out of here soon. You look better now, I guess that piece of chocolate did help you." Xuan gave a little smile, something that she had not done for a long time.

Thuy and three other girls carried Nguyen Tam out of the woods. They placed him on the white sand; waiting to see what the Thai authority were going to do.

Two crew chiefs were discussing what to do when one of the chief pointed his finger toward the fire, "The fire is spreading hard on the West side of the island, which burnt a lot of dead bodies there, and we don't know who these people are exactly. They can't be the good guys. Somebody must have killed these bad guys. I saw no resistance on the island. We're not sure that the bad guys are all dead. We should call the Navy and let them handle the search, after all our mission is rescue, what you think?"

Another crew chief thought about it for a moment, then reported to headquarters, "Big Bird… this is Dragonfly, over."

"Dragonfly…this is Big Bird, go ahead, over."

"Big Bird, half of the island is on fire, a lot of dead bodies lying around; we don't know who fought with whom. There is one injured individual with bullet wound to his shoulder, possibly a Vietnamese refugee. You want us to wait for the Navy to check it out, or are we to handle the search. We're not for sure that the bad guys all gone, we also have a lot of young women here. We have no idea where these women came from or how they got here. We can transport all the personnel out of here, and the Navy can come here and secure the island. One more thing, there's a vessel still untouched. We don't know whether anybody is still in there. This is the Situation Report from Dragonfly, waiting for your order over."

"Dragonfly acknowledged your situation report. Stand by for your order. The Navy will come to search the entire island. You and your company will stay there and secure the area. The Navy speed boat will be there in a few hours. Stay alert for any incoming hostiles. The area has been known to be infested with pirates."

"Dragonfly, roger out."

The crew chief of the Dragonfly was in charge of the operation. He left a medic and a coast guard agent to stay with the women and the injured individuals. Then both of the crafts went on their way to observe the situation on the rest of the island.

The Thai coast guard agent sat next to Nguyen Tam, light up a cigarette and gave it to him, and started to ask him questions about what is going on. They both only comprehended each other by using English which is their second language. They both barely comprehended each other. Nguyen Tam, while in the war, learned to speak English through his American counterpart. The coast guard agent pointed at his wounded shoulder, asked, "How you get hurt?"

Nguyen Tam used his finger to draw on the white sand the picture of the skull with the cross bones, the pirate flag, spoke in broken English, "The sea robbers, very bad people, I killed most of them with the M-60 machinegun."

The agent, with his eyes full of surprise, didn't really believe what Nguyen Tam just said, - "You!" he pointed his finger at Nguyen Tam. "You all by yourself?"

Nguyen Tam smiled, tried to find the word to describe the battle between him and the pirates, he pointed his finger at himself and answered with pride, "Yes, me."

The coast guard checked on his wound asking, "Who shot you? You're lucky! Are you O.K? By the way, where did you come from?"

Nguyen Tam, reluctantly answered the questions, the morphine working on him now, his eyes began feeling heavy and his voice was cutting off, "The mean guy…huh…he is the last one. I shot him in his leg…sorry, I'm so sleepy…" Then Nguyen Tam closed his eyes lid, exhausted he dosed off.

Xuan, the sick girl, could get up now but was still too tired to move around; so she sat on the white sand and looked at the clear blue sky. Thinking back to the day that she was home with the same white sand and the same coconut trees along the beach created a monotone music every time the light breeze blew through. The tranquility of the surroundings along with everyone exhaustion slowly put the people to sleep.

Xuan used to like to stay out on the beach late in the evening, looking at the blue horizon toward the West. She wished that she could fly over the water to land known as the rich country which was full of opportunities; which the people called "America". Born at the end of the South Government, Xuan's family owned a big business in the beach area. Then the northern government took over the country. They also took over her family's business. Becoming poor over night, her father went insane, her mother sold everything they had, and moved to the coast area.

They heard about the opportunities oversea like "America" or some other rich country from the west. Then one day her mother decided to take a risk and cross the ocean to find freedom and new opportunities. She sold everything they had and paid a connection that would help them to cross the Gulf of Siam then enter to Thailand. From there they might get selected to go to America. There were risks that they had to accept but still they went for it. Her mother ended up getting killed when the pirates robbed and destroyed their escape boat. They held Xuan captive until now. Watching the silver cloud freely floating, the tide beating on the shore, all seemed so free and peaceful now, finally Xuan could let out a sigh of relief.

****

The chopper hovered above the vessel and the pilot managed to drop two coast guard agents on the vessel to check its interior. They carefully moved around because someone might still be inside the vessel. Before they advanced into the cabin they yelled to warn anybody to give it up, "This is Thailand Coast Guard. We advise you to surrender immediately!"

After a short moment, a young voice responded to the agents in Thai, "Don't shoot! I'm coming out. I'm not with the pirates."

A young man came out with his hands on his head. He showed no sign of hostility or a rebellious attitude. He looked at the agents with obedient eyes. One of the agents ordered him to lie down on the floor, "Advance slowly and lie on the floor, put your hand on your head, don't move."

One of the agents carefully approached the young boy, cuffed his hands and ordered him to sit still. Before they went down to check the vessel, they questioned the young man, "Are you with the people who owned the vessel, does anybody still hide inside the vessel?"

The young man shook his head, answered, "No, only me here. They all left the vessel to go put out the fire. That's all I know. They don't tell me anything."

"Okay you stay here. We will go down to check around. When we get back, if nothing happens like you say, we let you go free."

The young man bowed his head low, a sign of respect and agreement, promising that he would not do anything stupid, "No Sir! I wouldn't do anything wrong."

The two agents carefully advanced down the stairway, and they found that people were in a hurry to leave their meals that were half finished. Then they found the Captain's cabin door was locked. One agent kicked open the door while the other pointed their rifles at it in case someone in there and would try to attack. They found no one in the room but discovered a lot of jewelry and money hiding in one of the old trunks. The agents looked at each other, confused, and asked, "What should we do with all the money and jewelry, are we going to turn them in to the government?"

Another agent suggested to his partner, "What do you think? This guy stashed a lot of money and jewelry, that's unusual for a fisherman who has a lot of money like him; this is not a normal fishing boat, what do you think?"

"Yes, I think you are right this is not a normal boat. Let's go down see if they have anything else."

Carefully descending the narrow steps, two agents entered the storage room which contained food, beverage, and some, weaponry. One of the agents screamed out loud in surprise, "Hey! Look here. Man, these guys were carrying heavy weapons M-72 Law. I bet you these as...holes were bandits! They probably were the ones who attacked the Coast Guard boat. With these weapons, they could easily take down the boat."

His partner couldn't believe the weapons they just found. He kept shaking his head, in disbelief. "Man, I cannot believe this. These guys must be drug smugglers...got stopped by the coast guard then they blew them up. We should report this right away."

"Yes, we will, but first, we have to check the rest of the vessel. We have to make sure that nobody is still hiding."

When they got to the storage room, they heard a noise in the corner of a darker room. One of the agents shined the flashlight and found two young children who sat close to each other. Their faces were caked with mud and sweat. Their small bright eyes were full of tears and fear, and their skeletal bodies were telling of days of starvation. When the light first hit their eyes, they covered up with their little hands, and screamed out loud for their parents. The agent slowly approached the children and gave them a piece of chocolate to insure that he wasn't the bad guy.

PART 3

"Team Alpha, we believe that we might have found those who sunk the coast guard speedboat. All those who are still alive will be detained and well guarded, over!"

"Team Alpha, acknowledge your transmission, will comply. We have one heavily injured…believe he is still alive; we will do our best to rescue him. Over."

"Is there anyone else still alive?"

"Yes, there is another one who is also injured. He claimed that he killed all these guys by himself. We believe that he is a Vietnamese refugee, can't understand him too well. The way I understand it, these guys are some kind of pirates. We saw a lot of dead bodies beside the stolen goods. It looks like they tried to move out of the fire. It's hard to believe one man could eliminate the whole gang of pirates."

"Team Alpha, message understood, we want to keep this man alive. He might be the fugitive who the Thai Police have been looking for."

"Team Alpha, will do. Over and out!"

The lieutenant in charge took another look at the casualties. The heat had roasted his face and it was hard to recognize that is was a human being. He looked at the motionless body and couldn't believe that he was still alive. "Headquarters wanted information out of this survivor, otherwise," the lieutenant mumbled to himself, "I wouldn't want to waste any effort on this guy anyway."

By now the two soldiers just found the route to approach Sami. They finally reached Sami's position and put him on the stretcher, then hauled him out of the burning field. One of the soldiers looked at Sami and said, "This is your lucky day. You're just about half roasted. If you make it, your mama probably won't recognize you either."

Hurrying to place the man's body on the stretcher, another soldier didn't want to waste any more time, "Come on man! Quit messing around, lets' get the hell out of here before you get your ass roasted like his."

Sami was still unconscious but at least he was spared, just inches away from death. Then the wind suddenly got stronger and black clouds covered most of this part of the island. A moment later a big rain swept in put out most of the fire in the area. After the rain, everything seemed green again although the hottest part was still smoldering. The island came back to an innocent and peaceful atmosphere, which also produced more fresh air.

Mai Lan and the girls sat underneath a big tree sheltered from the rain; watching the curtain of water showering the beachfront. Everybody was quiet. The rain reminded them the monsoon season at home. Being alone in this strange land which is so far from home, the girls were getting homesick. Mai Lan remembered after the rain, she and her brother folded paper to the shape of a boat then let it float down the water current. Now she had nobody to share with.

Tears silently rolled down her cheeks. Xuan, the young girl, looked at her sad face. She also felt sad because she lost her family, too. Both girls squeezed their hands tight together, sharing their hurt, hoping for a better day.

Now that the rain put out the fire, the soldiers could come close to the bodies and identify them. Some of the bodies were burnt to bones. One of the Navy investigators took pictures of all the dead bodies and gave his comment to the lieutenant, "Seems like these guys were slammed by the heavy caliber machine guns. They must have come to pick up their stuff and got ambushed. Who did all this killing?"

"I was told that it was one guy. A Vietnamese refugee shot all these guys with a M-60 machinegun."

"But where did he get it from?"

"That I don't know. Probably from the vessel, if the kid told the truth about what he heard yesterday, I wouldn't doubt that these guys were the ones who shot our Coast guard speedboat. If the injured people we just saved are lucky enough to live, he could tell us the whole story."

"You think he is going to make it?"

"He is hurt pretty bad. He is probably losing his leg. He applied a tourniquet, but waited too long."

"If the bastard is found guilty he will be hanged. What about all the girls, where the hell did they came from?"

"We don't know exactly, but they were held captive on this island for a few weeks."

"These fishermen must be pirates or drug smugglers. They will probably sell these girls to some whorehouse in Bangkok. They only speak Vietnamese.

"Yeah, I think they're Vietnamese all right. Boat people, I guess."

"Lieutenant, what do you want to do with the bodies?"

"After you take all your pictures, we will bury them all."

"That's a big job lieutenant. These bodies were half burnt. Wish we can get a hell out of here quick."

"As soon you get your job done, get our guys to bury these bodies, and then we can get out of here."

"Yes, Sir!"

The sun came back with its full intensity, vaporizing the rainwater, creating a humid atmosphere. Everybody wanted to leave the spooky island as soon as possible. The soldiers began digging a big grave to bury the corpses. The girls were busy bringing fruit to offer to the soldiers. In return they gave the girls some dry food. After the soldiers buried the bodies, the sun went down in the West taking with it the uncomfortable heat. A soothing breeze fanned the fresh ocean air. Some of the soldiers asked permission to get into the water to wash off their sticky bodies, "Lieutenant, can we get in the water. Man, I'm dying to swim the clear blue water."

"Yes, but we still have to secure the beach. Divide into two teams. One can take a break and do whatever, and another team still has to maintain guard duty. Remember, we have to get back to the ship."

"Yes, sir!"

Mai Lan sat on the beach, watching the soldiers indulge in the oceans peacefulness, she found it hard to believe that just hours ago, there was so much death. Mai Lan showed the soldiers to Xuan saying, "You know, I don't think the soldiers knew what happened to us. Now that we're free, this island seems prettier, before it was hell to me. I really thought that we might die here."

"Yes, me too, but do you think they're going to take us out of here?"

"I think so. I guess they won't leave us here alone. The Thai Government will probably keep us for awhile and then some country may want to take us. Hopefully the Americans will take us."

"Do you like America? I heard people are very rich and there are good jobs."

"How do you know?"

"Well, I heard my neighbor talking about it. Her sister owned a nail shop in California and she has a lot of money. She bought her mother a brand new house."

Mai Lan asked, "What kind of nails, our fingernails?"

"Yes, our fingernails."

Still skeptical about it, Mai Lan asked again, "How could she be rich, just doing nails?"

"Oh, no it's more than that, they make the nails look longer and prettier, too."

"I still don't get it, how did she get so rich?"

"I don't know, she said she saved a lot of money."

"You know, if we're lucky enough to come to America, we would be rich like her," Mai Lan finished. "Perhaps we'll be rich too."

The soldiers finished cleaning themselves off and got ready to return to their base. The lieutenant dispatched a team combined with Navy personnel and Marines to take the vessel back to headquarters for further investigation. In their mind, they have an idea who sunk of the Coast Guard vessel.

Because of the limitation of space on the Navy cruiser, the girls had to embark on the fishing vessel. They didn't want to return on the same vessel where their loved ones had died. Xuan was worried when the girls were told to embark on the evil pirate vessel. She whispered with Mai Lan, "Sister, where are they taking us to? Why on this spooky vessel. It makes me sick every time I look at it."

Mai Lan said, "That's all right. We'll be okay. I don't think the government has enough room for all of us. That's why we have to ride on this vessel. Besides, they don't know how we feel about this vessel. Soon we will arrive in Thailand and we'll be all right."

The women, who had lost their children, found them still alive and were so happy to see them again. They got down on her knees to thank God who had saved her children, "Thank you God, thank you God! I thought that I never see my children again. Oh God, please don't separate us ever again." Then she embraced her children tight in her arms with tears rolling down there eyes. With the assistance of the young man who had been here before, the vessel slowly departed away from the island taking the people to a new home.

Without the pirates, the vessel seemed more peaceful and returned to its original innocent. The girls asked for permission to go to the kitchen to prepare some food. The sergeant in charge released the young man so he could help the girls in the kitchen, since he claimed that he was once a cook. This was the first time that Mai Lan got to look at him real close, he has more Vietnamese in him than his native race, she thought. The young man suddenly looked back at her and smiled. Mai Lan quickly turned her eyes away. He is probably about her age, she thought, pretty good-looking guy. A moment later, she mustard all her strength and approached him. She bowed her head and said, "Thank you for saving my life. If not for you, that devil probably would have done something bad to me." Her eyes sparkled with tears while she spoke to him.

The young man didn't know what to say but he took her tiny hand and placed it on his chest, then spoke in her native language, "That's all right. I couldn't stand to see that man hurt you."

Mai Lan felt electrified when the young man held her hand. Beside her fiancé, nobody has ever touched her hands before. The young man, had never touched a girl's hand before, but to Mai Lan, he had some special feelings for her. He embraced her hand like a precious gem. Both were frozen for a moment after the initial contact, the young man let her hand go free.

Mai Lan was embarrassed in front of other women, but one woman praised the young man for his kindness, "He is a good man. He brought food to us when we were hungry. I don't think he is with the pirate anyway. He is good looking; I think that he likes you."

Mai Lan tried to look a different way. She felt that the young man had a special feeling for her. She tried to avoid his attention by staying busy preparing the meal with the other women. It wasn't that she didn't like him, but she didn't want to venture into another love affair, not yet anyway.

The women killed a couple chickens and prepared a simple but very tasty meal and offered some to the soldiers. The young man sat with the females, keeping his eyes secretly on Mai Lan. Xuan recognized the sparks in the young man's look and whispered to Mai Lan, "Hey sister, that handsome guy really likes you, I caught him looking at you several times. How does he know you?

Embarrassed, Mai Lan said, "Long ago, he saved me. I will tell you later. Right now, just ignore him, let's eat."

The young man had the feeling that he was being noticed by the females, so he stopped looking at Mai Lan. Now it was his turn to be stared at.

Xuan looked at him then looked at Mai Lan and suggested, "Wow, I think you would look good together. I know he's crazy about you."

Mai Lan, hit Xuan on her shoulder, "I like him too, but it is just not the right time. Anyway, I already have someone waiting for me back home. Besides, he is my savior. I don't want him to feel bad. So don't talk about it anymore."

Xuan nodded her head in agreement and said, "Yeah, you're right."

When they finished dinner it was getting dark. The ocean allowed everybody to enjoy the calm and peacefulness. Mai Lan pointed her finger at the huge moon that reflected a shining light on top of the water creating a giant tapestry put together with million pieces of silver.

It was getting late, the nice fresh breeze and the monotone sound from the ocean water beating on the hull of the boat relaxed everyone. They lay on the deck and watched the millions of stars sparkling in the sky. Xuan sat next to Mai Lan, pointed at the stars and asked, "Has anybody ever counted all these stars? I tried it once, I couldn't count them all."

Trying not to laugh, Mai Lan felt sorry for her ignorance and pretended, "Wow, you counted all the stars? I don't think I can do that."

Then Mai Lan closed her eyes and recaptured the scenario which included her fiancé in it. Such sweet memories that could never be forgotten. It would be nice if he was right here with her now. Xuan with her eyes wide open, counted the stars, again.

The chopper brought Nguyen Tam to the Navy hospital, where a surgeon waited for his arrival. They treated his wound immediately. Nguyen Tam lost a lot of blood but he was stable. His AB+ blood type wasn't easy to come by, so the staff asked around to see who would donate the blood. Finally, they found a sailor with the same blood type who was willing to donate some of his blood. Because Nguyen Tam was the key witness, headquarters gave the specific order to save his life at all cost. After making sure that the blood supply was sufficient, the surgeon began to work on Nguyen Tam. Waiting for Nguyen Tam, Thuy kept praying for him, she was worried about him. At least, she thought, they were in the Thai's governments hands. Although her body was tiny, she tiptoed trying to peek in the window to look at Nguyen Tam who was being treated. A half hour later, a nurse came to Thuy gave her a sign meaning that Nguyen Tam was okay. Thuy was so happy that she screamed joyfully and bowed her head to show her appreciation. The nurse shared in Thuy's joy by embracing her and wished them well.

The chopper transported Sami to the naval emergency hospital. At this time, nobody was certain who he was. Perhaps later, naval intelligence would find out his identity. Upon his arrival, they rushed him to the trauma center where they decided whether to amputate his leg or not. Sami was badly burned throughout his whole body. It was kind of hard to recognize who he was now because of the burns and blood oozing. After carefully releasing his tourniquet, the doctor decided to cut his leg off in order to save his life.

The vessel that carried the girls and its secret fortune was steadily moving toward its destination. The first sparkling rays of sunlight illuminated the dark blue horizon. Mai Lan sat quietly viewing the splendid show of nature. The sound from the flock of seagulls hunting for bait fish echoed from a distance. Along the edge of the immense horizon, suddenly appeared a dark line along its edge. Mai

Lan got up quickly and blocked the sunlight from her brow for a better view. She screamed, "Wake up Xuan. I see the land, I see the land. We are saved."

Xuan, got up and looked in that direction and was happy to see the land, yelling, "Wake up everybody, we see the land." Now everybody was waking up and looking at the land that you could now see clearly.

Not too far from the shore, another vessel was patiently waiting. Upon recognizing the pirate vessel, the captain ordered the crew to start up the engine and to be ready for the delivery of the girls that were promised by Sami. They weren't aware of the situation since there was no communications made since last night. Through his binoculars, he sensed something was wrong with the vessel. Because of the distance, the captain wasn't really sure about the pirate ship and had tried to radio but failed to reach Sami.

In the mean time, the oncoming vessel began slowing down while approaching the land. Now everybody was on deck looking toward the land. The girls, motionless, nervously looked at their new home full of hope. Xuan tapped on Mai Lan's shoulder, pointed at the land and said, "It looks like our country, right. But it is completely different. I heard that we may get selected to go to America if we are lucky."

"Yeah well, any country will be all right, I guess. As long as we are alive and well, I don't care. Just hope that we don't end up in some communist country."

"That would be awful. Try to run away from one then fall into another. I would rather return to my country than to live in another communist country."

"I heard that Communist China accepted some refugees, but I'm afraid to go there."

"Hey look!" Xuan pointed her finger at the coast line and shouted, "Looks like a vessel is coming toward our boat. I hope they aren't pirates."

Mai Lan looked in the direction Xuan pointed and saw a vessel speeding up to them. She didn't know what was their business was but the oncoming boat seemed like they were up to something. Mai Lan said, "You shouldn't be worried too much. What can they do to us? The Thai soldiers will be here shortly if anything happens, we're pretty close to the coast line anyway. Okay?"

The captain of the oncoming vessel observed the scenario of another vessel through his binocular and saw the women on the deck. He was pretty sure that these women were to be delivered to him. Smiling he ordered the crew be ready for the pickup.

The Thai Navy crew also noticed the strange ship approaching their vessel at a fast speed. They alerted the crew to get ready for the encounter. For the safety of the women and children, they were asked to move down below.

The senior ranking officer in charge immediately radioed to the headquarters to report, "Big Bird, This is Blue Water. Come in over!"

The response from Headquarters was loud and clear through the radio, "Blue Water, this is Big Bird, over!"

"Big Bird, we have an unknown visitor trying to intercept us head on. What should we do?"

"Blue water, the best thing is to avoid confronting them. We will send you more help right away, over and out."

It was foggy in that area, so the captain himself didn't realize that he was head on with the pirate vessel, which he thought was going to stop for the delivery according to their plan.

The former pirate vessel, governed by the Thai Navy personnel, veered in a different direction to avoid colliding with another vessel.

The captain of the pickup vessel realized the boat tried to ignore his presence, or maybe they didn't recognize him. Perhaps they didn't want to deliver as they promised. Sami has drawn the money in advance, so the delivery is a done deal. Confused by the act of the other vessel, the captain cursed in anger and drove his vessel around to follow it. Then drew his pistol and fired at the pirate's vessel. One bullet struck the cabin and shattered the glass into pieces.

The marines returned fire at the pursuing vessel with automatic weapons spraying the second boat with bullets. He had been doing business with Sami for a quite long time. Sami never broke his promises and left them alone. One individual got hit in the chest. The rest of the crew hit the floor fast and some tried to grab a weapon to fight back. Finally seeing the counter force on the other boat and the marine uniforms, the captain aborted the chase. He had no desire to confront the Thai army.

The officer in charge received a radio transmission from two helicopters approaching their way, "Blue water, this is Dragon Fire. We are two minutes away from you. What is your situation, over!"

"This is Blue water! We just returned fire and they seem to be getting away from us. They are armed. Check them out over and out."

"Roger out."

Acknowledging their targets, the crew chiefs prepared their armament for the battle.

The captain tried to veer away from the pirate vessel. However, two Navy helicopters were already in the line of sight. Next thing he knew two huge explosions rocked his vessel and two columns of water splashed over his boat, he knew then the Government had arrived. Two navy helicopters hovered on top of the vessel. They began calling out to the crew to drop their weapons and surrender. The crew themselves, weren't trained for heavy combat and under the pressure of the fire power, they quickly laid their weapon down and surrendered.

PART 4

Four agents in the Thai Navy uniform rappelled down, and seized the control of the vessel. They ordered everybody to sit still on the deck, and then applied restraints to all of them.

The women and children were gathered in the kitchen below when they heard some thundering noises from distant. They were all frightened and held on to each other. The huge shock wave created by the explosions shook the vessel, and all the can goods in the kitchen fell on the floor causing a big mess. Suddenly everybody heard a soft scream from one of the women, "Oh my God! Take a look at all this jewelry! These bastards must have hid them in here."

Everybody got up and moved toward the area where the jewelry was spotted. They helped pick the gold out of a grease can and Mai Lan recognized her little brother's necklace. She burst out crying, "This necklace with the small cross belonged to my little brother. I took it off and hid it in the boat before the pirates got us. Can I please have it back?"

"Sure, we're going to divide the jewelry equally to everyone here. We all lost something to the evil pirates. Here, you can have your brother's necklace, and may his soul rest in peace."

Holding her brother's necklace in her hand; Mai Lan felt like her little brother was still around and she knelt down to pray for her brother. Xuan knelt down by her side, and joined the group in prayer. Once finished, they divided the jewelry equally to all the people on the boat. The newly found treasure could be very useful to them in the future once they arrived in their new country. For the survivors, it seemed that all the hardships were over.

Thuy stood next to Nguyen Tam. She lightly blotted Nguyen Tam's face with a hot towel. He had been sleeping for quite a long time. The shoulder wound wasn't bothering him as much so the Thai authority allowed Thuy to take care of him.

Once Nguyen Tam regained his strength, the Thai government wanted to bring in a Vietnamese translator to investigate the whole mess. Thuy wanted to use this opportunity to reach out to her older brother who was in America. She wanted to let him know her whereabouts but she didn't know how. *Perhaps when Nguyen Tam got up he would know what to do*, she thought.

Sami was still unconscious when they brought him in. He had a third degree burn on his body, two broken arms and a severely wounded knee. The surgeon carefully examined his leg wound and decided to amputate his leg in order to save his life. They had orders from the Navy headquarters to do their best to save his life. Sami was the only one who could answer questions about the missing coast guard speedboat. The successful operation took about a half an hour and Sami was still left in a deep coma.

The former pirate vessel which carried the women and children safely landed at the Navy Bay. Waiting at the dock were the Thai immigration agents, the police and some Vietnamese translators. This was the first time that the Thai government had to deal with such a bizarre situation. There were reports about Thai pirates' in the Gulf of Siam, but no witnesses had ever survived. The women and children became nervous when they saw all the authorities lined up at the dock. Xuan squeezed Mai Lan's hand hard, "Sister, look at all the people who are waiting for us. Will they put us in jail? God, I'm so afraid."

One more time, Mai Lan calmed her down, "Here you go, crying again. Cheer up. At least we are safe. They may put us in a refugee camp for a while but we will be free. We'll be all right. Okay sweetie?"

Xuan, mumbling, still had doubts about the situation, "How can we prove that we're not one of them? We've been with them for so long."

"Yes, but we are Vietnamese. We don't belong to them." Mai Lan replied.

"I'm just, kind of afraid that they will put us all in jail."

"They won't." Mai Lan confirmed.

As soon as the vessel was tied to the dock, two Thai Navy policemen and a Vietnamese translator rushed up to the group of women and children. The police did a head count while the translator began to question the first woman that he saw. In Vietnamese the translator said, "Hi! I was told that you all are Vietnamese. How you end up here? Is everyone all right?"

The woman hesitated for a moment, and then she burst out crying when she heard her native language. Other girls in the group started to cry too, this was a very emotional moment for all of them.

The woman wiped her tears off of her face, regained her composure and said, "I'm sorry! When I heard you speak my language,

I remembered thinking that I would never live long enough to hear my native language again. So excuse me, what is your question?

The translator understood that she was emotional, so he slowly asked, "What happened to all of you, exactly?"

The woman pointed at the group of the young women and children, and slowly described her tearful adventure, "We snuck out of Vietnam and while at sea we were robbed and kidnapped by the pirates. They raped us and then locked us up on the island." She continued, "I don't know what happened to my family or the people on board. We heard some crashing noises and people screaming, and then everything went quiet. We have no idea where our family is right now."

The translator shook his head, feeling sorry for these people seeking freedom. "All of you are very lucky to still be alive. No one has ever survived being kidnapped by the pirates."

"I have prayed to God every day for our lives, and so many things happened to us since we left. Somehow we escaped death and are here to talk to you. Where do we go from here?"

The translator hesitated for a moment, then answered, "Well, they probably will relocate all of you to a refugee camp. The government is still investigating the incident that happened three days ago."

"What's incident?"

"Well, the government suspected that the pirates blew up a Coast Guard boat. They will probably investigate each one of you. I suggest that if any of you know anything about that, you should report. Perhaps they will find those criminals."

"I don't know anything about that. There were some people came to the island later; they may know something. I haven't heard them say anything about it. One thing that I do know is that those pirates who made slaves of us on the island do possess a lot of guns.

They used a big machine gun mounted to the front of their vessel to kill our people."

"You said they had a big machine gun? Are you sure? We never found a machine gun."

A woman who stood nearby heard the conversation and remembered that Nguyen Tam said something about taking a machine gun to fight to the pirates, "Yes, there was a machine gun, but Nguyen Tam our hero, took the gun off the vessel to fight the pirates. We helped him carry the ammunition."

The translator couldn't believe that one man fought the band of thugs, "You said that he killed all the pirates by himself? This is hard to believe that one man can alone do all that."

The woman confirmed, "Yes, sir, he did it. He even got shot by the pirate leader in the end. We beat him up before he could kill Tam. We nearly broke every bone in his body; he probably died in the fire."

The translator shook his head, and told them that the pirate leader was still very much alive, "The last I heard is that the soldiers saved a man who was burning. He was badly injured and they had to cut his leg off to keep him alive."

The women became terrified when she heard the bad news, "Oh God! He is still alive? He is going to kill us all."

"Don't worry. He only has one leg, and on top of that he was burned pretty badly. If the government ever found him guilty of piracy, they will execute him anyway. So you all don't have to worry about him, he's history."

The woman turned her head and announced the bad news, "Hey, ladies! The evil pirate leader is still alive!"

The women showed more concern then fear. Xuan couldn't resist letting out a scream, "What? Did she say the big evil man is still alive? Oh my God, he is going to kill us all."

The woman tried to calm her down, "Poor child, don't worry. I was told that this evil man was severely injured. Plus he only has one leg now. He will be dead if we can prove that he is pirate."

Everybody shouted in joy, "Yes! Yes! God looks after us! This evil man can't hurt us anymore."

Mai Lan patted Xuan's head, "You see, he got what was coming to him. I don't think God would let anybody hurt people for so long and get away with it. So don't worry, if you are nice to people, God will be nice to you."

Xuan looked at Mai Lan with a soothing appreciation and held Mai Lan's hand and said, "Thank you very much for being my sister. You know I didn't used to be like this. After what the pirates did to me, it changed me. I feel that now, I will always have fear in my heart."

"It is alright to be afraid, but just don't get panicked. You have to learn how to forget the past; otherwise you'll have a heart attack."

"I know. I'll try."

Now, the interrogator and the translator approached Mai Lan and Xuan, to ask them questions, "Hi, I have talked to some of the women, and they told me that you two were also held captive with them?"

"No, when we arrived earlier at the island. When we got to the island there were other girls already there. The pirates left and then came back with more people. When they started to execute the men; we started the fire so the pirates would stop the killings go put out the fire. Then, there was one man from who came from nowhere, and he killed all the pirates… well, except for one. I never met this man before, but he is our hero. We're free and still alive because of him. He stood up and fought for us all. We hope he soon recovers."

"I heard that he is doing well now. They're treating him at the Navy hospital," replied the interrogator.

An agent from the Thai police department interrogated the young man who still remained restrained with handcuffs, "You claimed that you were forced to stay with the pirates, why's that?"

Almost crying, the young man tried to explain his bizarre situation, "It's hard for me to explain why, but one thing that I know for sure is that they murdered all of the fishermen, including my parents. I am still alive because they thought I was dumb and deaf."

"You never tried to escape? Why?"

"They always kept me below deck. If I violated their orders, they would kill me. I had to obey their rules to survive."

"Did they know that they killed your parents?"

"No! I don't think they knew that I had parents aboard. I was pretending being deaf so they would leave me alone."

"Did you see them kill anyone?"

"A few times, I could hear screaming voices, but then they threw the bodies overboard. They never let me out on the deck when they did the killings, but I saw them rape a lot of girls. I did save one of the girls from the leader. Maybe she's still here and perhaps she can tell you what I say is true. There she is over there." Then he pointed at Mai Lan.

"Can you identify the leader? Yes if he's still alive?"

"Yes, I can."

"Would you be a witness in court if we prosecute him?"

"Absolutely, then I would avenge my parents and the fishermen's death."

"Do you know anything about the disappearance of the Thai government speedboat?"

"Yes, I heard some small arms fire and then a huge explosion, after that, they raced back to the island. I didn't see what happened, but they were in a big hurry to get away."

The investigator nodded his head and patted the young man's shoulder with a friendly gesture, "Well boy, we will need your testimony to bring this evil man to justice. For now, you will be held in custody until we sort things out. So I suggest that you will lay low and cooperate with us. Do you have any relative around here that we can contact for you?"

"I have some but they live far from here. We spent so much time at sea that we never had anytime to visit them. Perhaps when I am free I will go and look for them."

The police and the Navy gathered enough information to determine who's who. They had a good idea who was behind the disappearance of the coast guard speedboat. The police and government agents handed the refugees over to the immigration department. The group of women would relocate to one of the refugee camps, and from there, they would wait to be accepted by other countries.

The translator lined everyone up to board a big bus to transport them to the refugee camp. One woman asked the translator, "Sir, can you tell us where we are going? They are not sending us back to Vietnam, are they?"

"Right now, I don't really think so. They need you all to be witnesses for the investigation. If you have good reasons, you can then be chosen to go to some other country, perhaps to America or Australia; they sponsor a lot of refugees everyday. "Well, good luck." The translator waved to the women for the last time. The women waved back to the translator as they were getting into the bus.

Nguyen Tam opened his eyes and found his shoulder was wrapped in a bandage and that Thuy sat next to him. She was so happy when she saw that Nguyen Tam was awake. She excitingly grabbed his hands and she yelled, "Oh, my God! You're up. You've slept almost two days. I thought that you're never going to get up again. How is your shoulder? Are you hungry?"

Nguyen Tam smiled slightly at Thuy. He waived wis hand to tell her to slow down, "I'm Okay sweetie. I'm glad that you are the here. Where are we?"

"We are still at the Thai hospital. The police were here to talk to you but you were out, so they will come back later." Thuy tried to remember the details the translator had told her "Something about the battle on the island, and they were amazed about what you did to the pirates. The Thai soldiers rescued another man from the fire. They may want you to identify this man later. That's all that they would tell me."

Looking up at the water stained ceiling, Nguyen Tam tried to remember if there were any survivors from the island. The only one that he could remember was the leader. He couldn't remember exactly what happened to the man who shot him, "Do you remember anything at all about the man who shot me. I passed out when I shot him. Was he still alive?"

"Oh yes! That evil man tried to kill you, but the girls and I beat him down real bad. We left him there so I didn't really know what happened to him. Oh my God! I hope that is not him. He will never leave us alone."

Nguyen Tam's attention was drawn to a pair of geckos that were fighting in the corner of the ceiling. Nguyen Tam silently planned against this maniac who did tried to kill him before. Thuy looked at his serious face, and she knew that Nguyen Tam was worried about the man, "He was hurt pretty bad. They said that he probably can't do anything for a while yet; nobody was able to identify who's who yet. They're going to wait for you to do it."

"Couldn't you recognize his face? You beat him with the stick." Nguyen Tam joked with Thuy.

A little embarrassed, Thuy slightly squeezed Nguyen Tam's hand and said, "Yes, but I tried to save you. He scared me to death, if it were not for the other ladies; he would have gotten a hold of me."

Raising his eyebrows, Nguyen Tam said, "Really? Oh my love, I'm sorry for what happened to you. You could have been killed by this maniac. Thank you very much for saving my life."

"No! Thank you for saving us. You will always be our hero."

Nguyen Tam put Thuy's hand on his chest as he looked at her with a sea of love. He realized the love for her was so great; it was incomparable. Thuy sat beside him motionless. She felt his heartbeat in his chest. His heart beat faster and faster and was almost as same as hers. Nguyen Tam just remembered one thing important, "Sweetheart, we have got to get a hold of your brother somehow. He told us to get in touch with him once we reached Thailand. The sooner he knows we are here, the sooner we go to America."

"I know, but we have to wait until your shoulder gets a little better. You can talk to the translator when he gets here, and see what he can do for us."

Nguyen Tam looked at Thuy for a moment and nodded his head in agreement, "You are right. You have grown a lot since we got caught the first time. I can hardly believe that my sweet and innocent girl has grown so much. I hope that our future will pay you back some of the hardship that you've endured. If not for your growing courage, I would probably already be dead."

Thuy tried to hide her shyness and mumbled, "I'm still the same girl, it just that I have had to deal with a lot of evils. It was the natural instinct of a survivor that drove me. To tell you the truth, if I had known of all these dangers, I would have never left home."

Nguyen Tam caressed her hand and dreamed of a brighter future. He hoped to be with her in America, "You know, I've been told a lot about America, about its freedom and that there are a lot of opportunities for those who are willing to achieve it. I would like to get a job and go to school for the underwater welding. An American instructor told me about the job. He said that he would like to get that job when he got back to America. He said it pays very well."

"Yeah, then you would have to stay in the water a long time. Won't you get cold when you stay in the water that long?" Concerned, but curious about life in America, she asked him again, "What else do you know about America?"

Nguyen Tam took a moment to remember all of the good things he was once told about America. Then he slowly told her all he knew, "One thing that I know for sure is, if we work hard, we get rewarded. Everybody has the same opportunity, no matter who you are or what you are. Look at your brother, I think he's doing very well. When I first met him, I hardly recognized him. It took him less than six years to be where he's at. I promised myself that some day if I'm ever lucky enough to go to freedom land, I will work hard to achieve my dream."

Thuy squeezed Nguyen Tam's hand, smiled, and joking said, "Wow! I guess you'll be rich. You will probably forget me by then. There are so many beautiful women in America."

Nguyen Tam pulled Thuy's close to him, until her rosy cheek was close to his mouth, then he gave her a kiss, "You know that I love you more than myself. Unless, that is, you don't want me anymore."

Thuy kindly slapped Nguyen Tam's hand and said, "I will never forget my hero. Unless..." She pointed her finger at Nguyen Tam, "You choose someone else over me."

Nguyen Tam winked at Thuy and promised, "I swear I will never pick anybody over you, not for a million years."

The nurse came in the room to check on Nguyen Tam and bring some food for Thuy and Nguyen Tam. She knew Thuy couldn't afford to buy any food so she gave it to her.

The nurse checked Nguyen Tam's temperature. She gave the thumb's up that he was doing fine. The nurse patted Thuy's shoulder to tell her to eat the food, "You need to eat, little girl, you need some meat in you. He's okay. He's going to be getting up in a few days. I will bring some more food for you later, poor child."

This kindness of the nurse reminded Thuy of her mother. Thuy embraced the nurse's hand and while crying said, "Thank you very much for being so kind to us. We will never forget you."

The nurse lightly rubbed Thuy on her long black hair, and she comforted Thuy as if she were her own child. Even with the language's barrier, they still shared the love and respect of a fellow human being.

****

A vessel that was seized by the coast guard slowly docked at the Navy headquarters. Police and government agents were waiting to pick up the criminals. They wanted to find out why they were shooting at government soldiers. The police placed the captain in a separate room from the crew and began the interrogation, "Why did you shoot at the government soldier's? What kind of business were you running with the pirates?"

The vessels' owner realized that he was in big trouble. He could not let the officials know about his connection to the pirates. If the official were able to put it together, he would be brought up on charges for kidnapping, prostitution, drugs, and murder; they would throw him away for sure. So he did what anyone would do in that situation, he flatly denied everything, "I swear that I didn't know anything about a government seized boat, I was mistaking for another boat. You have the wrong person."

The interrogator didn't believe the statement from the vessel owner, so he threatened the suspect, "You know sooner or later, we are going to find out what you did. You will be charged and prosecuted for the attempted murder of government soldiers…not to mention the drugs which we found. You're going to prison no matter what, if you cooperate with us, of course the sentence will be lowered. Otherwise, you will get a life sentence, so take your pick wisely."

Facing a possible life sentence, the vessel owner had no other choice but to come out with the truth, "Well! He was supposed to deliver his promise, but he stood me up so I chased him down to find out what was going on. I lost my temper and took a shot at him, but I didn't know that the government took over control of the vessel. I wouldn't dare to mess with the government soldiers. I swear I didn't shoot at them on purpose, as a matter of fact, after we found out that we pursued the wrong boat, we split."

"What kind of promise?" The interrogator found a connection between the vessel owner and the pirates, so he squeezed some more information out of him. The vessel owner finally broke down and confessed, "We made a deal, and he supposed to deliver some girls and merchandise. I already paid for it, and that was why I got so mad."

"You said girls? What kind of girls? Where do they come from?" The interrogator asked.

"I don't know what kind of girl's, I don't know where are they are from. I don't get into people's business, you know."

"Can you identify any of them?" The interrogator asked.

The vessel owner hesitated a moment, then he agreed, "Yes, whatever."

Then he bargained, "What are you going to do to me and my crew?"

"That will be up to headquarters; probably some of your men will be released early."

"That is not their fault, it's mine. If I cooperate with you, will they be set free? They were innocent, you know."

"Yes! I guess. I will speak to headquarters about this. In the mean time, you are a material witness. We need you to testify in court, and when this all done; they will release you." Mumbling with a curse, the vessel owner was escorted to the jail cell.

Thuy and Nguyen Tam were eating their meal, when two policemen and a translator entered the room to investigate the incident on the island which they knew that Nguyen Tam had the main role.

Looking at Nguyen Tam with his shoulder wound, the translator who was also a Vietnamese refugee, felt sorry for him. He went to shake Nguyen Tam's hand, "Hi, how are you? Your shoulder still bothers you? Can we ask you a few questions about the incident in the island?"

Feeling a little tired, Nguyen Tam was still glad to tell them about what had happened, perhaps he could put that maniac in prison for life.

The policeman started up first by asking, "Where you came from?"

Nguyen Tam pointed his finger at Thuy, "We came from Vietnam. We escaped from the Vietnamese communist government."

"So how did you end up on the island?"

"We were stopped by the pirates; I knew something was wrong so I snuck on their ship. The pirates then murdered all of the men. A helicopter was approaching, so they took off."

The government agent gave a hand sign to stop for a moment, and asked him again, "You said a helicopter, are you certain?"

Lifting his brow, Nguyen Tam tried to remember but he wasn't for sure, "I didn't not know exactly whether it was a helicopter or not, I just heard the sound from far away." Nguyen Tam paused for a moment then continued, "When we arrived at the island, the pirates got ready to execute some more people. Then all of a sudden a fire broke out on the island. All the pirates except one ran onto the island to put out the fire. At that point I came out of hiding and killed the single guard that remained and told everyone on the boat to go find a place to hide on the island. Then I took the M-60 machinegun, set up a choke point to trap the pirates when they returned. I ambushed two groups of them and was able to take them out one by one."

The interrogator eyes know wide said, "How did you get hurt?"

Nguyen Tam took a sip of water, and felt his painfully wounded shoulder, "He took me by surprise. He was the last survivor; I did get him back though. The girls beat him up too."

"Who took you by surprise? Do you remember his face? We rescued a man from the fire. They had to amputate his leg and he had bad burns all over his body. I wonder if that's the one who shot you."

"I shot him in the left leg. He is the only one who got shot in the leg. The rest of them were all killed."

The investigating officer was truly amazed by this story, "I can't imagine how you killed these beasts all by yourself. Did you have any military training before?"

Nguyen Tam let out a long sigh, "Yes, I had a lot of military training during the war. It wasn't the military training that helped me on that island."

"What was it?"

"It was the will to survive." Then Nguyen Tam reached out and held Thuy's hand, "And for her." Thuy blushed with the joy of being loved, she bowed her head to hide a content smile. "Really," continued Nguyen Tam. "If it were not for her help in the end, I would have been killed. She beat him with a stick when he was going to finish me off."

The translator clapped his hand to cheer for the lady's courage, "Wow! That's the way, girl. You're so brave."

With her head still down, Thuy mumbled, "Thank you, I just tried to save his life. That man was very mean, and he killed a lot of people."

The police investigator, now paid attention to Thuy, asked her more questions, "You know this man too, don't you."

Her eyes began turning red, the shameful memory started to roll back, and she slowly told him everything, "After the pirates got all of us on board, and he made us undress. When we refused, he started killing the men. Then like he said, some kind of aircraft was approaching, so they put us in a small cabin and they hurried to get away."

Now, with matching stories, the investigator tried to get more details, "Did you see the oncoming aircraft?"

"No!" Thuy responded. "When they spotted the aircraft it was far away, I only heard a sound that was similar to a helicopter. They moved us down below before we could see what was going on."

"Do you happen to know how long it took the pirates to reach their island?"

"It took a quite a long time. They ran the boat at high speed for a long time."

Anxious about the story, the investigator couldn't help himself, "So, what happened next?"

A tear drop silently rolled down her cheek while she continued her painful story, "When we stopped at the island, they killed more people. The leader was about to rape me when then the big fire suddenly broke out, so they left us on the boat with one guard." She pointed her finger at Nguyen Tam, "From out of nowhere he appeared and killed the guard and freed all of us."

By now the police investigator was satisfied with her story. He stood up and shook their hands. Before they left the room, Nguyen Tam told the translator, "Her brother is a U.S citizen, perhaps if you can, please help us to locate him as fast as possible?"

The translator shook Nguyen Tam's hand and promised to help him, "We will keep in touch, I promise. Soon as they let me know anything, I will tell you. By the way, do you have any kind of letter or address, anything that we can contact with him that all?"

Nguyen Tam, shaking his head desperately, tried to retrieve all the possible information that may help to speed up the process. All the documents were lost during the get away, "We lost most of our belongings, including the phone numbers. I have no idea how to reach him now."

"Well, perhaps you can look up his name in the phone book." Nguyen Tam's eyes met with Thuy's eyes, and they were sparkling with hope. The best thing for them now is to somehow get hold of her brother.

Le Son went to meet his connection to find out about the escape. He was informed that the boat had left Vietnam, but nobody had any clue of where the boat was. Le Son was upset because this news. He had to leave Vietnam in a few days. It had been a week and a half since their departure, and if he didn't hear anything by the time he left, he planned on going to Thailand to all the refugee camps to look for them. It was getting too spooky to stay here, Le Son thought.

The girls got to stay together at one of the refugee camp. They were awaiting an interview from different countries with the possibility that they would grant immigration. There wasn't much room there, a small area for each individual on a concrete floor. The newcomers usually slept on top of some kind of pile of leaves which substituted for a bed. Later, people used shredded banana leaves weaving them into a mat.

Each day, a water supply truck brought the muddy water from the river to the camp. Each person received a small portion of water for both drinking and bathing. Life in the camp wasn't much, however, being qualified to migrate to America or some other rich country was the only hope which kept everybody here alive in this poor and trashy camp.

Mai Lan and the girls were assigned a small cubicle in a building which was built with an old tin roof. The tropical sun roasted almost everything inside, but somehow, people managed to sleep in it. The refugees were treated like prisoners. They had to obey strict rules and regulations. The Thai authority expected the refugees to absolutely obey them. The punishments were very harsh. The guards did not hesitate to whip the refugees with a cane. In most cases, the victim could barely stand up. Mai Lan and Xuan witnessed the punishment for the first time and it really shook them up. The most important rule is when the warden walked into the camp, no matter what people were doing, everybody had to stop and greet him by bowing their head. There was a young boy half deaf, who didn't hear that people were calling out that the warden was coming, so he didn't stop working and bow. The guards yanked him out into the court yard, and they tore his shirt off then whipped him with the cane. The boy cried in agony and terror and he tried to avoid the cane. The more he resisted the more the guard got excited. They whipped him until he couldn't move any more. The kid's mother was on her knees begging for mercy from the warden. She finally collapsed beside her young son. Mai Lan was terrified by the cruelty of the guards. She covered her face and screamed, "Oh, My god... they killed him! Oh my God, he is just a kid!" Then she turned and vomited on the ground. Xuan stood next to her, and called to Mai Lan, "Sister, are you all right?"

Mai Lan slumped down on the ground and she passed out. Xuan screamed for help. She bent down to grab Mai Lan to keep her from hitting the ground. Women nearby also gave a hand to help Mai Lan.

Disturbed by the noise, the warden turned around to find out what was going on. One of the guards came to the warden and reported the matter. The warden gave the guard an order to calm the crowd down. Facing the possibility of the riot, and he also ordered the guards to take both Mai Lan and the boy to the camp's clinic.

Sami, the pirate leader, finally woke up. He looked around the room and he couldn't believe that he was still alive. The last thing he saw was hell when the formidable fire engulfed his body and soul. Now with most of his body wrapped in bandages; the incomparable pain of the burning flesh has been driven him into insanity. Suicide began to run through his mind. He rather die than lay in bed suffering. When he founds out that his leg is missing; that probably will be the end of his desperate life.

Within the calmness of the hospital, he began to hear the crying voices of all his victims which were echoing from the deep of his sub consciousness. All through his days, Sami took life away from the innocent and it didn't seem to be a great deal for him. Now, all the atrocities were returning to haunt him. Consequently, he wanted to die rather than being tormented by the voices from the unrest souls. Unfortunately, he couldn't do anything to stop it.

Sami tried to get up to look around, but he felt like he had no control of his leg. He wasn't aware that the leg had been amputated. He reached down to feel his leg and found that the leg wasn't there anymore. He remembered that he had used the tourniquet to stop bleeding of his leg, and now he lost that leg forever.

The pain from his burning skin mixed with the pain from losing his leg was hitting hard on his mind. He let out a scream in anger and agony. In the deep of his emotional disturbance, he thought of the man who created all his anguish. The thought of vengeance suddenly boiled up inside him. He tried to visualize his enemy's face and realized how close he was to finishing him off. He wished to have one more chance to confront him.

A line of tears sudden rolled down his face. The thought of being a cripple from now on was just setting in. This was the first time he ever cried. Throughout his life, he never allowed tears on his face. So much pain and anger were troubling his mind, and it all drove him into madness.

Mai Lan woke up with a terrible headache but the feeling of nausea was gone. She didn't know what was happening to her but she was glad that Xuan was with her, "Xuan, where were we at? Wow, my head is hurting, bad!"

Xuan was happy to see Mai Lan waking up. She grabbed her hand and said joyously, "Sister, you're up. Are you all right, I was worried about you."

Mai Lan rubbed her head to relieve some tension. She tried to remember what caused her to past out, "I don't know." She said, "That's just too terrible what they did to that young boy, what happened to him?"

"They brought him to the hospital the same time as you, I felt sorry for his mother also. Why are they so mean to us?" Xuan asked with a sad face.

"Well, because we are the unwanted. Nobody really wants us to stay here or anywhere else. They have to accept us because they have no other means to get rid of us."

Just as they finished their conversation, the nurse walked in with the translator. She pointed at Mai Lan and said something to him. The translator turned to Mai Lan and interpreted, "Hi, this is the camp clinic. All the nurses and doctors, well, not exactly a doctor, but they are good. They come voluntarily to help the refugees here. They visit once or twice a week. The nurse needs to take a urine sample, the doctor thinks that you may be expecting." Mai Lan, very surprised by the unexpected news, lowered her brows, and tried to remember what, where, and how?

"Oh my God, I am pregnant? How's that happened?"

Xuan embraced Mai Lan, and comforted her the best that she could, "That's Okay sister. This isn't a bad thing. I can help you to raise your child."

Mai Lan thought back to before she left the country. The last night she spent with her fiancé, *that could be it,* she thought. Mai Lan let out a long sigh, and became angry with herself, wondering how she could let this happen. Now what she is going to do? She couldn't even take care of herself. Xuan is her best friend. Mai Lan didn't feel quite as lonely with her around. She looked at Xuan with her thankful eyes, "Thank you! I don't know what to do if you weren't around."

"Well when I need you…you will help me, right?" Xuan winked at Mai Lan.

"Yes, I promise." Mai Lan patted on Xuan's head while she spoke to her.

The refugee camp was so hot and humid during the day. People usually gathered under the tin roof to have some shade and to feel the breeze. Mai Lan stood by herself close to the barb wire fence and looked toward the small town far away. Saddened she thought about her belly getting bigger. What is she going to do with the baby? Mai Lan, most of the time, couldn't even feed herself sufficiently. She was so angry with herself to have let this happen. She missed her fiancé so much. He usually took care of her when she needed him and offered comfort to her when she was down. While she was floating in her world of worries and sadness, she suddenly heard somebody was calling her, "Hi!"

Mai Lan turned around to find where about the noise came

from. She heard the voice of a young man who was outside of the fence, "Over here!"

Mai Lan raised her hand up to block the bright sun light and looked toward the direction where the voice. She recognized a familiar face which was really surprised her. Mai Lan didn't really know how to act, whether she should or shouldn't greet him. On top of the troubles with her pregnancy, she had no desire to see anybody right now. Then she thought, he was her savior at one time, and he had some special sentiment toward her. That was why she couldn't really ignore him, so she hesitantly waved back to him to let him know that she recognized him.

The young man with no name seemed very happy. He ran to her with a big smile on his face. He spoke some of her native language which was not fluent but it was understandable, "Hi! How are you? I've been looking all over for you. The Vietnamese translator told me where they kept you. I came here and found you. Are you all right? You don't look so happy."

Mai Lan mumbled while trying to hide her sadness, "Oh, nothing. I was just kind of homesick. But, I'm glad to see you again. So they let you go free?"

With a faint smile, he answered, "They finally let me go, I agreed to be a witness in court for the prosecution of the pirate leader. Did you know that he murdered both of my parents?"

PART 5

Mai Lan was surprised that he told her that the same pirates killed their families. She said, "My little brother was also killed by the pirate, I know how you feel. I heard that the leader is still alive. Do you know anything about him?"

"Yes, he's still alive. They treated him in some government hospital and nobody is allowed to see him. He is badly burnt and only when his face is recognizable. The law is going to prosecute him."

"Do you think that they will ever free him?"

"No, I don't think so. If they find him guilty, he is probably going to get a death sentence," replied the young man. "If they don't, I will!" There were mixed feelings between her and the young man. A special sentiment was just about to bloom out of kindness, on top of that, it seemed like he always looked out for her. Right now, how she was going to explain to him that she was expecting a child? She felt ashamed. The young man looked into her troubled eyes. He knew that she had something to hide so he asked her, "Are you okay? Do you need any help? I will give reverend Si some food to bring to you. I know they don't feed you very well in here."

Mai Lan felt bad that she couldn't open up to him. She was mumbling the words thank you so low nobody was able to hear. Before she could say anything else the young man waved his hands to say, don't worry about it. The young man said good bye and promised to visit her again. Mai Lan looked at him and she thought, *I would like to be a friend... I don't know if I should tell you that I am pregnant, would you still want to see me again?* Instead, she waved to him with a smile, "Thank you very much for your kindness, I owe you so much already. I don't know when I will be able to repay you."

"Oh, don't worry. I would like to see you as my good friend." The young man held his hand across the fence and waited for hers.

Mai Lan hesitated for a moment, then reached out for his hand. They both could feel their hearts racing while they held each other hands. She stood motionless, watching the shadow of the young man fade into distant. The siren sounded, which was the call for food distribution. Awakening from the day dream, Mai Lan hurried to receive her portion of food for the day. It was not much, but enough to keep her alive.

When Mai Lan got back to the food distribution building; a long line of people already gathered in front of the center. Today's food was the same as yesterday and the day before. It was from some Japanese fishing industry who donated the outdated mackerel. People lived on fish day after day. Some knew how to cook and created different menus. The Red Cross sometimes donated different meals but the refugees would rarely receive any. While Mai Lan stood in line waiting for her turn, she heard somebody called for her name; she raised her hand up to respond to the call. She recognized that the priest was calling her name from a distance. Xuan stood by Mai

Thomas Nguyen

Lan and pointed her finger toward the priest. She shouted, "Look, over there…the priest is calling you, what is happening?"

Mai Lan, knew what it was all about. She left the line and went to meet the reverend This was the first time she ever met the reverend. She never had a chance to speak to a reverend before. She nervously approached him in a respectful manner and bowed her head to greet him, "Did you call me, Sir?"

The reverend gently placed his hand on her tiny shoulder, and told her some good news, "Yes, I did. A young man asked me to give some food to you. He spoke in Thai language, how do you know him?"

Mai Lan, sort of embarrassed didn't know how to answer the question, she smiled shyly, "Well, he saved my life. I was very surprised to see him again. He is a very good man."

The reverend took a good look at her face and he remembered her from somewhere, "Did they bring you to the clinic yesterday? I remember your face when the nurse told me that you're probably expecting a child."

Feelings of being ashamed and worry made her feel like she was tumbling. Feeling sorry for her, the reverend handed the bag of food to her and said, "That's okay don't worry. If you have any problems just come here to see me. Well, I will see you later." Then he added, "reverend Si is my name, everybody calls me that." The reverend guided her shoulder straight up while introducing himself.

"Yes, Sir."

She walked out the Chapel, with the mixed emotions lingering between hope and sadness. The hope was for a better tomorrow under a brighter horizon and the sadness was for her unborn child who might come into the world in such poor place. Xuan yelled

- 122 -

for Mai Lan from their assigned building, "Where did you go? You missed your portion today. Are you in some kind of trouble?"

Smiling, Mai Lan patted on her shoulder, and told her not to worry, "No, I'm Okay I got some food from the guy on the pirate ship. I couldn't believe that he still remembered us."

"Us? I don't think so, he remembers you. So what did he give you?" Xuan joked with Mai Lan.

"Food, I guess." Then she slowly opened the bag and found inside some dried fish and squid, a set of clothing and a pair of thongs. For Mai Lan this was a very valuable gift. Since their arrival, Mai Lan had had nothing but her old set of clothes. Xuan loved the set of clothing so much that she screamed, "Wow, it's so beautiful! I have never seen such pretty material. It felt like some kind of expensive silk. The color looks so good with your tone of skin, you're so lucky." Xuan rubbed the soft silky material against her face and wished that she could try it on, at least once. Mai Lan sensing Xuan's envy, let Xuan try on the new set of clothing, "Go ahead, put it on. It will look good on you."

Xuan she said with joy, "Oh, really! You are really going let me try it on? Thank you very much."

Mai Lan smiled and gave a go ahead gesture. She then tore a small piece of dry squid and began chewing. Xuan hesitated for a moment, then returned the piece of clothing back to Mai Lan and said, "Thank you for letting me wear this beautiful garment, but this is yours. I just don't feel right wearing it before you. Maybe later, after you wear it a few times, I will borrow it from you."

Mai Lan patted Xuan's shoulder promising, "Don't worry about it, I will let you wear it when the camp celebrates New Year. Okay?"

Xuan, with a big smile on her face, shook Mai Lan hands and said, "Really, you will let me wear it on New Year's? Thank you very much."

Sami got up in the middle of the night to find that his whole body was bathed in sweat. He awoke from a nightmare, seeing the conclusion of his life; a prosecution with a death sentence. It was past midnight, the hospital was so quiet you could hear a pin drop. Sami laid on the bed listening to the sound of the geckos. He could not foresee what was going to happen to him, nevertheless, a death sentence could be the way it would end. He wasn't worried about his life, he just wanted revenge. He wanted to take the man who caused him all these troubles down to hell with him. Within the silent night a sound emerged. It was the sound of someone approaching, besides the guard who came around to check the building; nobody was loitering about in these late hours. The footsteps were getting closer. Sami sat up quickly ready to deal with the intruder. At that moment the custodian walked by. He usually came to clean the floor a couple times a week. Beside him, nobody was allowed to be on this floor any time.

Sami called out for him while he cleaned the front of the room, "Hey! Who is out there? Can I ask you a question? Please?"

That was unusual for Sami to say please to someone, but now his situation has changed. He was at someone else's mercy and no longer could be the mean and tough pirate like before. The custodian first ignored the calls. The pirate kept calling him in a desperate voice. The custodian decided that he has no choice but to answer, "What do you want? I am not allowed to talk to you."

Sami tried to lure him in, "I need to let my mother know where

I'm at. She'll be worried if I don't. If you find her and give this letter, I will pay you."

As soon as he heard money, the custodian came to confirm that this was real, "How much?" the custodian said. He looked over Sami once more then said, "The way you look now, I think you need more money than I do."

Quite embarrassed by what the custodian had just said; Sami swallowed his pride and anger. He just wanted the custodian to help him, "When you give this note to my mother; she will pay you. I tell you what. If my mother does not give you any money, don't give this letter to her."

Thinking about the offer, the custodian still wasn't certain about helping the criminal. On the other hand, he thought, he could use the money if this were true. Standing silently for a moment, to justify between the do and don't, he finally agreed to help Sami, "I will help you to get a hold of your mother, but I want more money. This is a big job, you know, I may get into trouble with the police."

Sami, with a positive gesture, promised the custodian once again, "Hey, money is no problem. You name the price and we will pay it. Here is the address, it may be a little hard for you to find. My mother ran a whore house in Bangkok, she will treat you good. You just hand her this note, she knows my handwriting. Please, I need your help."

"Okay, I will do what I can. I'm not promising anything." Then the custodian left the room and took the note; the note being the last hope of the pirate.

After a long sleep, Nguyen Tam felt better. The shoulder wound didn't bother him as much. Thuy still slept on the small cot in the corner. Although she had been with him all this time in this small room, she never complained about anything. Watching her from his bed, Nguyen Tam heart was filled with love for Thuy. He really wanted to hold her tight and never let her go. Nguyen Tam tried to think of some way that he could get a hold of Thuy's brother. He regretted the fact that all his important documents went missing when they were captured.

The morning brought busy noises throughout the hospital. The commotion woke Thuy up. She rubbed her eyes to get used to the sun light that now lit up the room. Thuy looked over at Nguyen Tam, and she found the message of love in Nguyen Tam's eyes. She felt a little embarrassed when she met the stream of love in his vision. She quickly looked the other way to hide her blushed cheeks. Nguyen Tam also felt a little embarrassed, like a boy got caught peeping on a virgin, he diverted his eyes quickly to another direction then greeted her, "Oh! You're up. Did you sleep well last night?"

Thuy, slightly yawning, answered, "Yes, but I had a bad dream, it scared me half to death."

Nguyen Tam, really interested in her dream, lowered his brow asking, "A bad dream? What was it all about? Did you have me in there?"

Thuy got more serious, looking straight at Nguyen Tam. She began to narrate her dream, "Yes, you were in it. I saw the pirate tried to kill you. But…" Thuy stopped telling her story. Thuy had a look of scared sadness on her face, "Yes, but he killed me instead."

Nguyen Tam felt sorry for her. All he could do was try to change the subject, "Well, we will have to be more careful from now on. We have to try harder to locate your brother, in the mean time, we have to stay alert."

Thuy watched the singing birds perched outside the window. She wished she had a pair of wings to fly far away... so far away from here. She pointed out the pair of birds playing under the sun to Nguyen Tam and wished, "You see those birds? I wish that we had wings like them and that they could carry us far away from here."

Nguyen Tam, sharing in the peaceful scene with Thuy, hoped for a better future for the both of them, together, "You see, the sun always shines after the stormy rain. We have been through a lot of hardships; I think God is going to help us to get out of here, soon."

"I have prayed to God everyday to come and help us to be well and alive. I guess when the time comes; we will both get out of here safe, right?" Thuy, sort of waiting for the answer, since always asked questions.

Nguyen Tam replied, "I think you're right, I mean, we have been through hell and back. We are bound to get more luck at some point. At least I hope."

Thuy let out a long sigh. She imagined that a brighter day would come some day. Even now, they still live in fear. She sat next to Nguyen Tam and felt a little safer. She always felt safer when she was around him. She held his hand and whispered in his ear, "Every time I was close to you I felt protected. Even when you were injured, I always felt safer with you. I don't know what I'm going to do when you aren't around."

Smiling, Nguyen Tam slightly patted on Thuy's head, "You're silly. Where am I going to go without you? I promised your brother that I would return his sister to him without any harm. By the way, your image is engraved deep within my heart already."

Nguyen Tam then placed her hand on top of his chest to feel his heartbeat. The couple, who were sharing a moment of love quietly, forgot about the future whatever it may be.

The two coast guard agents who seized the gold and jewelries, returned to collect their treasure. They used caution when they got inside the vessel. They knew if they got caught, they would not lose all their goods; they would have to explain what they were doing in the vessel after hours. They rushed down the stairs and into the galley looking for the bucket of lard they had hidden the treasure in. They picked out the marked bucket and looked inside. Peering inside, they found that all of the jewelry was gone, triggering anger. They tore the kitchen to pieces trying to find their lost treasure. After turning the place upside down, they sat down and began think of a way to recover the lost treasure. "I think the young bastard, the one that was down here when the boat moved, is the one who took it; probably along with the refugees. We have to find him before he spends all the money!"

"Right we have to find him, the bastard must have knew where we hide the gold. They already released him a couple days ago," another agent agreed.

"Well, we have to look for him? I'll kill that greedy bastard," the agent cursed in anger.

"How are we going to look for his ass... shit?" one agent questioned.

"Hell, I guess we have to find out from headquarters," his partner suggested.

They suddenly heard footsteps on the deck and a flashlight shined down through the stairway, which lead to the kitchen. Then a loud voice rung out through the quiet night, "Hey, who's down there? This is off limits to everybody. Get out of there now or I will shoot you!"

A moment of silence fell back over the night. Only to be broken by the distinctive sound of a shotgun receiving a shell in the chamber.

The two coast guard agents froze and looked anxiously at each other. They were totally unaware of any pier security when they came to the boat. They both remained silent, waiting to see what the security guard was going to do. Cautiously the pier security guard stepped down the stairs into the boat and shined his flashlight about to observe the scenario. Into the darkness, the security guard pointed his shotgun. He carefully stepped down the last staircase and he called out loud, "Hey, you better show yourself or I will shoot!" Then suddenly something struck him in head and knocked him out cold. One of the coast guard agents came behind the unconscious security guard and put away his pistol he had used to bludgeon the guard with. Forgetting about the gold, both agents went racing up to the deck, "Let's get out of here before somebody else comes. Forget about the gold. We will find that kid," the agent remarked.

"Yes, let get out of here. I hope he didn't call for back up." The other agent agreed and soon they disappeared into the dark night.

Sami woke up in the morning to the sight of two policemen and a Navy agent who stood in his room. Sami felt uncomfortable when he saw the law surrounding him. He had a feeling that the police department found out something about him. He slowly opened his eyes, pretending that no one was there.

The Navy officer started up the conversation when he saw that Sami woke up, "About time, we thought that you're never going to wake up. So, how do you feel?"

"Better, I guess," Sami mumbled, pretending to be incoherent. "My face is hurting because of the burn. What is happening to me?

Why I'm here?" Then he moaned, "Oh my God it hurts. I don't know if I'm going to live." He played his role so well that the officer almost believed him.

One of the officers suggested that they should come back later. They figured that they couldn't get anything out of this man, "All right, man. We will come back later to check on you. It looks like you are not in any shape to talk."

Sami, smiled slightly at the police agents. He thought to himself, *this is just one more time I was still able to manipulate the law.* He was buying time. He wanted his mother to come and rescue him before they found out who he was. His priority was revenge. He knew that the man who took his leg away was around here in this hospital. He wasn't sure where he was located; but that shouldn't be a big problem for him to find out.

The more he thought about revenge, the faster his blood rushed through his body. Sweat started trickling down his burned skin which caused tremendous pain. Sami tried not to get too excited and tried to lay still. The best remedy for him right now was to fall to sleep.

******

The young man, after he met Mai Lan, thought he recognized a different look in her eyes, the kind of sadness and worry. He wanted to ask her what was bothering her, but he was too nervous to ask her. He planned on asking her during the next visit.

He felt the love growing in his heart everyday. He wished to someday marry and have children with her. He wanted a family of his own. He thought of buying more food for her next time. He felt sorry for the refugees that have to live in such a crummy place. He tried to visualize her wearing the costume. Her image always appeared so vivid in his mind; especially when he would lay in his room alone. He was waiting for the judgment day. He prayed for his parents to help him to bring their murderer to justice.

He found a new hope for the future. The girl who he saved from the pirate was indeed his reward. The young man looked at himself in the mirror and thought, *I'm not that bad, I have to give her more time.* Smiling, he looked out the window and watched a pair of birds play and sing; quietly wishing that his dream girl was here with him. He walked outside, taking a deep breath of the fresh morning air. He bowed his head to thank God for his freedom and his health.

******

Mai Lan got up early in the morning. The nausea induced by the pregnancy caused her great discomfort. Here in the refugee camp, the toilet facility was located quite a distance from the residential building. Mai Lan would rush to the facility whenever she felt morning sickness. When she got there, the nausea would dissipate only to be replaced by shortness of breath. Mai Lan didn't know how long this would continue. She wished this would never happen to her again. The odor of the latrine, carried by the summer breeze, hit Mai Lan right on the nose. The smell almost knocked her out; feeling dizzy she grabbed her belly and vomited. Mai Lan, beginning to blackout, called for help. She could just hear the voice of somebody calling her name from a distance as she passed out.

Mai Lan opened her eyes and saw Xuan. Other women in the camp, who saw Mai Lan pass out, came to keep her warm. Xuan looked sadly upon Mai Lan and began to cry while holding her hand, "Are you all right? Say something. I'm so worried about you and the baby. Tell me if you're okay." The women rubbed menthol balm all over her body. They massaged it into her skin in order to help her blood flow.

Suddenly Mai Lan opened her eyes and looked around and saw everybody caring for her; she asked Xuan, "Oh, my head feels like it has a thousand pounds on top of it. What happened to me?"

Xuan, with a serious look on her face answered, "You passed out just outside the latrine. It is lucky for you that I heard your voice. I bet you the smell of the latrine knocked you out...wasn't it?"

Mai Lan now embarrassed, shook her head and gestured to Xuan meaning, it's gross to talk about it, "I don't know... it did smell bad. I don't think that is why I passed out."

Xuan tried to make a big deal out of it, "Yes, but it makes me sick every time I go in there. I'm sick of this whole place. Are going to be here forever? This is the worst place I ever lived. I really miss my home." Tears were silently rolling down her cheeks.

Everybody felt the same as Xuan. Some of the other woman also started to shed tears. Mai Lan, succumbing to sadness held Xuan in her arm and comforted her, "I know what you mean, but let's hope that we will get out of here someday. We're not going to live here forever. Matter of fact, you may leave here before I do."

Xuan wiped off her tears and started shaking her head. She looked at Mai Lan and said, "No, I'm not going to leave you, especially when you're expecting a child."

Mai Lan gave Xuan a big hug as if she were her little sister. After all they've been through. All the hardships together; they were even closer than sisters, "I love you like my little sister, but if they let you go," shaking her finger she said, "you will go. Okay...I will find you later."

Xuan silently stared at the blue sky. She wanted to stay with Mai lan, "I'm afraid of being in a strange place alone. I don't know if I can make it without you. It would be nice if we could all leave at the same time. God, I don't know what I'm going to do if I go to America. I'll probably starve to death."

Mai Lan looked at Xuan. She didn't really have any idea what she was going to do either, plus her child? Mai Lan always had a strong mind, and a will to survive. Now she even has to have to find more strength, "You know life is not easy... for everybody... especially us. We have fought hard for survival, and we made it here alive. We have to thank God for guiding us here." She continued, "Now we have to be patient for our turn to be interviewed. If you happened to get it first, don't you dare to turn it down. You hear me? Mai Lan paused for a response. She wanted to let Xuan know she was serious. She continued, "You will be all right. Now, if I go first, I will find a way to help you. Okay?"

Xuan nodded her head and agreed with Mai Lan, even though she didn't want to leave Mai Lan... ever.

Le son arrived in Bangkok and brought with him the picture of his sister and Nguyen Tam. The first thing he did was to stop at the U.S. embassy in Bangkok. With their assistance, he might be able track down Nguyen Tam and her sister faster.

The U.S. embassy agreed to help him locate his sister. That is if she ever made to Thailand. They couldn't promise how long it will take to find her. The embassy suggested that Le Son might want to stick around since there were a large number of refugees in each camp. It might take weeks to locate one.

Disappointed, Le son returned to the hotel to rest for a while. Trying to think of a better way to find out the whereabouts of his sister and his friend, Le Son reached the decision to go to the camp to find them himself.

Le son wanted to go back to the U.S embassy to request permission to search for his relative inside of the refugee camp. To enter the camp, it required the authorization from the Thai Government. It is not impossible, but it takes time for the paper work to get approved. It was the same time Le Son didn't have. So, he thought about bribing the camp's authority for a list containing the names of the refugees. If they're in there, he would find the way to get them out. Pretty satisfied with the idea, he fell sleep.

This was the third day Nguyen Tam spent in the hospital. The wound seemed to be getting better and it didn't bother him as much anymore. The nurse told him, when he got better, the government would send him and his girlfriend to the refugee camp. Nguyen Tam got up with a good feeling. He lightly touched his shoulder wound and it didn't feel as bad. He felt like trying to walk around the hospital today, first to get some fresh air, second to look around at the scenery. All this time in bed, he could only see the outside through the window. Right about the time he tried to get out the bed, Thuy walked in and found him almost off the bed. She yelled at him to stop him, "Tam, where are you going? My God, you're going to fall on the floor. Your shoulder, are you okay?"

Nguyen Tam reluctantly put his legs back on the bed. He begged Thuy to let him go outside, "I just want to breath the fresh air outside and take a look at the scenery. I don't want to bother you I want to try by myself. It's not too bad."

Thuy slightly slapped on Nguyen Tam's hand joking, "You almost fell off the bed. You should wait for me."

Nguyen Tam could only smile back, because he knew that she was right. Now that his life was so attached to her, and her maturity grew more day by day, he begged, "I want to breathe fresh air so bad. I'm willing to do anything for you, please."

Thuy felt pity for Nguyen Tam, "Still, you are not strong enough to be outside all by yourself. Next time, you have to wait for me to help you, okay?"

"Okay" Nguyen Tam responded, in a soft voice he apologizing, "Sorry my dear, I will ask you to help next time." Nguyen Tam was so glad that now he has someone to look out for him. He then remembered those lonely days when he lost his whole family. He would sit outside the restaurant, drunk, and had no future to look forward to. Now a whole new future awaits him. Plus with a beautiful girl at his side; what else he could ask for?

Thuy slowly guided Nguyen Tam back into his bed, "I will take you out there after I ask the nurse if it's okay for you to go. I don't mind taking you around. I don't want you to bother that shoulder wound, it needs time to healing."

After adjusting himself on the bed, Nguyen Tam reached for Thuy's hand. He placed her hand up to his mouth and gently kissed her. At first, Thuy jerked her hand back. Then she relaxed and let him to hold it. They quietly stood by each other and felt their blood flowing fast through their veins.

The sound of someone approaching the room quickly broke the couple apart. Thuy pulled her hand back and waited for someone to enter the room. A moment later, a translator and two investigators entered the room. They were glad to see Nguyen Tam was up. The translator patted Tam's shoulder and greeted him, "Hey, how are you buddy?"

"I'm fine, how are you?"

"We're doing well. These gentlemen are investigators from the Navy Headquarters." He pointed at the two agents as he introduced them to Nguyen Tam.

The two agents shook Nguyen Tam's hand then they opened up the conversation, "Hi, we are here to ask you one more time about the incident involving our speedboat at sea. We calculated the time of the last transmission from the coast guard speed boat and the location of the pirate boat. The pirate boat could have been the one which sunk our boat. We have two suspects in custody. We did not get much out of one of them. The other is unable to be questioned at this time. Do you think you could point out the person who kidnapped you?"

Nguyen Tam agreed to help to identify the suspect. Still he had doubts that he could identify this man. He only saw him from distance. When he was shot in the shoulder, he only tried to return fire as quick as he could without even looking at his opponent. He turned and looked at Thuy, maybe she will be able to recognize the suspect, "Thuy, you would probably remember this man better. I have no chance to look at him clearly. I thought that you may have gotten a good look at him.

Thuy, second guessing herself nodded her head and agreed, "I think I may able to identify this man if I get close to him. Was his face burned pretty bad, Sir?"

The agent nodded his head, "Yes, they wrapped bandages on his face. It would take a while to take it off. All of his skin was burned off. I don't know how he survived. We would rather let him die, but he is the only key witness that may know what happened to the coast guard boat."

"How you are going to make him talk? He knows that once he confesses he will be sentenced to death," said Nguyen Tam.

The agent agreed with Nguyen Tam. They also believed that with ample witnesses; they could squeeze the truth out of him, "Yes, we know that he is not going to voluntarily admit to the crime. He may show us the location of the sinking boat, if we offer him a lighter sentence. Our main goal is to find the boat and the people in it."

Nguyen Tam, sort of understood what the Department was trying to do. It may work if he can positively identify the suspect, "Yes, I see what you are trying to do. I will do my best to help out in the search for the boat."

The agent shook Nguyen Tam's hand. In return the Department will offer better care for his injury and provide more security. The important thing right now for the both of them was to find Thuy's brother. Nguyen Tam then shook the hand of the translator, and asked, "Please, sir. Help me find her brother. The sooner we find him, the sooner we will have some help. Thank you very much."

The translator spoke with the agents about Nguyen Tam's request. They promised to help the couple find her brother. They all admired his courage. Before they left, Nguyen Tam asked about the security of the hospital, "Do you think the injured pirate can do us some harm. What if he finds out that we are the key witnesses?"

The agent promised as soon as the shoulder wound healed, they will move him to a different location. With a friendly smile the agent said, "Don't worry, we will keep this guy under tight security. He is really in pretty bad condition. We understand your concern and we will not to let anybody contact with him without our supervision."

Nguyen Tam waved back to the agent and knew that he has no choice but to wait. Nguyen Tam waited for the agents to leave the room and then he asked Thuy to sit next to him. He gently held her hand and spoke softly to her, "I wish we could find your brother soon. I have the feeling that he is looking for us, too. If somehow we can post our names in all the refugee camps, perhaps he can find out where we are. What do you think?"

Thuy, brightened up with a big smile and said, "Yes, you are right. He will probably find out that we already got out of the country. You know, most refugees stay in the camp. We are the only ones who are staying here under a special condition. If he is looking for us, there is no way that he will be able to find our names. We have to find a way to list our names on all the camps as soon as possible."

Nguyen Tam surprised that Thuy could make a good solid decision; looked at her with respectful eyes, "Wow, I got to say that you are getting good, compared with the Thuy of old. I guess after all these mishaps you have really learned to beat the odds."

Thuy agreed with Nguyen Tam. She has grown from mental to physical challenges they have had to endure during these death trips to freedom. She sat next to Nguyen Tam, and ran her fingers through his hair to untangle it. She asked about his war career in Viet Nam and about the bloody night when he saved her brother's life, "Was it horrible in the war? Did you kill a lot of people?"

Nguyen Tam out looked at the blue sky through the window. His mind lazily drifted back to the same blue sky during the war. He looked at Thuy and said, "You know you do look like your brother. You remind me of him the morning before we got attacked. The day started out beautiful, just like today. We sat around and played cards, and talked about taking some time off together to go do some fishing in Saigon river."

"You two were close friend?"

"Yes, your brother was under my command. We had to look out for each other's back."

"During the war I had hardly saw my brother. My family prayed for him all the time. When he left Vietnam for America, my family thought that he had been killed. We had no news from him. My mother was so sad from the news of his death. The new communist government confiscated her business and then the new money system exchange. My mom had nothing left to live for and she died a year later. After her death a few months passed when I received news from my brother. When he found out that our mother was deceased, he promised to come back and do whatever he could to get me out of the country... Sorry, I am getting carried away. So, what happened to you and my brother?"

"Well, the communist pushed hard in the front line to cross the Saigon River. We tried to stop an amphibious tank from crossing trying to advance to the city. Your brother and I were assigned the duty to stop anything from crossing. We blew up one Pt-76, but your brother's diving equipment got shot. I had to bail him out and let he breathe through my equipment. We both got out of there. When we returned to the unit only to find out that everybody had already left, including the Commanding Officer. The Communist army already broke the defense line and your brother was hurting because the bullet had pierced through the tube and shredded his skin. I told your brother go ahead and leave. I told him that I would stick around a little longer to see if anybody came back. That was the last time that I saw him. I tried to look for him later but I never saw him again. When I met him years later, he told me that he got in one of the American transport barges in Khanh Hoi and got out of the country."

"So nobody from your unit showed?" Thuy curiously questioned.

Quiet for a moment, Nguyen Tam tried to bring back those last horrible days of the whole mighty Southern Army, "Yes, a few returned to the unit. I was told that the lieutenant in charge was shot and killed. On top of that, President Thieu had already left the country and all the generals disappeared. The new government was declared in a hurry. We were in chaos, we didn't know what we were supposed to do. The new government called for a peaceful solution, but that was a joke."

Thuy was pretty interested in listening to the story, because she was a little young when the war happened. Nguyen Tam continued his war story, "When the new government was declared, we pretty much knew that the war almost over. The South Regime was just about to finish when the president gave the order to lay down our arms. Some of the top ranking commanders committed suicide. That was the worst moment for all the arm forces. We sat for hours waiting for the order to surrender."

"That is sad. I can't believe the regime fell so quickly." Thuy added.

"Do you know why?" Until now, Nguyen Tam still felt hurt and angry of the abandonment of the United States Army, "We fought hard for freedom. When we lost the support of the American Army, the South lost the confidence. It was the younger generation, like us, who really fought hard for our freedom."

Thuy asked, "Why did the American people abandon us?"

"I don't really know, I guess people got tired of the war. It went on for so many years. One thing is for sure, the younger generation, like us, wanted to win the war and we almost won." Nguyen Tam let out a sigh full of sadness, "Millions of people had died for nothing." Nguyen Tam added, "Because of this war, every family lost at least one of its members. Two of my uncles were killed in the battle field. The sad thing is, they both served on different sides."

Since the story was a little bit bizarre, Thuy couldn't help but to ask for more details, "How did it happen? How could a family fight one another…they were from the same family? That is awful."

"Different beliefs, I guess. After the Geneva Convention, we were assigned to divide the country at the 17th parallel. After that my uncle was recruited to the North. We never heard from him again… well, it wasn't until the end of the war when we heard from his wife. She told us that my uncle was killed during the Southern invasion of the Tet offensive in 1968. A year later, my other uncle was killed as well. My poor grandma was so upset that she almost killed herself."

"That is sad," Thuy said.

Nguyen Tam continued, "You know, so many of my friends had died in this war already. Even though the communist took over the South, we still have the spirit to fight for our country."

"We heard a lot about what the communist did to people. We never thought of being poor. After the invasion, we had virtually nothing. If it were not for my brother, I would have had nothing to live for." Thuy told her story with tears in her eyes. Nguyen Tam felt bad for her family and for all others including his. He remembered the last days of his army career. He didn't know what was going to happen to him. He had returned home to find his family buried underneath rubbles of his former house; the thought of his horrible past, caused tears to roll down his face. The deep scar of the war has implanted into his memory.

Thuy found a towel to blot the tears on his face. She tried to change the subject in order to divert the sad story of his life, "I think we should go outside for a little bit, before the sun gets up to high. Would you like to?"

Nguyen Tam nodded his head and used Thuy's shoulder to lean on so he could slowly merge from the bed. Thuy took his right arm and crossed it around her shoulder, then slowly guided him to the hospital's courtyard.

The morning fresh air and multi-colored flowers surrounded the couple. The fragrances somehow seemed to be soothing their bad feelings. To Nguyen Tam, this was the most peaceful time he could remember; to be able to sit down and to enjoy a beautiful scene without hearing the sound of artillery shells or rockets. He took a deep breath of the fresh air and let out the stale air from his room. Listening to the sound of the tropical birds, he smelled the fragrance of the colorful flowers. Sitting next to his beautiful girl, for a moment, Nguyen Tam thought he was in the paradise.

The night custodian went to find the mother of the patient to relay a message. He didn't know who Sami really was nor what he does; but as long as they pay him good he didn't care. To look for someone in Bangkok, it took time, especially this patient's mother who ran a whorehouse in the most dangerous area; an area where people are regularly robbed and killed.

Finally finding the place, he wondered what kind of people live here. He thought to himself, *that patient's mother must be some tough woman to run a whorehouse in this slum neighborhood*. He avoided the pot holes in the small alley that lead to the house. He couldn't wait to get out of the area; he had a bad feeling as he approached the place. When he first met the patient's mother, she refused to see him. Then he showed the piece paper to one of the girls. It seemed to convince her that her long lost son was in some kind of trouble. The madam was sort of reluctant to show her relationship to Sami, not that she didn't care for him, but the police had been looking for him. Although he didn't appear to be the police, she still kept a certain distance between her and the stranger, "You said this man was injured pretty bad? How bad was he?"

"He has been burned almost all over his body, plus he has lost one of his legs. I don't know what he did, but the government has isolated him. You are his mother, aren't you?" The custodian asked in a doubting voice.

"He is my son but he never did live with me. So what do you think about his condition?" She sounded curious but with less concern.

The custodian began to get impatient, "Well, he is hurting pretty bad, otherwise, I guess he wouldn't need your help. I didn't have to come over here to look for you either." The custodian retorted.

Sensing the custodians discontent she explained, "Well, I haven't seen him in a long time. I don't even remember what he looks like, tell you the truth. He has gotten me in a lot of trouble in the past. I'm kind of keeping distance between him and I."

The custodian becoming anxious said, "You know, I don't know exactly what happened to the relationship between you two, but the man promised me that you would pay me good. I am risking my job to come here. So, what's going to be? I can't stay here too long."

The madam shifted her voice from a mild to a harsher tone, almost belligerent, "Look, mister…I don't know what you are talking about. What kind of money do you think you are going to get? I haven't seen him in years." She paused, "Well, since you came here to do my son a favor, I will offer you a sweet deal. You can choose to sleep with any of my girl, free, and I will give you some money to get home."

Frustrated and with the feeling of being cheated, the custodian pointed his finger at the madam and cursed, "You and your crippled ass son. You all are nothing but a bunch of scumbags and liars. I'm not coming all the way over here just to fuck your nasty whores.

The madam ordered the thugs outside the building to remove the custodian, "Hey, come here and get rid of this crazy son of a bitch!"

The custodian saw two muscular thugs racing in his direction. Realizing the approaching danger, he whipped out his pocket knife and grabbed the madam, locking her body with his left arm. He positioned the knife on her throat and threatened, "Look, bitch! You better tell these a…holes to back up; otherwise I'm going to slit your throat wide open. I will take your ass out along with me, I promise!"

The madam was helplessly confined by his strength. She tried to free her throat to get some air. As her face turned from red to pale white the custodian cut with the tip of his knife on her jaw line causing a thin line of blood to trickle down her throat. The old woman waved her hands to the thugs signaling them to back up. With the upper hand, the custodian demanded his money, "All I want is to get paid, but no, you want to jack me around. If we're going to die then we're all going to die together. Or if you want to live, you better pay." The custodian released his grasp a little so she could breathe. He knew how to squeeze these types of people, "Well, where is the money? I don't have all day."

The madam seemed to give up, she waved to the thugs to go get some money. The thugs, like tigers ready to tear up their prey, looked for a good moment to attack. The only thing kept them back was the threat on their boss's life.

One of the thugs stared at the custodian and warned him, "Hey, you think that you can get out of here safely? How far do you think you can go?"

Spitting on the floor, the custodian used the madam's body as the shield, "What ever you do, she will go first, I promise you that."

The woman, fearing for her life, gave the hand gesture telling the thug to back up. She ordered them to bring out the money. One of the thugs went inside to get the money and brought out a wooden box full of cash. He looked at his boss who was restrained and asked, "How much do you want to pay him?"

PART 6

The woman, mumbling from her throat, begged for some relief so she could speak. Her face had now turned pale white from poor circulation. The custodian slightly relieved the pressure on her throat so she could speak. Leaving a small gap between her chin and his arm; she lowered her mouth and quickly bit into his arm. The woman sank her teeth into the custodian's flesh like a mad dog and his blood trickled along her jaw, which made her look like some kind of vampire. The sudden pain drove him insane. The custodian panicked from the pain and in the process drove his knife into her. Blood spewed from her cut covering the two of them.

Despite being stabbed, the old woman wouldn't let go with her jaw. One of the thugs rushed to the custodian attempting to free the woman from the knife. The other one ran behind the custodian and gave him a blow to his lower back. The blow was so powerful it knocked the custodian out in a second and laid him flat on the ground. While he was down on the ground, the thugs continued to beat him savagely.

The woman stood there to watch the beating. She wiped the blood off her mouth and spat on the poor man's motionless body. The thug's continued to pound on him with hatred then they realized that they had killed the man. One of the thugs continued to kick the dead corpse. The other thug finally stopped his raging buddy and said, "All right man, he's dead. Come on, let get rid of his body."

Around this area murder happened every day. Another body would probably go unnoticed. The thugs took his wallet and the money then rolled the body up in an old piece of canvas. They covered the canvas in plastic and hauled the body to a swamp to be dumped. When the thugs returned from disposing the body, the madam called one of them in and said, "According to this s.o.b, my son Sami was injured and is being treated at the Navy hospital. They will execute him when they find out who he is. I want you to get in there and find a way to get him out. You think you can handle it?"

The thug said, "Sami, he's in trouble? Man, I haven't seen him in years. Is he doing okay?"

"I don't know what has happened to him, that's why I am sending you over there. Be careful, they will probably keep him in tight security. I tell you what, take the custodian's ID and see if you can get inside."

"I will try to help Sami out. When do you want me to go?"

"Right now! We don't have much time, be careful." She opened the cash box, and gave him some money and a small revolver. She instructed him with some last details on how to get there and sent him on his way.

Le Son traveled for about a half of a day to get to one of the refugee camps. When he got there he talked to the warden of the camp to ask for his assistance in searching for one of his family members. The warden was reluctant to give the list of names to Le Son. Le Son bribed him with a few American dollars and then the warden agreed.

Le Son went through the list but couldn't find the names of his sister and Nguyen Tam anywhere. Disappointed, he gave the list back to the warden. Now, he will have to wait for news from the U.S Consular. Le Son gave the warden the phone number from his hotel. Just in case, the warden could contact Le Son if he found the whereabouts of his sister.

The longer he stayed here the more money he would have to spend. Le Son didn't think that this trip would take so long. He didn't know about all the dangers that came along with it. Le Son asked permission to go around the camp and talk to people. Maybe he could find out something about them from the refugees here. He had to bribe the warden again for permission to get around the camp. The warden signed a temporary permit for Le Son and gave him three hours to talk to the people there.

A guard escorted him to the gate and turned him loose. Feeling like he was being thrown into another world, Le Son tried to avoid staring at the crowds of people. He didn't even know where to start. Then he thought, *what if I ask around to find out who were the most recent arrivals*. Confident with the idea, Le Son approached an older man and said, "Hi, how are you doing? How long have you been here?"

The old man, surprised by the question, didn't know what kind of trouble that he was in and tried to avoid answering the question. He pointed out another young man who stood not far from him and said, "I don't know, I don't remember exactly. You can ask the young man over there, he can tell you more than I can."

Le Son quickly said, "Oh no, you are not in any kind of trouble. I just want to find my little sister, or someone who may know something about her."

The young man heard the conversation and volunteered some information, "Yes! I know a couple girls just arrived last week. I can take you to meet them, if you want."

Le Son took a few dollars and gave to the young manand said, "This is for you. Would you take me there?"

"Thanks. Yes, I will take you to see them." The young man gestured for Le Son to follow him. He led Le Son to the last building in the camp. The deeper he traveled into the camp the more he recognized the living conditions. He felt sorry for the people who lived there. The only thing they lived for was the hope to migrate to America or some other country.

Le Son finally entered the building which housed Mai Lan and some other women. The young man brought Le Son to Mai Lan and introduced him to her, "Hi, this man wants to ask you something about his sister. I know just arrived so I think you may know something." Then he turned around to Le Son and said, "Sir, I think she can help find your sister, good luck." Le Son shook his hand in appreciation of his kindness. Le Son shook Mai Lan's hand and introduced himself to her, "Hi, my name is Son. How are you?"

Mai Lan stood up and bowed her head to greet the stranger. She was embarrassed by the condition of their living quarters, "Hi Sir, my name is Mai Lan. Sorry that we don't have much room here for a guest. Is there anything that I can help you with?"

Le Son waiving his hand said, "Oh, don't worry about it, I understand this is only the temporary shelter. I was told that you just arrived here and wondered if you happen to know a girl named Thuy, she is my sister."

The name sounded familiar to Mai Lan and she tried to recall the girl's face. She turned to Xuan and asked, "Xuan, was she the one who accompanied the injured gentleman to the hospital? I think her name was Thuy but I'm not sure."

Xuan, with her hand over her forehead, also tried to remember the girl, "Yeah, I remember her. She was with the group of ladies who arrived to the island after us. Let me go find the woman who was with her. She may be able to tell you more about her."

Le Son, ignited with new hope, had the feeling that his sister would soon to be found. He shook Xuan's hand with joy and said, "Thank you very much for helping me out."

Xuan, smiling back said, "That's okay we want you to find your sister as soon as possible. I'll be right back."

Le Son looked around the building wondering how people could live here in such a small space. Being spoiled by the mild temperature in the United States, Le Son began sweating; his body was unable to tolerate the heat. He wiped the rolls of sweats from his forehead, he felt like taking a shower. The heat made Le Son feel a little dizzy.

Xuan returned with an older woman and said, "Sir, this lady was traveled with Thuy. She can tell you more about her."

Le Son was so glad that someone knew the whereabouts of his sister. He gave Xuan a big hug and then offered her five U.S. dollars. First Xuan didn't want to accept the money but Le Son insisted that she could use the money to buy some food. So she finally accepted the money with great appreciation and said, "Thank you very much for the money. I just want to help out. I hope that you will find your sister soon."

"You're very welcome, I hope so, too. I have the feeling that I will find her soon. Thanks again."

Then he bowed his head to greet the woman who could lead him to his sister, "Hi madam, how are you doing? You know something about Thuy, my sister? It would be great if you could tell me where she is now."

The woman wanted asked, "Yes, I know Thuy and her boyfriend, but who are you?"

Le Son, smiling, pointed his thumb at his chest, "I'm her brother. I'm here to find her. I heard they got caught but later they were freed. I tried here to see if, with any luck, I can find her and my friend Nguyen Tam."

The woman opened up to Le Son, "I guess you are her brother. You kind of look like Thuy. We heard that the pirate leader is still alive. That is why we have to be careful to who we give out the location of Thuy and Tam to."

Surprised by the news, Le Son couldn't wait any longer to find out the story, "What kind of pirate, they really exist? Were my sister and Tam in any danger?"

The woman shrugged her shoulder and confirmed, "Yes, they were real pirates, and they were armed to the teeth. Nguyen Tam killed them all by himself. He got shot by one of them but he is still alive."

Le Son became excited and said, "Oh, my sister is still alive. I'm so glad that's she is okay."

"Yes, the last time I saw of her was when she got in the helicopter with Nguyen Tam and sent to some Thai Navy hospital. I haven't heard anything about her since then."

"Were they all right? I heard that Tam was hurt but he is he still alive?" Le Son asked.

"He was shot in the shoulder and had lost a lot of blood, but the Thai Navy came to his rescue. Then they were flown out. Thuy was allowed to go with him to the hospital. We don't exactly know where the hospital is, but you can ask the Thai Government, probably the Navy."

Le son embraced the woman's shoulder then he pulled out a ten dollar bill. He took the woman's hand and squeezed the money in it before she even knew it. When she opened up her hand and found the money, she screamed with excitement then bowed her head to Le Son.

Now that Le Son has found out about his sister and his friend, Le Son headed back to Bangkok to go to the U.S embassy. He had a good feeling that he would soon reunite his family.

Reverend Si, who took care of the camp, had Mai Lan come to see him to discuss her future maternity. Perhaps she would have to give the baby to the church so she could receive the help from the Church. Mai Lan was nervous about the deal that the church offered. She really did not have any other options. Still tears kept on rolling off her face. Father Si, with a comforting tone of voice, soothed her emotion the best that he could. He understood how a mother felt about losing her child, "Child, when you process for departure, the church will give you back your baby. You can still take care of your child."

Wiping the tears off her face, Mai Lan still had doubts about the future of her son. She said, "Reverend, not that I don't trust you… but I have been through a lot of hardships, I don't know what to think anymore. Would I ever have my child back?"

"Of course, you would. All we want is to give your child a little more nutrition than you can find here so that he or she can be healthy. As you see, the camp's budget does not provide the necessary supplements for a child. So the Church has provided a small fund for an infant as long as he or she belongs to the church. Once you get ready to leave the country, you will get your child back…I promise."

Mai Lan bowed her head to show respect to the reverend. Her trust in him started to grow, "You are very kind to our people," Mai Lan said, "but I never expected this to happen, I trust you with my heart. I pray to God for your blessing."

Reverend Si patted on her shoulder to ensure the safety of her future child.

Before she left the office Mai Lan asked, "Sir, do I have to sign anything?"

Reverend Si waved his hand goodbye, "Bye, don't worry. Once you have your baby then we talk about it. You know if you pass the interview you may not have to worry about that."

"I hope so, Father," she said from the deep part of her mind.

The thug from the whorehouse arrived at the Navy hospital at dawn. The hospital was quiet at night. No one was around except a couple custodians who were cleaning the floor. Every now and then a nurse would walk around to check on the patients. The hard part was to locate the wing where they kept Sami. The thug put on an old uniform to match the custodian; then began to infiltrate in the hospital. Except for the sound of crickets there was no activity in the hallway whatsoever. The only thing that he could do now was to look for another custodian and try to ask for directions, *have to be careful*, he thought. Down the hallway he saw an old maintenance guy fixing a light switch. Acting like a new custodian who had got lost in their first day, he approached the maintenance guy and started a conversation, "Hi, Bi is sick. I am here to take his place until he gets well. I'm kind of lost in here. Can you show me how to go to his area, please?"

It was hard for him to speak politely to someone, most of the time, he spoke with his fists. The maintenance guy looked at the big muscular body of the thug and asked, "You don't even come close to looking like a janitor. Do you practice kickboxing?"

For a moment the thug thought that he had blown his cover. He quickly regained his cool and said, "Yes, I used to. Now I work all the time. I didn't really have much time to practice."

The maintenance guy observed the thug closely. There was something about him that didn't quite make sense, "Man, look at that big scar on your jaw. What happened to you? I think I've seen you somewhere before."

The thug began to get aggravated. If it was in his territory, he would punch this guy right on the nose; but he had to back down, "No, I don't think so. Would you like to show me how to get there before I'm late for work please?"

The maintenance guy stopped checking on the thug and pointed at the different building, "Over there, but you have to report to the security desk first. Your partner usually worked in the high security wing. See you around."

The thug shook hands with the maintenance guy and then rushed toward the pointed direction. "It isn't easy like I thought," the thug mumbled, "I have to find the way to get around the security." He carefully approached the wing where they kept the high security patients. Observing an alternate route without getting caught, he figured out how to take Sami with him. He entered a dark corridor that led to the security desk. There were some windows that didn't close all the way, he thought of climbing up to the top floor. Perhaps he could trace where they kept Sami. The risk of getting caught was still great.

Before he approached the desk, he stood there for a moment to study the situation. Should he climb to the other level and how he is going to make it? He could see the desk from where he stood and a security guard still sat there. After determining the risk of being caught by the desk he decided to climb up to the window. While he tried to find a way to climb up the window, a sudden hard tap on his shoulder caught him off guard. He took a defensive position and was ready to strike back. As it turned out, it was the maintenance guy who had snuck up on him to play a joke. The maintenance guy stepped back, waving his hands to show peace, "Hey, hey, take it easy man, just playing."

The thug, now recognizing the maintenance guy, also acted like he is playing to try and divert the possibility of being exposed, "Hey man, you gave me a heart attack. I heard a lot of ghost stories about this hospital."

"Hell yeah, there are a lot of ghosts around here. What are you waiting for? The desk is over there, go to work man," the maintenance guy said.

"Oh, I will just wait for my co-worker, somehow, he's late," the thug falsely responded.

"You can go in with me," the maintenance man insisted.

Hesitating for a moment, the thug knew that he didn't have a choice but to follow the maintenance man. He said, "Yes, I guess I can go in with you, thank you very much."

The thug slowly followed the maintenance man. One thing certain and that was that he had been through a lot more dangerous situations than this, so he was able to act normal without any signs of nervousness. The two men approached the desk and signed in the log; the maintenance man introduced the thug to security guard, "Here is the guy to take over the job of one of your custodians."

The security guard glanced at the thug and saw his identity card attached to his pocket, then pointed at the hall that lead to the security wing. The thug was accompanied by the maintenance man who was pretty well known in the hospital, so he managed to avoid some suspicion from the guard. He couldn't believe that he could easily pass this security desk without a lot of hassle. He found a storage room down the hall and took out the cleaning equipment. The whole business had been pretty smooth, now he had to locate Sami's room before getting caught. Somehow he has to move him out of this hospital.

The young man came to visit Mai Lan again. This time he brought more food than clothing and saw her in person. The reverend allowed her to meet him in the chapel. Mai Lan felt embarrassed because her belly had swelled a little bigger than before. She was avoiding looking straight into his eyes, the eyes that contained a lot of love for her. The young man felt the uneasiness in her and carefully approached her with words of comfort, "Hi, how are you doing? You look pale. Do you have enough food to eat? I brought more food this time. I like seeing you healthy, both you and your baby."

Stunned at what he said, she felt even more shameful because the not yet born baby had no father. In her country that was even more shameful for the family when a child was born without paternity. The young man understood her uneasy feeling and kindly held her hand, caressed, then comforted her, "Don't worry, you just take care of yourself. Your pregnancy does not change my feeling for you. I would be very happy if you let me help you."

Mai Lan didn't know what to do except to leave her hand to rest in his. She felt the tingling sensation from the heat of his flesh. She also felt her heartbeat escalate along with his. Both of them sat quietly for a moment, sharing each other feelings. Then Mai Lan quietly pulled her hand away from him. She couldn't explain her troubled mind to him. She had not yet erased the memory of her fiancé who was the real father of her child; the one who she still loved. The young man wasn't just an ordinary man, he was her savior and he helped her when she needed it the most. Mai Lan couldn't easily refuse his special interest in her, besides, he was the only one who could help her in her present situation. She will need a lot for her baby. The young man saw her troubling face. He raised her chin up and looked straight to her eyes and spoke softly, "Hey, hey, smile. This is not the end of the world. You should be happy so your baby will be happy, too."

Feeling a little easier with his kindness, Mai Lan smiled at him and then rubbed on her tummy. This is the first time she would speak to him a little more freely, "When the baby grows up, he or she can call you uncle."

"I would be delighted," the young man replied in joy.

Then, he lightly kissed her on her forehead. All this time he had been dreaming about her. This was the first time that he was able to be close to her beautiful face.

Mai Lan asked, "Sir, I do not know your name. Would you mind telling me? My baby should know his or her uncle's name."

The young man, sort of thinking for a moment, then answered, "You know, I don't even know my real name. I remember my parents used to call me by my nickname. Then when they died, they took it with them. My mother was Vietnamese so she always called me Be Ti. So that is my name, you can call me that, if you want."

Mai Lan, sort of surprised by his simplistic nature, kindly spoke, "That's all right, we will find you a good name. Now, we just call you Anh Hai. Okay?"

They now both felt the comfort between them. It made the conversation seem more exciting. The young man, as if he just found a new family of his own, was as happy as a child who just received a toy. "You know all these years of being a slave for the pirates; I never found anybody that I could really talk to. Just like being in prison, sometimes I thought about killing myself. The will to avenge my family has kept me alive. Plus, I had to pretend to be deaf and dumb so the pirates would let me alone."

Quietly listening to the horrible story of his life, Mai Lan shared in his pain of his relatives who perished because of greed. Her innocent little brother also was killed for the same reason. The thought of her brother caused her tears to begin to crystallize in her eyes. The young man took out a handkerchief and blotted her tears and felt badly for getting her upset, "I'm sorry, I don't mean to make you sad. I never had anyone to talk to before. I think the time to exact revenge is close. The pirate leader has to pay for all his crimes and for a lot of people who were slaughtered by him."

Mai Lan wiped the tears from her eyes and said, "I thought that he was burned in the fire. I couldn't believe that he lived through that. My little brother does not rest in peace until the pirate gets punished to the full extent of the law. Now, we can help the government to bring this horrible human being to justice; until then, the crying souls will be at rest."

The two of them now shared the same thought, the same deep feelings which they haven't been able to share with anybody. The more Mai Lan came close to him, the more she felt more comfort, and for now, he was welcomed to be one of her good friends. Sitting quietly for a moment, they wanted to tell each other a thousand stories but the thoughts couldn't make into words; so they just watched the sparrows playing in the yard. Outside, the brightening sun began shifting lower to the West, yielding less heat in the camp; and the breeze was sifting throughout the area somehow adding a little comfort to the population. Realizing that it was getting late, the young man had to leave the camp. He stood up and promised to come back to visit her soon, "It must getting late. I have to go to work. I will be back. If you need anything just let me know, I don't mind. Now we are like family, so don't be afraid. If you want to just talk to the priest, it's okay."

After he finished talking, he raised his hands out to Mai Lan to initiate the good-bye. Mai Lan also stood up and placed her hands in his. The young couple silently stood for a moment hand in hand without exchanging a word. Their hearts exchanged signals. The sign of a new relation was just born. Mai Lan did not feel strange with him any longer. Instead, she experienced new emotion tingling in her heart every time he touched her. She really couldn't deny the sentiment that silently attacked her heart and she tried to avoid to looking into his flamboyant eyes. Mumbling the word good bye, but deeply, she enjoyed his company. When he walked away, she sat back down in the empty room, feeling lonely once again.

It seemed like all the men in her life always left her. The calmness in the room added to the solitary atmosphere which reminded her of her brother. She thought of him every time she was alone. She always blamed herself because she was unable to save his life. The picture of him being drowned replayed in her memory; she missed her parents at home. One day she had to tell her parents that their son died a horrible death at sea without a decent burial. Every time the memory revived, tears just poured out of her eyes. Her family had built a great hope for her brother's future, and now he was gone forever.

The bright orange ball slowly descended to the horizon and reflected the blue scales of clouds in the sky. Rubbing her tummy again, Mai Lan tried to imagine the face of her child. Will he look like her fiancé or maybe she will look like her? *No matter who the child looks like*, she thought, *this is her future*. She slowly got up, gathered the food given by the young man, and headed back to the building.

The two agents tried to find out where the young man lived. They had to find him soon to retrieve their lost treasure. They knew he was released but couldn't find his address. They knew that the boy would have to return to testify in court so they have to find him before then. Navy Intelligence had the document that told of his whereabouts. It was kind of hard for them to get into the headquarters files to search for the information. One thing which the agents didn't know was that their treasure was gone forever. It belonged to the refugees so it had been returned to the refugees.

It was nice in the evening around the Navy hospital. The cool breeze from the ocean fanned through the room. Nguyen Tam just finished his dinner. It was a small portion but just enough for him. Nguyen Tam waited for Thuy to get back so he could ask her to take him outside. He sat by himself in the old white room feeling lonely. Now he could really appreciate the presence of Thuy. She always brought joy to his life and without her, his life would be so lonesome.

The footsteps in the hallway awoke Nguyen Tam from his

daydream. He looked out of the door to see if Thuy was coming back. Perhaps he would ask her if she wanted to go outside. The sound of the footsteps reached the outside of the doorway and Nguyen Tam peered out the door and said, "Thuy, you're back early." He didn't hear a response, so he looked out the door to see who was coming. He could see a strange man who he had never seen before. The man pushed a mop bucket and some cleaning equipment, *must be a new custodian*, he thought. Nguyen Tam got an uneasy feeling about the new custodian. The man didn't look like the type of person who would push a broom. Nguyen Tam missed the old custodian who had been nice to him. The thug glanced at Nguyen Tam then quickly disappeared down the hall way. His attitude seemed real nasty compared to the other one.

About that time Thuy came back with a couple of bananas. She looked around the room then asked Nguyen Tam, "I heard you speaking to someone. Who were you speaking to?"

"Really, you heard that? It was the new custodian. He probably replaced the other one. This guy looked mean and nasty. I have a bad feeling about him. Did you see him?" Nguyen Tam asked.

Thinking back, Thuy said "Yes, I saw him with the maintenance man down at the security desk. Yes, he does look like one of the pirates."

"By the looks of this guy, he is not an ordinary custodian. He is up to something. We will have to watch this guy closely. We have to report him to the security officer. They may want to check this guy out."

"Don't you think the security guard already checked him out? I wonder what happened to the old custodian, he was so nice to us," Thuy said, sounding regretful.

"Maybe this guy just took over for a few days?" Nguyen Tam wondered aloud.

"This is such a nice evening. Would you like to go outside?" Thuy invited.

"Yes, you read my mind. I was going to ask you that." Nguyen Tam was glad that Thuy had the same idea.

Thuy fixed his hospital gown to try to look nice and neat. Sitting in the courtyard looking out of the clear blue ocean; the couple enjoyed the fresh breeze fanning over their bodies. It felt so good to be outside since he had been locked up in the small room all day. Nguyen Tam felt like a free bird that had just gotten out of its cage.

Thuy sat next to him on the old stone bench. She watched a flock of seagulls hunt for baitfish and wished that she had wings to fly wherever she wanted. Thinking about her brother, Thuy asked Nguyen Tam, "After your shoulder gets better, do you know where we will go from here? We can't stay here forever, you know."

"I don't really know, but we have to wait for the Thai government to make a decision. We may have to stay here a little while longer to be witnesses for the prosecution. Then we will probably be off to one of the refugee camps, where we will wait for an interview," Nguyen Tam answered. "Somehow, I feel like something may go wrong," he added in a concerned voice.

The gorgeous evening soon distracted the young couple from their worries. The natural beauty of relaxed them. The coolness of the ocean breeze soothed their minds and the peaceful atmosphere calmed their anxiety. Thuy said, "Look at the beautiful sunset Tam. I wish that life could always be this simple and peaceful. The ocean looks so innocent. It's a shame that so many people were killed in this beautiful scenery." Then she sighed, "How long will it take to erase this horrible memory?"

Nguyen Tam said, "You know, we don't realize how valuable freedom can be until we lose it. Then we end up paying a great price for it."

The thug was getting close to the room which housed Sami. Most of the rooms were empty so the thug didn't have to spend a lot of time to find him. The thug had forgotten what Sami looked like. He felt as though he would recognize him. He carefully approached each room and checked them out. He found Sami lying motionless on his bed with bandages covering half of his face. The thug carefully looked around to see if anybody was coming. He quietly approached Sami's bed and whispered in his ear, "Shhh…Sami wake up it's me, Songkhu."

Sami slowly opened up his eyes and tried to focus on the individual who spoke to him. He finally recognized the thug, "Hey Songkhu, is that you man? It has been a long time. How are you doing? You still work for my mother?"

"Yes, I still work for your mother. That's why I'm here, to get you out," the thug answered with a grin on his face.

"What happened to the custodian? Did he get paid? I didn't see him working tonight. By the way, how you get in here, man?" Sami questioned.

The thug gave the hand signal for him to slow down, "Hey, chill out, man. He's dead, that is how I got in here. Now, let's figure out how to get you out of here."

Sami, still surprised, asked again, "You say the custodian is dead, how?"

"Yes, he's dead," the thug answered. "What's up with you, man? Why you are worried about that ass….?"

"No, but I still owe him a favor," Sami reluctantly answered.

"Yeah, that bastard nearly choked your mom to death. We had to kill him to save her," the thug explained. "Anyway, I used his I.D. card to get in here."

"He attacked my mother for real? Did she pay him like I told him she would?"

"I don't know. That's between your mother and him. We just had to kill him because he hurt your mother, the hell with him, man. I will try to find a way to get you out of here before somebody finds out."

"Wait! Did you bring the toy with you?"

"Yea, why? Your mother gave it to me in case of an emergency."

"I need it." His voice now became cold and determined.

The thug thought that he heard wrong so he said again, "What did you say? You want the gun? Are you for real, man? You and I are never going to get out of here. Your mother never told me to let you have the gun. Come on, man. Forget it."

Sami begged, "Come on, man. This s.o.b took everything from me, including my crew. I have to kill him so they can rest their souls. Find me a wheel chair and let me have the gun and you can leave. I rather die here than leave dishonorably."

The thug understood Sami's feeling. If caught, he could possibly spend a long time in jail. If they found out about the murder of a government employee, he was sure to catch a death sentence. He tried to convince Sami one more time, "Listen to me, let's get out of here now. When you heal up, then we can go kill him. It's already going to be hard to leave this place quietly. You go and shoot somebody and make a lot of noise, we are going to get caught for sure. Let go, man."

Sami was determined to kill him, nothing would change his

mind, "Look at me, man. I don't want to live like a beggar. You know me. This is the end for me. This is my last chance to repay the debt to my shipmates. You just leave me the gun and go, my mother would understand. Tell her this is my decision. I would rather die here rather than live my life a cripple. I appreciate you coming here to help me but you have to understand my situation. I don't want to see you get caught. Leave me the gun, and get out of here. I will find my way out later."

Not able to change his mind, the thug took out the gun and checked the pistol's condition, put on the safety, then stuck it underneath the blanket for Sami, "Here is the pistol your mother gave me, use it wisely. I will wait for you outside for one hour. After that, you're on your own. Good luck."

"Thanks, man. If I make it out of here, I will owe you." Sami waved to the thug then lay down with a serious look on his face. The thug looked at Sami one last time before he left the room. He had the feeling that Sami would never get out of this place alive. He shook his head then left the room quietly.

Now lying alone in the small white room, Sami relived the last moment when he encountered the strange man who shot him in the leg. He tried to recall his enemy's face. According to the dead custodian, he knew the man was still alive in this hospital. He sort of remembered the face, and with a shoulder's wound, he couldn't miss. Sami put his hand on the cold trigger of the pistol. Determination boiled up inside him. Now he had to find a way to get to this man, to put him away forever. He regretted that the custodian had gotten killed. A thought sparked in his head, he must patiently wait for a right moment to strike. To kill this man would also eliminate a potential witness in court. Satisfied with the idea he hid the gun inside his clothes and went back to sleep.

Le Son returned to his hotel in Bangkok after a long day at the refugee camp. Exhausted, he laid naked under the air conditioning unit to try and cool off while he thought about the people at the camp. He really felt sorry for the children who have to live in such horrible conditions. They were treated more or less like prisoners. Tomorrow, he planned to go to the U.S. Consulate to request a permission to get into the Navy hospital where his sister and his friend were staying. He imagined they would be very happy to see him. Then he would try to start the process for them to come to America where they would start a new life.

Mai Lan, with the package from the young man, slowly walked back to her building. Xuan spotted Mai Lan from far away, waving and screaming, "Hey, sister. You have more food? He is really a nice guy, isn't he?"

Mai Lan signaled her to be quiet. The young girl realized that she was a little too loud, covered her mouth up, "Oops, sorry! I was a little too loud. Wasn't I?"

Mai Lan, patted on Xuan's head smiled and said, "I don't really know what to do. He keeps giving me food, and I don't have anything in return."

"I don't think he expects anything," Xuan reasoned.

"We can't even feed ourselves, much less…" Mai Lan answered.

Xuan said, "Hey, you know what. I have an idea."

"What, buy a lottery ticket?" Mai Lan joshed back.

"No, we don't even have a lottery here," Xuan debated without realizing that it was just a joke.

Mai Lan apologized, "Hey, it's just a joke. Of course, there is no lottery here. Sorry."

With a serious look on her face she said, "No, listen, we can sell the clothes and some of the food, and…"

"Then what?" This time, Mai Lan got a little more curious about the idea.

Xuan hesitated for a moment then slowly spoke, "Well, I think we can take the money and start up some kind of business. He can bring you some stuff from the outside. You know some of the people who live here have money sent from overseas."

Mai Lan was surprised by the young girl's idea. Maybe she wasn't dumb after all. Mai Lan tried to reason, "There is no way for me to ask for that kind of favor from him. I already owe him a lot. By the way, what are we going to do with the money?"

"Oh, don't worry about that. I see a lot of people like to drink coffee in the morning. The coffee around here is no good, so…"

She paused and Mai Lan, who was interested in the idea, rushed the girl to finish her sentence, "So what? Go on. Who is going to make the coffee?"

Xuan added, "I do. I used to filter the coffee at home. We had a small coffee shop and I used to get up early in the morning to make it. Don't worry, I can handle it." The girl sounded very convincing.

Mai Lan thought about how much money she could generate opening a small coffee shop, "I don't know how much it takes to do that. This is not a bad idea. I'll tell you what, you go around and ask people who wants to buy this stuff. In the meantime, I will ask reverend Si for advice, I'm willing to take a chance if you think that you can handle it."

The young girl said, "Oh wow, you're going to do it. Yes! I have a gold ring I can sell for some money."

"No, don't sell it yet. Let's see how much we can get out of all this stuff. Then we will talk about that."

Xuan, happy with Mai Lan's decision, embraced her then quickly disappeared out the door. Mai Lan sat quietly by herself rubbing on her stomach to check the growth of the fetus. She tried to guess if there is a boy or a girl who is doing the squirming in her tummy. She felt sad that the baby being born will be without the care of the father. Moments like this reminded Mai Lan of her fiancé. The struggle to survive and the distance have somehow faded the image of her fiancé in her memory and it was replaced by the strange faces of the surrounding neighbors. The mad love for him had once driven her into an indefinite pleasure but now remained with shame and loneliness. She did not regret offering him her virginity but felt ashamed to bare the dishonor for her family and herself. What is she going to tell her family about her baby? The strictness of her family's code of conduct never permitted a decent woman being pregnant without being marriage. These sadden matters, which piled up in her mind and linked with the worries for her future. Together it would breakdown her state of mind. Then a sudden idea just swept through her mind telling her that she has to get up and forget about her past and be strong for her baby's future. She got up and went to look for reverend Si to ask his opinion about the small business she planned to start.

Sami, with so many thoughts rolling in his head, kept turning on his bed. He would like to get to his opponent as soon as possible, before the hospital discharged him, and this is the only chance which he had to get his revenge. According to the custodian, his opponent's room wasn't too far from where he's at. After he killed the man; he would be able to save himself. Then a sad but solid thought sparked in his head, he rather end his life here instead of living like a cripple. Touching the cold steel of the revolver was like the last insurance policy, providing him the last assurance of his wish. While he was lying on the ground with the fire surrounding him, it was so hot he thought he was in hell and that he would never get out. There was time that he wished he had died with his team mates, but destiny kept him alive to fulfill his vengeance. Soon he would be able to get himself into wheelchair and then he would go find the man who destroyed his life. Sami never did actually know what he looked like or where he came from and he never allowed any male survivor. This man single-handedly wiped out his entire crew and almost killed him, too. Sami had no clue how the man got on the island or when. Normally, they made sure everybody in the boat drowned before they left the scene but Sami wasn't so sure himself about the last boat that they robbed. They were rushing to leave so he didn't have enough time to check. Perhaps his enemy snuck on the vessel about that time. He concluded the man has to die. He lightly squeezed the cold steel of the revolver again before he reentered his frequent nightmare which engulfed him with fire.

The young man with no name walked home with plenty of hope and joy. It was the first time he was able to be close with his dream girl. He loved her so much that he smelled his clothes to recapture the sweet moment with her. He looked forward to meeting her again soon. It was getting dark when he got to his little shaggy room which he paid a small fee. It wasn't much but he called it home; something which he didn't have before. Upon entering the room which was getting dark, he wasn't aware that someone was waiting for him as he headed for the light switch in the corner. Then he felt someone yank hard on his collar pushing him down on the floor. Then he heard a voice, "Stay down on the floor, don't move. I will kill you."

The young man, obeying the order, remained sitting on the floor and reluctantly questioned the intruder, "What did I do? Did I get in some kind of trouble?"

The man answered with hatred in his voice, "Sorry? You're a little thief. You steal all the jewelry that we hid in the kitchen, that we hid in the kitchen. You better give it back to us, or we're going to hurt you real bad." Before he finished the sentence, he kicked the young man's ribcage. The young man screamed in pain, rolled on the floor and tried to avoid another blow. He convinced the intruder that he had no idea of what they are talking about, "Please don't hurt me. I didn't take any of your jewelry. Believe me, I am telling you the truth." Then, he remembered the people that found the gold in the kitchen, he told them, "Oh, I remember now. The refugees found some hidden gold in the kitchen but they said the jewelries belonged to them. So they gave it back to the rightful owners. I swear on my mother's grave, I didn't have anything to do with the jewelry. Besides, I wouldn't live in this dump if I had the money."

The two agents listened to his convincing voice and determined that he's telling the truth. They threatened the young man, "Perhaps you're telling the truth, we are still investigating the facts. You will be in prison for life. We will ask the people on the boat, if they say something different, we'll be back."

"I would never tell you lies, I swear," replied the young man.

The two agents quickly disappeared into the dawn and left the young man lying on the ground in pain. After they were gone, the small room returned to its silence and darkness. The young man still lay on the ground holding his rib cage. He didn't bother to get up to turn the light on. The sense of happiness now being replaced with a lonesome sadness, and somehow, the lovely image of the girl just appeared in his mind, which somehow soothing his pain with love and hope. The young man slowly got up and sat on his favorite bamboo chair. Alone in the dark, painting a romantic future for them two; *some day*, he thought.

Le Son got up early in the morning and went to the U.S consular in Bangkok to ask for permission to enter the Thai Royal Navy base to search for his sister. The response from the consular was that it would take at least two days before they could grant him a permit from the Thai government to enter their premises. However, the process might take longer because, according to the U.S Consular, they kept these personnel in the restricted area. Now, he had to spend more time which he didn't have in Bangkok to wait for permission to enter the Navy hospital. Despite all the obstacles along the way, Le Son still had high hopes he would meet his sister and his friend. Only one thing he wasn't aware of was that they would get transferred as soon as Nguyen Tam's shoulder wound was healed up. It might only take a few more days.

Le Son stood outside the hotel, looking at the heavy traffic in Bangkok which was very similar to Saigon's heavy congestion at noon time. Motorcycles were zigzagging everywhere which puffed out the very dense smoke. Being spoiled with the nice clean air in the states, Le Son was choking with the gasoline odor being cooked by the hot tropical sun. Aborting the idea of touring the city, Le Son retreated back to his room which had much cooler air and waited for the evening to explore the city of Bangkok.

Mai Lan sat in front of the tin building to catch the evening breeze, thinking of the small coffee business which Xuan had discussed with her before. If she sold all the stuff, she would just have enough money to buy some coffee to start with. She remembered that the water is very scarce in the camp. They only have so much water to use for everything, condensed milk, and sugar...etc. Then the voice of Xuan from distant woke her up, "Hey sister, what are you worrying about? I think you are afraid that we don't have enough money for the business?"

Mai Lan kindly smiled at Xuan's and avoided answering her question, "No, I was just thinking about how we can find enough water to make the coffee, and condensed milk, and..."

Xuan cut off Mai Lan's sentence and added in the kind of voice which Mai Lan had never heard from Xuan before, "You don't have to worry too much about that. We will pay more for the water delivery guy. He will let us have more portions of water and we will try to cut down the cooking and washing. I think we should have enough water for the business. Don't you think, sister?"

Mai Lan commented, "Hey listen to you, a business girl. You are surprising me every day Xuan. Well, if you can get what we need to start out the business, I'm in."

"But..." Xuan patted on Mai Lan's shoulder.

Mai Lan thought Xuan was trying to tell her some bad news, "But what? We have more problems? What?"

Xuan slowly replied, "No, I don't have a problem. You have the problem."

Mai Lan, pointing her thumb at her chest, didn't have any idea what Xuan was talking about, "Me, I have a problem? What kind of problem are you talking about?"

Xuan, smiling, tried to avoid offending Mai Lan's feeling, "I mean, you know…!"

This time, Mai Lan was even more anxious to find out what Xuan tried to tell her, "Know what? Come on, you better come out and say it. Don't worry I'm not going to get mad at you."

This time, Xuan held Mai Lan's hand and said, "I mean you have to ask for help from that guy. I know that he will be glad to help you. Anyway, we will pay him for everything. What do you think?"

This was a sensitive subject to Mai Lan. She didn't know if she had the strength to ask him for anything. She knew that he's always willing to help her but to ask him for any favor was something that really bothered her, even a small one. Mai Lan, hiding her weakness in front of Xuan, made a quick promise which she really didn't want to, "Yes, let me think about it, I really hate to use people like that. He was so good to us already."

"But we are going to pay him back. This is business, you know." Xuan still tried to convince Mai Lan to venture in the business. Finally, Mai Lan promised to do it just to get Xuan to quit talking about it, "Well, I guess I'm going to ask him but it's up to him to agree. I'm not going to force him to do anything. Now we won't talk about this anymore. I have to go to Father Si to ask his opinion. We have to ask permission from the warden before we can start anything. So don't get to excited."

Looking at the disappointment on Xuan's face, Mai Lan patted her shoulder and promised that she would do her best to get the business going quickly, "Oh, come on now. This is not the end of the world. I'll be back with the good news. By the way, we have to find someone who is willing to buy our stuff."

The happy smile soon returned back on her face, Xuan stood up and ran out of the door yelling back to Mai Lan, "Good luck, sister. I won't let you down." Then she disappeared through the tin buildings.

Mai Lan slowly got up from her wooden platform which was a substitute for a bed and headed to the camp's administration building to seek the assistance of reverend Si.

After waiting for Sami for a few hours, the thug left the Navy hospital and returned back to the whore house to meet with Sami's mother, telling what's happening to her son. Upon seeing him return she said, "You're back already, was he hurt bad?"

The thug nodded his head, "Yes, he is hurt pretty badly. They cut one of his legs off. Plus he was badly burned. He wanted to stay there a little longer so he can finish some business."

The old woman who seemed to have a little more concern for her long lost son said, "You know he is in bad shape, why didn't you stick around to help him, where is my gun?"

The thug, reluctant to answer the question said, "Well, I told him to get out but he kept telling me he has to stay and begged me to give him the gun so he can protect himself. I had no choice."

"No choice my ass…" the woman said angrily.

"You gave him the gun so he can go to kill somebody. You're a water buffalo head son of bitch, I hope the cops don't trace down my gun. You have to go back over there to take my gun back."

PART 7

"I have to go back overthere over there? You mean it? I'm going to get my ass caught this time for real." He tried to get the madam to change her mind, but she kept on demanding that he go back to retrieve her gun. She ordered him to go back right away before Sami used her gun to kill somebody. "You better go back over there quick and tell him that his mama wants the gun back right away and get the hell out of there before you get caught with my gun."

The thug still tried to get out of going back to the hospital, he said, "You know your son is very hard-headed, he's never going to give up the gun. What I am going to do then?"

The woman grunted at the thug then said, "I don't care what you have to do, I just want my gun back. I know my son, he is going to kill somebody. Don't waste time standing here arguing with me. When he kills someone the government is going to kill him. How he is going to get away with one leg? You would be better off kill him."

The thug had no choice but to agree with the madam, "I guess you are right, I have to go back to help him with what he is going to do then I will take the gun back."

The woman, as she walked off waved her hand and said to him, "I don't care what you have to do, as long I have my gun back and no police knock on my door. If you have to, get out of there clean. I don't care what you have to do, and don't come back here empty handed."

The thug stood there for a moment, he didn't know what to think. The madam wanted to get rid of her son, her only son for the gun, shaking his head in disbelief he whispered, "Can't believe it!"

Mai Lan went to meet Reverend Si to discuss her small business. The reverend greeted her at the door smiling, "Hi, how do you feel today? Do you want to see me for something?"

"I'm doing okay, reverend. Yes, I need your opinion about the small business we're about to open," Mai Lan nervously explained her plan to the reverend.

Reverend Si told her, "Come on in, you can tell me more."

Mai Lan carefully explained what they were planning to do, then asked the reverend for the assistance in their business. Reverend Si agreed to help her to start out the business. He explained that he had to ask the permission from the warden to bring in the supplies from outside the camp. He suggested that Mai Lan could use some help from the young man who visited her sometime before. He said, "I see more and more refugees come here every day. I think that it would be a good idea to start out the business now. At least you can make some money to buy things for your baby, and it keeps you busy."

Mai Lan bowed her head and said, "Thank you very much for

your help, reverend. I pray that God always blesses you with good health. We always need you."

Reverend Si kindly patted her on the head and gave her a blessing, "That's all right, child. I want to help those who want to help themselves. I believe that you can succeed in your business. I will do my best to help you. Come back and let me know when you get ready to start. God will be with you."

Mai Lan bowed her head to say goodbye to the reverend before she left the building. Once outside, she looked at the fence which separated her from the real world and imagined what is happening on the other side. The feeling of being a prisoner kept haunting her since the first day, ironically, searching for freedom inside the barb wire fence. The image of the young man standing outside the fence reminded her of his existence in her life. Now she felt lonely without him and she missed his soft voice, "perhaps", she sighed, "one day."

Mai Lan returned to the building and found Xuan waiting for her. With a big smile on her face, she didn't bother to wait for Mai Lan to approach she started yelling, "There you are. I got good news. I found…"

"Shuttt…!"

Mai Lan waived her hand meaning to be quiet and to wait for her. Recognizing that she was being loud, Xuan quickly covered her mouth telling Mai Lan that she understood and patiently waited for her. Being pregnant, Mai Lan could not move like before. She finally approached Xuan and sat down. Xuan, unable to wait, opened up the conversation right away, "I'm sorry for being so loud, I am just so excited."

"I know, but we have to keep it down. We still have to wait for the warden's decision. Reverend Si agreed to help us by speaking with the warden about the business. So, what is your good news?"

Xuan, crossed her arm around Mai Lan's shoulder, spoke with a soft voice in her ear, "I found people who will buy some of your stuff, plus I can sell my gold ring. That should be enough for us to buy a coffee filter and some coffee. Plus, I can get some small cups from the security guard."

Mai Lan, surprised by how Xuan can buy things from the guard, asked Xuan one more time, "Security guard? How did you get acquainted with security guard? Are you sure that we are not in any kind of trouble?"

Xuan hugged Mai Lan in her arms and confirmed that everything will be all right, "Hey… don't worry. He promised to help us if we need it. He spoke a little Vietnamese." She covered her mouth, then whispered in Mai Lan' ear, "I think he likes me."

Mai Lan, unable to help herself, smiled, "Look at you, a big girl in love, I can't believe it." Then she got serious and warned Xuan, "Don't get in trouble. If you get an interview, what are you going to do then?"

Xuan knocked on her head and said, "Yea, you're right. I don't think we are going to get serious, that is against camp's rules, thank you sister." Then she hugged Mai Lan again before heading out the door, "Right now, all I'm thinking about is the business, nothing else." Mai Lan watched the girl disappear out the door.

Le Son got up after an afternoon nap, walked outside to check the temperature and went to find something to eat. He strolled along the sidewalk to do some sightseeing. While looking for a good restaurant, he passed a small restaurant which was decorated with a bunch of glass jars which contained different highly toxin venomous snakes; among them were King Cobra. Curious, Le Son stopped to check it out and he saw that most of the customers were older but were accompanied by a younger date, "This is not a hot place for dating there must be something else," Le Son observed.

So he walked in to find out what the snakes were for. The owner pointed at the king cobra explaining, "You drink his blood, your dick gets a lot harder, good boom, boom tonight."

Le Son, embarrassed, heard people talking about it before and couldn't believe that it was true.

People have been telling him that snake meat tasted like chicken meat and he wanted to try it out but still felt a little funny. And to drink the fresh blood from the live and extremely lethal reptile in the Orient, he had to think again. He waved to the owner, promising that he would return to try it later. Le Son took one last look at the King cobra. The venomous snake seemed harmless in the glass cage, but if it had its freedom, the King would be a fearful opponent. Le Son thought about coming back to eat the snake to see what its meat really tasted like, but he was looking for a seafood restaurant.

He was hungry for a nice crunchy fish fry dipped in a spicy sauce. He finally found a popular fish fry restaurant. It smelled good from outside, but when he got inside, the strange way they fried the fish almost ruined his appetite. They took the live fish in the tank, wrapped it with wire mesh and then slowly dipped the fish in the hot oil frying it while it was still alive. Le Son asked the owner, "What is the purpose for doing that? Do you have to fry the fish like that? It looks inhumane."

The owner said, "Hey where you come from, man?" shrugged his shoulder and answered, "Yes, kind of looking rough, but people like it. Hey, you don't have to look at it. It's good and fresh, guaranteed."

Le Son stood for a moment, deciding whether he was going to have some fish or not. The fish fry smelled great, really attracting his demanding appetite. The cook suggested that long as he does not look at it, he won't feel bad.

"You come back in a few minutes. We have the fish ready for you. See?" The cook waved his hand to tell Le Son to leave the cooking area.

With his stomach growling, plus craving for fish fry, Le Son walked out of the restaurant for a few minutes. When he came back, the waiter showed him to the table with the fish ready to eat. The golden skin was still piping hot sending out a terrific smell and the dip sauce with bright red color from the floating hot pepper; it was really hard for anybody to turn away. Le Son had to admit that the fish was really good, the way to fry it may be a little inhuman, but it was the best fried fish that he ever had.

After dinner, Le Son walked along the sidewalk, looking for a massage parlor. *It's a waste if you don't get a body massage while you are in Bangkok*, he thought. The streets were lit with colorful neon. Having no idea where to go, he finally thought of getting a taxi to take him where he wanted to be, a nice and relaxing spa. The taxi's driver spoke a little English and took him to a nice massage parlor. He warned Le Son about the Thai girl's and how devious they could be, "This is very nice place, very relaxing, but watch out for the girls. They're very pretty, they will get you."

Le Son, smiling, told him, "Yes, I heard about Thai girls long ago. Let see how good they really are. Say, come back here in a couple hours, will you."

"Yes, I do that," replied the driver. He winked his eye at Le Son and said, "Have fun, man. See you in a couple hours."

Le Son waved back, approaching the massage parlor, eager to find out what was going on behind the deep red heavy door.

The thug got back to the hospital quite early. He sneaked inside Sami's room while he was still sleeping. He looked around to see if anyone was around, then woke Sami up, "Hey, hey. Get up man. I have to tell you something," he whispered while shaking Sami's shoulder.

Sami, deep in his usual nightmare, woke up with sweat all over his face. Facing an intruder in the dim light in the room he panicked while reaching for his gun. The thug quickly grabbed Sami's hand to stop him from firing the gun, "Hey, it's me Sami. Cool it man."

Now Sami, recognizing the thug, took his finger off the trigger and asked, "What are you doing here? I thought you were gone."

"Yeah, I came back. Your mother told me to help you with whatever had to be done and then take the gun back."

Sami, surprised, didn't know how to explain. He didn't really want anybody to get into his business, especially this, "I don't know, man. I just don't want you involved in this. You're never going to get out of here. Look at me, I have no future. I just don't feel right letting you get into my problem. So tell my mother I would ask her for this last favor for me."

The thug waved his hands and explained his situation, "Sami, you have to understand my situation. Your mother wants her gun back no matter what. Let me help you to finish what you need to finish then give me back the gun and I will split, I swear."

Sami felt that the thug was inconvincible and had no choice but to let him in. Sami began planning the execution with the thug and he knew that once he fired the gun, the guard would probably return fire and kill him. He told the thug to stay out of his way and to escape with the gun as soon as he took care of his business, "Here is the deal. You will push my wheelchair to him then leave me alone with him. When I finish the job I will toss the gun away. You pick it up and leave. Does that sound all right?" Sami asked.

The thug answered, "Yes, it sounds all right. I don't think the both of us can get out of here safely. Can you just forget the whole thing and just let it go? I will take you home and your mom will take care of you. At least you will still live to see her, right?"

Shaking his head, Sami still decided to go ahead with his plan, "You know what, lying here in this small room, every night is the same nightmare like living in hell. I'm sorry that you had to get involved in this but I just can't let that go. I don't want my mother taking care of me the rest of my life. My life is over, man. Don't you understand? I will make this quick so you don't have to get involved, all right?"

The thug seemed to understand Sami and he didn't have any more suggestions. He knew that Sami will never change his mind about his vengeance. On top of that, he knew that Sami will never accept the life of a cripple. So he said, "Well, I guess you've already made up your mind. So, what do you need to get the job done?" the thug asked.

"I need a different set of clothing. I need to change my look so nobody can recognize me. I need you to find out where he lives and for you to take me to him. That's all."

Nodding his head, the thug having no other choice but to agree with Sami's request; he said that he will return with the stuff which Sami wanted, then he quickly disappeared in the still dawn of the early morning.

It was more than two weeks since the young man had stopped by to visit. Mai Lan didn't know what happened to him and she didn't understand her real feelings for this man. She wouldn't admit herself that she missed him but the strange feeling of the loneliness kept rolling his charming face in her head. Being here with no family around, he is the only one who visited her giving her the warm and caring feeling of having her own family. She felt like she was betraying her fiancé whenever she thought of the young man. Then the loud and usual voice of Xuan rung on her ears, "Hey sister, what are you thinking about? I know you miss him, don't you? That's okay, I understand."

Mai Lan mumbled in her throat denying, "Shuttt…you're wrong. It's not what you think. I was just thinking about the business. I don't know if we can handle it."

Xuan knew she was thinking about the young man and said, "Oh no, you know that we can handle the business. It is him that you are worrying about. He hasn't stopped by in two weeks, I know. Don't worry, I know he loves you. The first chance he gets, he will come to see you. Trust me."

Mai Lan couldn't help but smile at Xuan's remarks and shyly admitted her feeling for the strange young man, "I guess I was a little worried about him. I think he is in some kind of trouble. I just have a bad feeling, that's all."

Xuan sat down next to Mai Lan, put her arm on Mai Lan' s shoulder and whispered in her ear, "There is nothing happening to him, I guarantee it. He will be here in a few days. See, I know you missed him. That's all right, he is a nice guy."

Mai Lan slightly squeezed Xuan's nose and said, "Just keep this between you and me. I don't like people gossiping about me. Anyway, I don't want him to think that I love him or anything like that. Beside, when I go to another country I can't take him along. So…"

Mai Lan stopped for a moment and Xuan continued her sentence, "So you don't want to start up something you can't finish."

Mai Lan shook her head agreeing with Xuan, "Wow, listen to you. I can't believe that you have grown up so much. This is not a big thing but I don't want people thinking that I…you know, with him."

"Don't worry sister I'm not going to tell anybody about that. Besides, I don't know anybody around here. Hey, I have some good news; the guard can get some good coffee for us." Xuan sounded very happy about the fact that they could get some coffee, she was pretty proud of that.

Mai Lan still didn't think it was a good idea to have a relationship with the government official. She looked at Xuan's happiness and she didn't want to be so skeptical. She still warned Xuan, "I just want to tell you to be careful about getting both you and the security officer in any kind of trouble. If something bad happens, they will bar you from the interview. I love you like my little sister, that's why I'm telling you all this. Don't focus too much on the business. We are just going to be here for a short time. I would like to see you and me get out of here at the same time."

Xuan held Mai Lan's hand and gently pressed it against her cheek and said, "You are right, sister. I'm just so anxious to have a business starting up. I forgot all about the interview, I promise not to do any wrong thing. Okay sister?"

Xuan sat quietly for a moment and squeezed Mai Lan's hand and said in a deep, weak tone of voice, "What if you…get to the interview before me? I don't know what I'm going to do then… when you leave…"a roll of tears silently trickled down her cheeks.

Mai Lan gently wiped the tears off of Xuan's cheeks and held on tight to her little hands she said, "Hey, we're going to be here for a while. I'm not leaving you yet. I just don't want you to get hurt. Well, another day is here, let's get our business started up."

Xuan rubbed her red and teary eyes upon hearing what Mai Lan said. She stood up quickly and yelled, "Yes, you're right sister. Let's go and take care of some business. Let's find a good place to set up the coffee stand. We have almost everything. Tomorrow he will bring us some coffee. Do you want to go with me to find a place? You need the exercise, come on. I hate seeing you sit here all day."

Since the day Mai Lan found out about her pregnancy, she very seldom went anywhere in the camp. The farthest she went was the front of the building and sat there for some fresh air. Mai Lan just didn't feel comfortable walking around the camp with her round tummy. So this was the first time she went with Xuan and she felt a little strange when people looked at her. Mai Lan tried to avoid some of the older women who sat around gossiping. The more she tried to avoid people, the more people kept looking at her. Xuan noticed Mai Lan avoiding the crowd, so she convinced Mai Lan that being shy won't help much for business. Anyway, nobody even knew who Mai Lan was. So they tried to mingle with the crowd and Xuan added, "Trust me, these people don't even know who we are. By the way, to be in business we have to be in their business. Once they know us, they will come to us for more. I know because I was in this business since childhood. I used to bring a single cup of coffee to my mom's customers quite a long walking distance. After awhile we gained more customers because of our good service. So I learned one thing, we have to reach out to people and give them what they want."

Mai Lan said, "Xuan, I have got to say. You're surprising me every day. I think you're going to handle the business all right."

Xuan, while waving to people around, let out a big smile to Mai

Lan, "Another important thing for business is the big smile. Even though sometimes you have some other problems, you still have to keep a big smile on your face."

Mai Lan patted on Xuan's shoulder and said "All right, I think you're right. How about I stand behind you and let you run the business. I will supply everything you need."

Xuan pointed her finger at the corner next to the food distribution center to Mai Lan and said, "I think this corner has a lot of business potential. People like to gather around here. If we can get the permit from the warden, this is the place. I guarantee it."

Mai Lan seemed to have little doubt about getting this location. She said, "I like the place, too, but I don't think we can get it. You know how strict they are. This is an official place of business. They don't want to see a lot of people hanging around here, especially a coffee shop. Let me speak to Father Si and see what he has to say. May be, I say…may be; he can ask the warden. You know that we may have to provide the coffee to the security guards too."

"That's okay we are glad to give them the coffee as long they're taking it easy on us. I don't really care to make a lot of money. I would just like to keep myself busy and get to mingle with everybody. That would make the day go faster."

"Yes, but we have to make some money to keep the business going, right boss?"

Xuan lightly slapped on Mai Lan's shoulder joshing with her, "Now, you're talking. I don't mean we give everything away free. Just give them a little."

"Well, let's see if we can get this corner and set up a small table with a small wood stove so we can keep the water hot, and a place for the ice. Yes, the ice. We have to find a real tight container to keep the ice cold. Now you see it isn't easy to have a business going, isn't it?"

"Yes, but after we get all these problems taken care of, it's time to make money right?" It seemed like nothing would change her mind about starting the business. She would step over all obstacles to get to it. Mai Lan vowed to give it to Xuan, "I am impressed of your willingness to achieve your goal. I will help with whatever you need. I wish…" Mai Lan just stopped her sentence for a moment, realizing that she shouldn't even think about it but the image of the young man just suddenly appeared in her mind.

Xuan noticed the slight embarrassment shown on Mai Lan's face and tried to squeeze out the rest of her thoughts, "Wish what? What do you wish, or…"

Xuan stopped and looked at Mai Lan's more reddened face, adding, "Or who do you wish?"

Mai Lan tried to hide her emotions by looking in a different direction and she diverted the conversation into a different direction, "Oh no, it's nothing like that. Maybe we can head back and I will go see reverend Si about getting the corner that you want. Okay?"

Xuan hugged Mai Lan and let out a big smile, "Sister, I love you. I don't know what to do without you."

"That's okay, my baby sister. I will be behind you all the way." They both returned to the building speechless, but in their mind a whole lot of thoughts and plans for their future business were rolling.

Nguyen Tam got up in the morning and felt that his shoulder wound was getting better. The sharp pain had somehow decreased and he could stretch his arm out a little longer and managed to get out the bed without any help from Thuy. When Thuy entered the room with the breakfast tray, he screamed out joyfully, "Thuy look, I can stretch my arm out with only a little pain. Pretty soon we will get out of here. When we get to the camp, we will have more access to find your brother. Or perhaps, with a lot of luck, he'll be there waiting for us."

Thuy, more concerned about the wound, said, "No, no, slow down will you? Don't be so excited. The open wound isn't completely healed yet; it still could possibly start bleeding, besides, I kind of like it here."

Surprised Nguyen Tam said, "Thuy, you really want to stay here? Why?"

"I just like the peaceful scenery around here. I got a job in the kitchen helping out in the morning and at lunch. So you won't see me at noon time. But for that, I can get you more food."

Nguyen Tam questioned, "You really want to stay here? The Thai Government is not going to let us stay here for a long period of time. Besides, how we are going to trace your brother down if we stay in this facility?"

Thuy fixed Nguyen Tam's hospital gown, straightened up his bed sheet then gently held Tam's hand and spoke in a soft convincing voice, "Don't worry about that for now. I heard rumors about the refugee camps. They don't have good hospitals or food there. People are starving and the living conditions are very poor. Your wound may get infected because of no available medication. The nurse told me that if your wound still bothers you, the Thai government will let you stay here a little longer. Besides, they may need you to be a witness in the case. So they want you to be one hundred percents healthy. Since I got a job in the kitchen, they don't mind me letting you have a little more food. Now do you see why I want to stay here?"

Nguyen Tam looked gratefully at Thuy and said, "You work in the kitchen now? How did you manage to do that? I'm very impressed. My shoulder is getting a lot better. If it were not for you being around, I really don't know what I would do. I just feel bad letting you work hard just for me."

"Tam, don't worry. I just can't stand around here doing nothing. Besides, this is a good place to work, I help the cook with whatever she needs. Before long, I will get fat. Don't you want to see me get fat? Well, I have to go back to work now. I see you a little later with some more food."

Thuy, smiling at Nguyen Tam, seemed so happy with the temporary occupation. She was so proud for what she was bringing in. To her this was the first step to earning something in the strange land. Nguyen Tam felt a little awkward, in his country the man had to provide a good living to his family, or perhaps his girlfriend. With mixed emotions, happy because he saw the smile on Thuy's face and sad because he felt so helpless; the old days of being young and healthy were now replaced by a tiresome and fatigue body.

The thought of being free from the hospital bed has been always on his mind. Nguyen Tam slowly moved his upper body to find out how much the pain would restrict him from getting out of his room. Being outside and breathing the fresh air was all that could he wish for right now. For him being outside to enjoy the peaceful scenario would be of help to his wound. Thuy thought that for fast healing, staying in bed and to rest all day was the only option. Nguyen Tam didn't agree with her opinion but wasn't opposed to her idea and he didn't want to get her upset. Being laid up in bed all day didn't help him much; it was rotting out his back.

Nguyen Tam was ready for some action and wished that he could somehow return to the old days of soldiering. Back then, he had all the potential and strength to be one of the best. He survived all of the difficult tasks and did them in a minimum time. He was a fearless war machine against the enemy. After the war, the unbearable sadness which was caused by the loss of his family and his unit, had deteriorated his might.

He used the heavy liquor to bury his memories of being a good soldier and a good husband. Nguyen Tam lost his dignity and health all at once. The healthy body had been replaced by the rotting organs caused by the alcohol. Nguyen Tam remembered the time he lay on the street like a dead corpse and almost out of his mind. The pedestrians avoided him like a dreadful disease. Nobody bothered to try to help him and the business flushed him away like a stray dog. His body was so numb which he couldn't even recognize himself as a human being.

While he was daydreaming, somebody knocked on the door and woke Nguyen Tam from his thoughts. The same two agents and the translator were at the door. Nguyen Tam waved to them and invited them into the room, "Hi, come in. How are you doing today? What can I do for you today?"

The translator waved back to Nguyen Tam and said, "How are you doing? We stopped by to see if you were doing all right. We have a few questions that we want to ask you. If that's okay with you?"

"Yes, anything that you want to know," he replied.

One of the agents asked a question then told the translator to ask Nguyen Tam. The translator turned to Nguyen Tam and asked, "They want to know how many men you killed and do you think if any of them may have lived besides the one in the hospital?"

"I don't really remember the exact number of people I have killed, probably all of them except the one here in the hospital. It was so intense… I would think about fourteen or fifteen. Why? Is something is wrong?"

"No, the Navy wanted to know how many outlaws exactly, so they can try to trace the rest of the bandits. According to one of his connections, they are still running drugs somewhere in Bangkok. We have to identify this pirate leader before we can prosecute him. Without enough evidence we can't prove his guilt to the jury and of course he can go free. According our calculation and the time that was recorded, the Navy is pretty sure that the pirate ship was responsible for the attack of the coast guard speedboat. However, we have no potential witnesses that can testify in court that they in fact, saw what happened. We have people who claimed, including you, that they just heard the sound an explosion. Besides, nobody has been able to identify the leader yet. Once the bandages are off his face, people might be able to recognize who he is, but that will be some time. His teammates might be here before the prosecution, who knows, they may be here already. We do recommend that you look out for any strange activities. We do have security but there is not enough manpower to cover the hospital."

"How will I know if there is one of them around here?" Nguyen Tam didn't understand the real situation here, but there is a possibility one of the remaining pirates may still be roaming around the area. Nguyen Tam was sure that he killed almost all of them, but there could be more. Nguyen Tam planned not to tell Thuy about this, and he didn't want to ruin her happiness too soon; maybe he would tell her later. Nguyen Tam had a little doubt about the identity of the last survivor. Nguyen Tam asked the translator "Is there any way to leave a message containing our names so my friend can find us here? My girlfriend's brother is probably looking for us right now in the refugee camps. If our names are not on the list, how could he find us? Can you help us?"

The Vietnamese translator relayed the question to the agent. The agent suggested that they would forward their names to the U.S. Consular. If any person requests a list of names it should show their names on the list. Nguyen Tam was very appreciative for their help and he politely bowed his head to them, "I don't know how to show my appreciation for your help. May God redeem you for everything you have done for us."

The translator said, "Hey, don't worry. We will do anything we can to get you out of here. We will forward your name to the U.S Consular as soon as we get out of here. In the mean time, keep a watch out for any intruders."

"Yes, sir," Nguyen Tam sincerely replied. Then he suddenly remembered that Thuy saw a new custodian with a mean face. He called the agents back and told them about him, "Sir, my girlfriend told me last night that she saw a new custodian and that he didn't look like a real custodian. She said he looks more like a thug. I don't know what she meant because I haven't seen this man yet. It may help."

The translator conveyed the message to the two agents about the new custodian. They said that they would check into it immediately.

After they left, Nguyen Tam tried to sit up straight and work out his upper body. Then he got out of his bed to work out his legs. He had to regain his strength back somehow, in case he had to defend Thuy and himself. The shoulder wound still bothered him. With a little effort he tried to overcome the pain, and began to get used to it. While he was on the floor exercising, Thuy walked in with a lunch plate. She yelled when she saw Nguyen Tam moving his body around, "My God Tam, what are you doing? You're supposed to be resting in bed. Be careful before the wound starts bleeding again. My God! Are you out of your mind?"

Nguyen Tam replied, "Calm down, I have a reason to do this. Listen to me. The agents and the translator just came to warn me to look out for a possible attack from the rest of the pirates. Remember what you told me last night about the new custodian? Well I reported it to the security police. The reason I am doing this is to get ready for whatever may happen."

Thuy stopped yelling and asked, "Are you sure? What did they want to know? Don't we get to leave here?

Nguyen Tam quickly answered to Thuy before she could come up with any more questions, "Okay now slowing down, let me tell you. They are warning us that the rest of the pirates might have survivors and are going to harm us in some way. I told them about that guy you saw last night. They said they are going to look into it. Oh and another thing, they are going to forward our names to the U.S Embassy so your brother can trace us down. Hopefully, he can find us quicker. Now we have to watch out for these people, they can be a threat to us."

The look on Thuy's face showed some sadness, Nguyen Tam knew that Thuy didn't want to leave this place so he gently held her hand and in a soft promising voice said, "Soon we will get hold of your brother. Then we will settle in America. There you will have a better job. Here it's just temporary. Now we only have to manage to stay alive. Okay? Don't be so sad. I have the feeling that we will get out of here soon."

Thuy now had doubts about their safety and looked at Nguyen Tam with her weary eyes, "I am really tired of these people. Will they ever leave us alone? I wonder if they will follow us for the rest of our lives. Why didn't the government didn't do anything to these outlaws?"

"They can't do anything yet because of the lack of evidence. Nobody is able to identify him because of the bandages covering his face and all his shipmates were dead. Only we will be able to identify him, probably only you. But…" he stopped there for a moment. He didn't want to get Thuy more worried.

Thuy wanted him finish his sentence but she knew that he didn't want her to get any more upset. She wanted to know exactly what was really going on, "But what, Tam? You can tell me, nothing really scares me anymore. I need to know so I can look out for it."

"We are the key witnesses and we are not for sure that he is the man. If he is, then they will try to kill us all."

Thuy had tears rolling down her face. She tried to hide it from Nguyen Tam. She turned away from Nguyen Tam and asked, "When are these animals going to leave us alone? All we want is to live in peace."

Nguyen Tam pulled Thuy into his arms and wiped the tears off her pretty face and said, "Come here, my queen. We are not even sure that this guy is one of them. As a matter of fact, the police will be looking for him. If you suspect anything you report it to the security guard. They probably don't even know who you are."

"Tam, I am just worried about you. You can't even defend yourself. They can find you easily because you are restricted in this room."

Nguyen Tam, full of emotion and love, pulled Thuy closer to his body until he felt a sharp pain in his shoulder, then he gently kissed on her forehead. Thuy leaned her head on Nguyen Tam's chest and listened to his raging heartbeat. She thought that it would be so horrible if she doesn't hear those beats anymore. She hated the pirates who had taken away everything she had, including her peace of mind.

"You know," Thuy added. "I'm pretty sure that he is the one. By looking at his face, I know he is not a regular custodian."

Nguyen Tam had the same feeling about this individual, especially since he hasn't seen the old custodian in a few days. "I haven't seen the regular custodian. I don't know what has happened to him. It must be the guy who you're talking about replacing him. If you ever see him again, you will need to let the security guards know right away."

"I certainly will," Thuy confirmed. After encountering all sort of scumbags, she is not about to put up with them anymore. "Now I have to get back to work. Don't overdo the exercise. The wound will bleed again. Okay my love?" She blew a kiss to Nguyen Tam and made sure that Nguyen Tam knew that she meant business.

Mai Lan stood at the side of the fence looking at the end of the bluish horizon. She felt like something was missing in her life. All the men have somehow left her. The sun slowly went down, reflecting its bright orange rays through the colorful clouds. Mai Lan used her imagination to draw shapes with the clouds. Then the face of the young man just appeared within the shape of the cloud. Mai Lan couldn't believe that the image of the young man was the first thing she saw. She was afraid that his image had already been imbedded into her mind so deep she couldn't remove it. She was confused about his position in her life right now and the question was… how she is going to accept him? She is still bearing a deep love from her fiancé. Then the shape of the cloud slowly moved toward the horizon, and brought with it the image of the young man once and again.

Through the mist of the evening, she saw a familiar person approaching the camp. Mai Lan couldn't believe her eyes, although she did not expect to ever see his return, it was the young man. The young man also saw her from distant. He waved to her when he first recognized her but this time, she noticed something was wrong with him; it seemed like he was hurt or something. She waved back to him and wondered why he came so late, but as he got closer to the fence, she noticed his gesture was different. She asked him, "Hi, how are you? What happen to you? You are hurt?"

"Yes, a little bit," he answered with a little hesitation. "But I am okay." His eyes weren't sparkling as before, instead they were filled with fatigue and redness.

Despite his soreness, he still tried to come to visit her; just to look at her face or to listen to her sweet voice; that's all he ever wanted. Mai Lan told him, "You know it is kind of strange but I was just thinking about you and then there you are."

"Really, you were thinking about me?" he said.

She blushed and pointed at the silver cloud and told him, "That silver cloud has the same shape as your face. Yes, it reminded me of you. You showed up as it floated away. I thought I would never see you again. All the men in my life have left me and now you came back. Maybe it's a good sign."

The young man looked at Mai Lan with a lot of love and hope. Right now, she is the only one who he could talk to. He reached his hand through the fence and tried to touch her beautiful face. But Mai Lan stepped back and told him not to touch her in front of the public. She explained that it may get them both in trouble, "Be careful! If people saw that you touched me, we would be in a lot of trouble. Besides, a lot of gossips are around here." The young man didn't really understand what she really meant, but he withdrew his hand after she moved away.

"I'm sorry. I don't mean to scare you like that. Wait, let me go inside and ask for permission. That way we can talk more freely. Okay?" Mai Lan shook her head in agreement. She needed to ask him for a special favor, and she was glad to see that he's was here.

The thug returned to the Navy Hospital with a white nursing gown pushing a wheelchair. He changed from being a custodian to becoming a male nurse; heading to Samis' room. He managed to steal one of the nurse's gown and the wheelchair, now he could move around more freely with a less of a chance to being caught. He got in Sami's room then went straight to his bed to wake him up, "Hey, wake up Sami. It's time to go man, look at me; I'm a nurse now. I have to find a way to sneak you past the Guard. No, first of all, we have to locate the guy. Do you have any idea where his room is located? We have to hit him fast. I have to leave before they find that the old custodian is missing."

Sami stared at the thug in disbelief that the thug managed to become a nurse, "You're good, I thought that you left far from here. Once you find out where he is at, you can take me there and I will do my thing. Don't worry about me, you can take off as soon as it is done. You will never get out of here with me. I can find a way out later."

Doubtful with the plan, the thug asked Sami again, "Really, how? You know they are going to execute you?"

Sami shrugged his shoulder, and with a careless tone said, "So let them. At least I'm not going to see my friends in shame when I die."

The thug understood, he didn't have much to say and would do the same if he was in Samis' shoes. The thug said, "Don't go anywhere or talk to anyone until I get back. This may take a few hours, but when I get back, be ready to go. So, pretend like you are sleeping. Let's make this thing go smooth."

Sami waved his hand to the thug; he really counted on the thug to help him through this. It seemed like this was going to be the end of his life and he was determined to accept his termination. He was willing to die rather than to live.

The U.S Consular sent a message to Le Son at his hotel, stating the name and location of his sister. After receiving the message Le Son prepared immediately for the trip; he could not wait any longer. Soon the sun broke the horizon and Le Son set out to the hospital. He was excited to meet his sister.

Mai Lan went to the chapel to meet the young man. Somehow she felt a little happier, a little more secure, as is he was one of her relatives. One who would stick around. The young man also felt as if Mai Lan was like one of his family members. During the years he spent with the pirates he never spoke to anyone. Now that he met Mai Lan, she is everything to him, like a light shining through his life; despite the aching body, he still came to visit her just to listen to her voice.

Now they both sat down to see each other eye to eye. As they sat there bodies spoke to one another and they never said a word. Mai Lan broke the silence to ask, "You have a bruise on your neck. Did somebody hurt you? You look so tired. Are you okay?"

This was the first time in his life he had heard a sweet voice from a beautiful lady who was concerned about him. The warm feeling she portrayed, pacified the anger buried deep in his mind. His eyes wandered toward the cross at the altar. He didn't know whether to tell her the truth or to hide it. He didn't want to get her all worried, so he said, "Well, I fell another night. It still hurts a little bit. But I'm okay now. So, how are you doing?

"I'm okay, but I haven't seen you for a while. I thought you moved." Mai Lan opened up her feelings to the young man.

The young man's eyes changed from tired to being full of joy and he moved a little closer to her and he whispered, "Did you miss me? Did you really miss me?"

Mai Lan didn't want to mislead the young man into a deeper relationship which they may both regret. She couldn't predict what her future will bring and to drag him into her troubling life wouldn't be fair for him. She knew that she couldn't forbid him from loving her, if she only could stop herself from loving him.

Mai Lan avoided answering his very personal question and instead diverted the conversation to a different subject, "I been so busy trying to open a small business in the camp. Since you are helping me, you are including in the business too. My partner and I talked it over and already decided, so you can't back out. We will pay you a percentage of whatever we make. I hope you approve our invitation."

The young man was stunned by the gesture at first said, "Wow, you have a business opening up soon? I cannot believe it. Yes of course, but you don't have to pay me anything. I will help you with whatever I can, anything…really." The young man was so happy. He could not believe that Mai Lan was including him in her business. Now he could visit her more often. To be included in the business with the woman he loved, it meant more than anything to him. He then said, "Now that I'm in, do you need anything right away to startup the business? By the way, what kind of business is it? I'm sorry. I was so excited that I forget to ask."

"That's okay. We're going to open a small coffee shop for the people in the camp. Maybe we will add some kind of breakfast to it later."

Mai Lan knew he had some special feelings toward her, but she couldn't believe that he was accepting her offer so quickly. The young man asked "Would you want me to get some things for you right now? I can do it, really. I can get the coffee for you, only the best kind."

Mai Lan felt very emotional because of how excited he is to get involved. She silently thanked to God who has brought him to help her. Mai Lan held his hand in hers and softly spoke, "Thank you very much for your desire to help, but it's not convenient for you to come here every day. I would really feel bad if you had to come here more often than you already do."

The young man softly squeezed her tiny hands and shook his head, "Oh no, no, don't you worry about that. I think I will move closer. I have a little money saved up and I would like to help you get supplies. You can pay me back later."

The sudden offer caught her off guard. She didn't know if she would rather accept his money now or wait a while longer. She didn't want the young man to get the impression that she really needed the money, "May be a little later. We're still trying to settle into a location and are waiting for permission from the warden. It's great that you want to help us. The main thing we need is water. I will let you know exactly when we need it."

The young man, a little disappointed, wanted to get involved in her business; so he said to her, "That's okay. I will find a place that is closer. I can bring water to you every day. I would like that very much. I never had an offer like this from anyone. You make me feel important. Thank you very much for allowing me an opportunity to be with you."

PART 8

Mai Lan, speechless from the young man's kindness, admired his inspiration and bowed her head to say thank you. The young man quickly held her hands and told her, "Oh no, that's okay I just want to help you. I am the one who should say thank you. Well, I have to go now. When I come back, I will bring you more stuff. He gave a big bag of dry food to Mai Lan and proudly told her, "Miss, this is dry deer meat. I killed a deer last week and cured the meat myself. I saved the best for you. I know you don't have a refrigerator in here so that the meat can keep without spoiling."

Mai Lan felt a real burden because of all his offerings. She felt badly trying to ignore his love. She couldn't vacate her heart so quickly and accept him into her life. She knew that this is a temporary place and she might just leave here and never return. The young man looked at her troubled face trying to understand her thoughts. He then held her hand and by using his warm blood to convey his deep feelings for her, he said softly, "Don't worry about trying to repay for me. I don't expect you to fall in love with me right away. I just want to help you. I have no family or relatives and so I consider you to be an immediate family member. So don't you worry about it. Okay?"

Mai Lan, astonished by his straightforwardness, felt a little better because he took some of the burden off her shoulders. She began accepting him as her family member also.

Everyone who resided in these refugee camps had very little knowledge of what was to come into their life. They lived here day by day awaiting their chance to come up with an interview. There were rumors that many would be forced to return to their country if the Thai Government closed the camps. No one could be certain about their life if they had to return to their government. The people lived in fear and worry. Most of the refugees here had either sold all their belongings or they were lost at sea. Only a few received money from relatives living abroad. If they were forced to return to their native country then they went back empty-handed and would most likely be punished by their government for fleeing.

Mai Lan couldn't afford to return to her country being pregnant. If worse came to worse, she would stay here with the young man and raise her baby. Noticing the worry still on her face still, the young man couldn't help but to ask her, "You are worried about something else? You can tell me. If I can help you, I will."

Mai Lan hesitated for a moment. She didn't know whether to tell him or not. She didn't want to hurt him. The young man didn't let her have a chance to hide anything and he looked straight at her eyes asking, "You are hiding something, I know. If you don't tell me; how I can help you? I already told you I am your family."

Mai Lan, eyes reddened with moist tears, told him about the rumors she just recently heard, "We… I just heard a rumor that the camp may close down and…and we will be forced to return to our country. I am just worried about my child, if…" Mai Lan stopped for a moment and wiped the tears off her face. So much emotion festered inside her that it almost stopped her breathing. She broke down crying.

The young man guided her to lean on him then he embraced her. He could feel her body trembling and couldn't resist gliding his hand through her silky hair and attempted to calm her down, "Don't you worry about that. The worse that could happen is that you would have to stay here with me in Thailand for a while, at least until you give birth. Then we will find some other way to get to another country. I will take care of you and your child, I promise."

Mai Lan leaned her forehead against his chest and said, "You really are going to do that for me? This is a big responsibility. I don't know what to do. I already owe you a lot already. I don't want to be a burden."

The young man lightly kissed her forehead and said, "You are my family. We are supposed to take care of our family. I'm going to get to the bottom of this. If there is any truth to this then I will ask the priest to marry us. That way I can legally get you out of the camp. But, you will lose the chance to get an interview. Let's see what is happening. Then we will find a way to deal with it. Right now just concentrate on your business. Okay? Well, I have to go to work now. I will be back soon to help you." Then, he held her chin up and asked, "Are you not going to worry anymore? Everything is going to be okay, trust me." He kissed her one more time, got up and then disappeared beyond the fence.

Sami had thoughts of suicide. If it were not for his oath to enact his revenge; he might have already pulled the trigger. To him, prolonging his life would be worse than any other punishment. He hated the nightmares, the sweating, and the fact that nobody was there to help him. The silence of the night became one of his worst enemies. It brought with it the horrific sounds of the people he had killed and it was driving him insane. The longer he lived, the worse life would become. He figured the sooner death came, the better.

Suddenly, he heard the footsteps outside his door. He got in position to be ready to go, but it turned out to be the nurse checking her patients. The nurse entered the room and turned on the light. She approached the bed and asked, "Are you doing okay? You still feel the pain. Do you need anything? The doctor will check on you later on today." With no response from Sami, she turned to look at him and asked him again, "You don't talk much do you?"

Sami without speaking, pretended that he was hurting bad and nodded his head. Then a moment later, he said slowly, "Hi, no I don't feel good. It hurts all over. Can I have some water?"

The nurse felt sorry for Sami, she didn't know that he was a cold blooded murder at sea. The nurse thought that he was just a victim of some terrible fire. She poured a glass of cold water and gave to him. She started checking his bandages and his temperature and tried to cheer him up with some good news, "You are okay the bandage seems pretty dry and the doctor probably will take it off tomorrow. Before long, you will be healed and go home. Are you glad?"

Sami didn't know what to say, he just nodded his head. He didn't want anybody to see his real face, not anytime soon anyway. When the nurse asked him if he needed anything else, he pretended like nothing else would be necessary, and then asked the nurse, "Did somebody else get hurt like me? That was a big fire."

The nurse, not knowing the intent of his question, told him about his enemy, "Yes, I think so. Another man was injured on his shoulder, you know him?"

"I don't know. I will go and see him when the bandage gets taken off. Where is his room?"

"Just down the hall from your room. I will take you down there when they get ready to let you go. Well, take care."

The nurse hurried to leave the room. She had no idea what was going to happen to the poor innocent man. After Sami found out the location of his enemy, he waited for the thug to return with the wheelchair. Now he felt so close to his enemy. He took a deep breath, and then closed his eyes. Sami concentrated on the plan which he hoped to execute. *Nothing is going to change now*, he vowed to himself.

After helping to serve lunch for the hospital, Thuy picked up a couple plates for her and Nguyen Tam then hurried back to the room to see him. She wanted to eat with him in the garden. She knew that Nguyen Tam had wanted to do that and now his wound was healing so Thuy wanted to surprise him. Nguyen Tam was napping when she entered the room. Thuy silently approached his bed and brought the plate close to his nose. The aroma rose from the hot food was the best in the kitchen, and it infiltrated his senses and quickly woke him up. Nguyen Tam opened his eyes to check where the aroma was coming from. He found Thuy standing next to him with the plate full of food; she was so beautiful and shining like an angel. He screamed out in joy and said, "Oh Thuy, you are so beautiful. I thought I had just seen an angel. Thank you very much for taking care of me. These are the best moments of my life."

Thuy began to blush but acted like she didn't hear the words from Nguyen Tam, "Yes…an angel with food, that's strange. I think that you are seeing somebody else. Come on, let's eat. The food is getting cold."

Nguyen Tam stared at Thuy like some kind of Goddess with the vision of love and happiness until Thuy slapped him on his wrist, "Tam, what you're staring at? I don't look any different than any other day. You are embarrassing me. Come on, the food is getting cold. Later, when it gets a little cooler, we will go to the garden."

Surprised Nguyen Tam couldn't believe that Thuy was going to take him to the rose garden which she loved so much. He took a bite then asked Thuy one more time, "You are really going to take me to the garden? Am I in the heaven with all of the angels around me?"

Thuy smiled, then took a piece of meat and tasted it first then ate it; bragging on herself she said, "You know I helped the kitchen to cook the meat. It's pretty good, right?" She continued, "Everybody loves it. They like Vietnamese food too, that's what they said."

Ignoring the food, Nguyen Tam looked at her in such a passionate way. He reached for Thuy's hand and gently pulled her closer to him. Thuy was also surprised by Nguyen Tam's behavior today, but she showed no resistance, she just let her body glide to him, and closed her eyes; waiting.

Nguyen Tam's soul was attracted to Thuy by the strong force of love. It erupted like a volcano with hot desire. With his hand crossing her waist… he placed a hot kiss on her red lips. Her whole body started trembling from the initial contact; this was the first kiss in her life. Nguyen Tam's manly tongue explored her lips. Tangling with her tongue she could feel her heart pumping the hot stream of blood throughout her body. Suddenly the sound of a wheel cart approached their room. Thuy pushed herself away from Nguyen Tam who was still dazed from the kiss. She listened intensely to the sound realizing that someone was coming. They both regained their composure, pretending like nothing ever happened, and were ready to greet whoever appeared. Nguyen Tam still looked at Thuy with desire, but Thuy pushed his face away, "What is wrong with you? Somebody is coming, behave." Then she bent down and kissed him on his forehead. Thuy stood up and straightened her clothing. She then got into position to be ready for whoever came.

When Mai Lan returned to her cubicle, Xuan was waiting for her. As usual, she yelled to Mai Lan, "Here you are. I have been waiting for a long time. Where have you been? I have good news. Listen to this!"

Xuan spoke so loud and fast, it was like a whole string of fire crackers bursting in her ears, she quickly gestured for Xuan to slow down and be quiet, "Okay…okay…slow down. Now, what do you want to tell me?"

Xuan, looked around and stuck out her tongue, meaning she knew that she made a mistake. She bent down and whispered into Mai Lan's ear, "I got the place picked out. Everybody likes to hang out there. That would be a good place for the coffee business. By the way, did you see that guy?"

Mai Lan nodded her head, and motioned for her to sit a little closer to her, "Yes, I just met him. That's why you didn't see me here. He's ready to help us whenever we need him. I told him that we may be forced to go back to Viet Nam."

Xuan grabbed Mai Lan's hands and asked, "What did he say? Is he going to do anything? I will marry the guard to stay here if I have to. I don't want to go back. They will put me in jail."

Mai Lan didn't answer. She nodded her head. She wasn't sure

that the young man would be up to what he promised. She let out a long sigh then said, "I don't know for sure. He said he would help me, but you know things change all the time. I just hope that we get an interview before the government closes the camp."

Xuan didn't seem to worry, she had confidence in her business, "Well, if there is an opportunity out there for us, I'm going to get it. I don't want to sit around and worry about it. It's just a rumor, we don't know anything for sure." Xuan shook Mai Lan's shoulder to bring her back to reality, "Come on, Sister, wake up. Money is waiting for us. Don't worry about that yet. Do you want to go ask the priest about the place to see if we can get it? Oh by the way, there's a woman who lives in the other building and she wants to buy your new garments, if you want to sell them?"

Mai Lan nodded her head and said, "Yes, I want to sell it. We need money for the business. I guess we will make the money back. Here, take it over there and show it to her and try to get the best price."

"You know I will. I'll be back to let you know how much we will get before we sell it."

"Okay," Mai Lan answered. She got up and went to see the priest.

The thug returned with the wheelchair bragging to Sami, "Look, I stole this wheelchair from the warehouse. Do I look like a nurse? Man, I am in charge of a lot of jobs around here. So far, nobody's been able to recognize me yet. If I stick around long enough, somebody is going to check me out, man." He continued, "Oh, I asked a nurse about this guy. She told me that there was another guy who came in the same time as you, except that he was injured in the shoulder or something. I think this is the guy you are looking for. Don't you think?'

Sami was in his own world and didn't hear what the thug had just told him, "What do you say? Oh, you found him. I think you are right. The nurse also told me the same thing. It's time to go. You wheel me to his room and let me take care of the business. Then you can take the gun and leave. Don't worry about me. Without any evidence, they can't do anything about it. The man is dead. They can't get anything out of a dead man, I reckon.

The thug now understood the real reason why the man wanted to terminate his enemy. Beside the revenge, he was after the elimination of any potential witnesses. The thug clapped his hands to congratulate the pirate, "You are getting rid the only witness, you are genius, man. You can kill two birds with one stone. You are a devil. I didn't even think of that. I wondered why you wanted to get him so bad. Well, for your sake, I'm with you on this. Let's go before he moves. Did you say you know where he is?"

Sami pointed his finger toward the end of the hall and told the thug, "I think his room is right down the hall. This is a restricted wing, so we have to make sure that nobody sees me out of here, especially the security. Are you nervous?"

"Hell yes, I'm nervous. But let's do it fast." The thug went back outside to check the security desk, and saw that the security officer was busy joking with a female nurse; both facing another direction.

The thug silently retreated back to Sami's room and carefully placed him in the wheelchair. Sami dealt with great pain when the thug moved him out of the bed. As soon as he sat comfortably in the wheelchair, the thug covered Sami with a blanket then pushed the cart to their target, Nguyen Tam. Underneath the blanket, Sami held on tight to his gun. He checked the gun several times to make sure that it will function smoothly. The thug bent down to check Sami one last time before he rolled him the door. He placed his hand on

Sami's shoulder for the last time and said to him, "Well, man, this probably will be the last time I see you. Are you ready to go?"

Sami nodded his head then said to the thug, "I really appreciate what you are doing. If I make it out of here, I will repay for what you have done."

"Let's go!" The thug rolled him out the room, and quickly disappeared down the hall.

Mai Lan walked to the chapel to talk to reverend Si about her business. She bowed her head to greet the priest, "Hi reverend, how are you? I would like to ask you something, if you have time?"

The reverend guided her to the chapel, patted her on the back and asked, "How are you doing? You feel all right? Now, what do you want to ask me?"

"Thank you, sir, for seeing me, I'm doing okay except for some morning sickness. I'm doing all right now. We found a little corner next to the guest house. Perhaps we can open a small coffee shop there, if you think that... if it's all right with the warden."

The reverend stayed quiet for a moment, then responded, "Well, I think it should be no problem as long you don't interfere with security. I will ask the warden for you. Do you think you can handle it?"

"Actually, there is another girl helping me with this. Otherwise, I would never think about it."

The reverend said, "I promised that I would help you to do what you want, but you have to take care of the business the way the warden wants. Okay?"

Mai Lan bowed her head to the priest to show her respect and appreciation. When Mai Lan got back to the building, Xuan was there waiting for her, and she showed Mai Lan the money she got from sale of the clothing, "I sold your new clothes like you wanted. The woman liked the material so much she paid pretty good. Here is the money I don't know how much he…the young man, paid for it. But compared to the price from our country, we got more money for it."

Mai Lan wasn't happy with the money they got from the woman, but she didn't want to get Xuan upset, so she just accepted it without saying anything. Xuan looked at Mai Lan for a moment, and said, "You don't look too happy about something. Is it bothering you?"

Mai Lan smiled and assured her that everything was all right, "Oh nothing really. I just have a lot on my mind. I am not sure that we can have the business at that location. The priest promised to ask the warden for us, but in my condition, I don't know if you can handle it by yourself." Xuan grabbed Mai Lan's hand, gently squeezed and said "You know I can take care of the business all by myself. I have taken care of a business before."

"Yes, I know you can handle it, but if they call you for an interview, I don't think that I can take care of it myself. I guess we can start out small and if you happen to go before me then I will just shut it down." Mai Lan said.

Xuan started to realize the burden of the business but she had made up her mind; she convinced Mai Lan, "Now I know that you are worried about that, but the list for the interview is quite long. By the time we come up we will be able to make some money for us. At least we don't spend time just sitting around doing nothing."

Mai Lan couldn't help but to smile. Most people here have nothing to do for themselves. It is fortunate for them that they have enough money to start out something small, even if the business is temporary. Mai Lan nodded her head and said, "I know you are ambitious. No matter what, I'm with you."

Xuan hugged Mai Lan and said, "Now that's my sister talking. I know we can handle it. Okay, I will go around to check things out. I'll be back in a little while."

Mai Lan patted on Xuan's head and said to her before she headed out of the building, "Take good care of yourself, all right?"

Xuan waved her hand before disappearing out of the door and said, "Yes! I will."

Thuy stood by the side of the bed and positioned herself for the oncoming guest. She thought that is would probably just be a nurse dropping by to check on Nguyen Tam's condition. When the wheelchair rolled into the room, Thuy thought they were in the wrong room. She looked at the male nurse who pushed the chair and realized that he looked similar to the custodian who she had seen another night. Her sixth sense alarmed her that something was wrong. From behind the bandages on his face, she met the eyes of the man sitting in the wheelchair. Thuy suddenly recognized those evil eyes. The last time she saw those eyes they belonged to the man who tried to kill her. Thuy screamed, "Tam, that is the custodian who I saw another night! The guy in the wheelchair is the pirate who tried to kill me on the island, watch out!"

Sami heard the woman screaming and quickly drew his gun and aimed it at Nguyen Tam, who was already out his bed. He squeezed off the first round at his prime target.

Thuy saw the revolver and despite the danger, she rushed to the man in the wheelchair to take his gun away. By the time she heard the thundering noise and saw the flash from the gun, the bullet already struck her in the chest. Blood instantly poured out and dyed her white shirt with the color of crimson red. She staggered for a few more feet, holding her wound and then fell on the floor a few feet from the wheelchair. Sami cursed and squeezed the trigger one more time while aiming at the man who was now lunging toward the woman. The round didn't go off the second time due to a weapon malfunction. Before Sami could pull the trigger again, Nguyen Tam got up and dove toward his assailant. Succumbed by rage he grabbed the revolver and twisted it in another direction before the gun could be fired. Nguyen Tam could only use his left arm to wrestle with his opponent who was also injured. Luckily he was stronger than the shooter. During the confrontation, Sami pulled the trigger again, but this time, the muzzle pointed at the thug's direction and it spat out the .38 bullet right into the thug's chest. The impact of the bullet pushed the thug's body backward. The thug screamed then staggered for a moment before collapsing on the floor.

The security guard heard the shots coming from Nguyen Tam's room and raced down to investigate. He saw Nguyen Tam wrestling to try and take the gun away from the man in the wheelchair. The security officer took out his pistol and whacked Sami on the head, knocking him out cold.

Nguyen Tam jumped back to Thuy and checked on her wound. He found the blood soaking through her white clothes. He called out her name in a desperate voice mixed with tears. Thuy, who was losing consciousness, tried to say something to Nguyen Tam, but wasn't able to. She gripped onto Nguyen Tam, her lips were moving but they made no sound and tears were rolling along side of her eyelids. Gasping for air, Thuy lost her grip on life as her head fell to the side and her whole body became limp in the arms of Nguyen Tam. Nguyen Tam's whole body numb for a moment and his brain stopped functioning. The pain from losing his lover was so great that it turned him into stone. Then he suddenly realized that her body had given up so he held her tight to his chest and screamed.

The security officer restrained the pirate and saw Nguyen Tam holding onto Thuy's body. Realizing that the girl was injured he started yelling for a nurse.

Nguyen Tam suddenly reverted to his training as a former combat soldier. Nguyen Tam carefully placed Thuy on the floor and quickly started C.P.R to try and retrieve the lost pulse. He applied pressure to the main artery to try and slow down the blood flow from the open wound. He took a deep breathe and forced it into her lungs. At first, Thuy's eyes remained shut and her body still had no pulse. Tears rained down on her face, but Nguyen Tam didn't give up the C.P.R. He gave her another deep breathe then pumped on her chest again. After a full cycle, Nguyen Tam stopped for a moment to check her pulse, and he screamed, "I feel a pulse!"

Nguyen Tam continued to try and resuscitate Thuy. He could feel life began to reemerge in her body little by little. Despite the pain in his shoulder, Nguyen Tam tried over and over to save Thuy's life.

Nurses raced to try and rescue Thuy once they heard that she was badly wounded. The whole wing was now on alert. Everybody was guessing as to what was happening because of the gun shots. When the two nurses arrived to the scene, Thuy slowly opened her eyes. She had not yet fully regained consciousness but she her life might be spared. The nurses hurried to secure her on a stretcher then stormed to the emergency room.

Nguyen Tam was trailing right behind them, anxious to find out about Thuy's condition.

Mai Lan got permission from the warden to open the coffee booth. Xuan was so excited when she heard the news. They paid a little money for some camp residents to build a small wooden table. The young security guard brought Xuan four small chairs and some plastic cups. *Well! That's a good start*, Xuan thought. Xuan went around the camp and found some old aluminum filters. Now they needed a kettle to boil water and were hoping the young man would bring the rest of the goods. Xuan used word of mouth to advertise their new business and promised that they won't let people down. Both Xuan and Mai Lan were very excited. Xuan kept asking Mai Lan about the young man, "Sister, when will he come? We need him now. What if he won't come? What are we going to do?"

Mai Lan patted on Xuan's shoulder and calmed her down with her soft voice, "Hey, hey, calm down girl. He'll be here, he promised." Xuan still worried that the business might be delayed couldn't sit still, "I just … I don't know. Tomorrow we open the business, but we don't have anything now. I don't know what to do, people are expecting us to be open for business tomorrow. They will think we are liars."

Mai Lan couldn't help but to laugh at Xuan's childish misery. She assured her that the young man would be here soon, "Calm down girl! He will be here. Even if he doesn't show up; we can wait for one more day. I know you are anxious to open the business, but you act like you have ants in your pant.

"I'm sorry! I'm just worry, you know."

"Well, I'm worried too, but you don't see me jumping up and down, do you?"

Sitting down beside Mai Lan and Xuan pretended like she was calm. Then she stood up and walked toward the door and said, "I just can't sit still. I am going to go to our neighbor's for a moment. Otherwise, I will go crazy. I will see you after awhile."

Then she disappeared. Mai Lan shook her head, thinking of Xuan's flamboyant attitude. It was good to think that she was excited about the business, but how long would the fire last?

After a long journey from Bangkok, Le Son finally stood in front of the Navy hospital and prepared to meet his sister and Nguyen Tam. He showed his permission slip to meet his family to the front desk officer. The front desk officer looked at Le Son for a moment then he told him the bad news, "We're sorry, sir. Your sister is in the emergency unit extensive care. She has lost a lot of blood. When we clear your admittance, we will take you there. I'll be right back."

Le Son felt like he had just been struck by lightning. He had no idea how his sister got hurt right here in the government property. He mumbled to the staff, "Sir, it couldn't be....How could she?"

The staff showed Le Son the list of the patient's names, "If this is your sister and I'm sure that it is... I'll be right back."

After the staff left, Le Son still stood there motionless. He still had no idea what had happened to Thuy. He could only silently pray for his sister and wait for the staff. When the staff returned and confirmed that she is the one, Le Son felt cold all over his body once again. Then he burst out in tears when he heard the news from the staff, "Sir, you are granted permission to enter the hospital. I'm sorry that your sister is the victim from the shoot out. I will take you to see her. She is still in the coma." Le Son silently followed the staff.

When he got close to the room, he saw that Nguyen Tam was sitting outside waiting. Right then he knew for sure that this is definitely his sister. Nguyen Tam turned around and saw Le Son, he said in a sad tone of voice, "Le Son, how did you know… I can't believe it's you. I wish you were here a day earlier then you could talk to your sister. We were talking about how to get hold of you and then…"

Nguyen Tam couldn't finish the sentence before tears started rolling down his face. Nobody could have predicted the incident that just happened to Thuy. He felt sorry for his sister's tragic life; she was just about to start a new life in America. Le Son said, "I heard people at the other camp talking about pirates. It happened here in the Navy hospital? I just can't figure that out."

Nguyen Tam slowly explained the whole event to Le Son, "We never did expect the leader to survive. He just wanted to eliminate me only, and Thuy tried to save me from being killed….and she ended up getting shot instead of me. Somehow, the pirate found out exactly where we're at.

The both men entered the room and sat next to Thuy. Le Son held his little sister's limp hand with his heart aching. He doubted that his sister was going to make it. Le Son looked at Nguyen Tam, and curiously asked, "I heard people say that you're the one who killed the whole gang. Is that true?

Nguyen Tam nodded his head, and humble explained, "It was pure luck with God's help. I had to kill them all to prevent them from hurting more people, especially Thuy, but they got her in the end anyway. I could have terminated him then, but…I felt bad killing a man who is already on the ground. Nobody imagined that one day he would return to haunt us."

Le Son placed his hand on Thuy's forehead and said to Nguyen Tam, "You know there is still hope that Thuy will make it through this. We just have to wait. It is all up to her to fight for her life.

Nguyen Tam stared into nothing trying to envision the moment that Thuy would get out of the coma and began to ask him all kind of questions. Nguyen Tam said, "Before all this happened, Thuy was very brave. She beat him with the stick and saved my life and now she tried to take the gun from him but took his bullet for me. I just don't know what to say. I feel so badly. I pray to God to spare her life so I can hear her voice once again. Twice she has risked her life for me…" He couldn't even finish the sentence before he broke down crying. Le Son came over and placed his hand on Nguyen Tam's shoulder and said, "I didn't know that you two had been through hell throughout this trip, and you did a lot for her too; I reckon."

Nguyen Tam nodded his head, "Thuy has survived all the horrible situations. She has matured and has been quite brave. I was surprised myself. I couldn't believe that she was so courageous. I really think that she is ready to start her new life in America. In one short moment, she gave it all up…for me."

Le Son saw the special connection between the two people, a kind of connection which bonded their two souls. He felt a deep sorrow for his sister and his friend. Le Son stood up and patted on Nguyen Tam's and said, "Tam, you need to rest and watch out for her. We still have hope for her life. I will go to check on her condition and then I need to apply for your visa. I should be back shortly."

Nguyen Tam stood up and shook Le Son's hand and said, "I will stay here until she gets up."

After Le Son left, Nguyen Tam sat beside Thuy. He had more hope now for their future than a few hours ago. Now all he could do was just waiting for Thuy to get well. He bowed his head to pray to God for Thuy to wake up so she could meet her brother.

Nguyen Tam still couldn't believe that Le Son was here now. Neither of them expected to see Le Son any time soon. Then out of nowhere, he is here. Nguyen Tam squeezed Thuy's hand a little bit. He really wanted to share with her the good news.

Mai Lan walked out close to the fence. She stood quietly watching the colorful butterflies hover over the red velvet flowers. She still wondered about the young man's promise. He should be here but he wasn't. *This might be a bad omen for the beginning*, she thought. The future wasn't as bright as she thought it would be. It seemed like they had a lot of hopes in the beginning, but a lot of disappointments came in the end and she hated being a skeptic about the future. The fact is, she wasn't certain about anything anymore. There was a time that she wished that she had never left home, a place where she was close to family and friends and especially with her fiancé. She was homesick the day she arrived to the camp. Mai Lan hadn't realized what the long hot days in this camp with nothing to do had done to these people.

Someone from the front door called Mai Lan's name. She had a visitor. Waking from a daydream, she got up and let out a big breath to unload all the burdens of her mind. She got up to go meet the young man in hopes that he was the bearer of good news. Sure enough, he was waiting for her at the guest house with a load of supplies for her business. He stood with his head held high and said, "Is it enough for you?"

Mai Lan was stunned by the overwhelming number of supplies that the young man offered. He soon realized that she had been overcome with joy as the tears broke from her eyes. The young man approached Mai Lan and held her hand. His grip tightened softly as he looked into her eyes and without words said, don't worry about it. Mai Lan felt a tingling sensation all over her body. If not for the baby in her womb and respect for the baby's father, she would have leaned on his body and cried. The young man pulled Mai Lan close to him and wrapped her body with his muscular arms. He placed a kiss on her cheek, then another kiss on her forehead.

Mai Lan was shivering like a little bird held in the hand of a human being. Her body was frozen by the power of the young man. Mai Lan regained her composure and gently pushed the young man away from her. She blushed and said, "Please, not here. Somebody may see. I will get a lot of trouble for it. Besides I'm expecting. There are a lot of ladies out there better than me. It's not that I don't like you; it's just that right now… I can't return my love to you. Perhaps when I get out of here, things will change. Please don't be mad at me."

The young man moved away from Mai Lan. He felt a little embarrassed by her denial of him. He respected her wishes and said, "I'm sorry, your lovely eyes are just so… inviting. I can't help it. I will wait for when you are ready." The look of disappointment clearly struck his face. All he could hope for was to one day win over her love.

The young man held her hand and guided Mai Lan through the supplies. He proudly showed her every item, "Here is the condensed milk, fresh black ground coffee and sugar. I think you will have enough to start the business. In a few days, I will return to see how things are going. Then I will get you some more. Okay?"

Mai Lan was emotionally touched with his sincere attitude. She bowed her head to say thank to him. She felt ashamed because she couldn't do much to return the love he showed with his flamboyant heart. She wasn't in any position to offer him anything, not right now anyway.

He carefully guided her to the chair and said, "Lan, you don't have to do that. I'm just glad to help you. Besides, I'm your partner. So don't you worry about it, okay?"

Mai Lan nodded her head *yes* to answer the young man. She knew that she owed him a lot and she wanted a chance to repay him. Somehow, her heart was still closed. The young man said, "You know, every time I look in your eyes, it is like looking into a different world. It is a sad world containing a lot of mysterious thoughts that I will probably never understand. Perhaps someday…hopefully, I will. The only thing that I have to say is that you have to live for your coming baby. I will always stay beside you and will help you anyway I can. Right now you are the only family I have and together, we will make it." The speech rolled from the bottom of his heart.

Suddenly a rush of tears flooded out of her eyes. She looked up at the young man. Her natural pink lips softly said to him, "You are so good to me, even though when I'm at my worst. I want you to be there when I give birth to my child. I want you to name him or her. Okay?"

The young man came closer to her, knelt down and held her hand. He caressed her hand and gently kissed it and then said, "I will be there right beside you no matter what. It will be an honor to name your child."

Suddenly, someone knocked on the door. The young man stood up to go open finding a young girl standing outside waiting. He greeted her politely and invited her to come inside. He remembered seeing this girl somewhere, but couldn't recall exactly where.

Mai Lan smiled and said, "Xuan, it's good that you are here. We need to take all these to the building so you can start your business tomorrow. Well, do you have any more doubts, young lady?"

Xuan smiled and bowed her head to return her greetings to the young man. She ran to the supply goods and screamed, "Hey, wow, look at this! We are ready for the business. Thank you very much. Thank you very much."

The young man smiled and stood up to say good bye to Mai Lan. They were silently facing each other as the young man stared deeply into her eyes. Mai Lan was little embarrassed and tried to look a different direction. He reached out and kept her face in place and then placed a kiss on her forehead. Xuan who knew that Mai Lan was embarrassed by her presence said, "Oops, I'm sorry. I'm out of here." Then she quickly disappeared out of the door.

The young man also didn't want to leave but the time was up. He hated the thought of going back to his empty little place alone. Mai Lan sensed the young man's grief and approached him. She placed her hand on his chest and slightly caressed him. It was the first time Mai Lan had ever touched him of her own free will. The young man grabbed a hold of her hand and pulled her close to him. He quickly placed a kiss on her beautiful inviting lips. He enclosed her body in his steel like muscular arms until he felt her throbbing heart against his chest. The close contact began to mount a level of desire that they both knew they could not follow through with. He gave her another hug, and left.

After he was gone, Xuan came back and teased Mai Lan, "Wow, all I can tell that he is in love with you. I saw his big muscular arms. You won't be able to get out of those, not by choice anyway."

Mai Lan, embarrassed, spanked Xuan on the buttock, and said, "You're bad girl, sneaking up on me. Now, help me bring these supplies back to the building. You always wanted to start a business, here it is."

Xuan apologized to Mai Lan and bent down to pick up the supplies; this was probably the best moment of her life.

Nguyen Tam still sat next to Thuy and held her hand. He felt no sign of life in it. To him, life was so meaningless without her smile, her radical reasoning and her endless questions. Her questions sometimes aggravated him but now he really missed them.

The footsteps of the agents and the translator at the door brought him back to the reality. Nguyen Tam turned to greet the agents knowing exactly what they came for. He was anxious to find out what is going to happen to the pirate who shot Thuy. The translator came and patted Tam on his shoulder to share some of his pain. He pointed at Thuy and asked, "How is she? My god, I couldn't believe what happened to her. The guy that shot her claimed that it was in self-defense. We know that he didn't tell the truth. We don't have enough evidence to conclude that he is guilty…" He stopped for a moment to see Nguyen Tam's reaction, and then continued, "And the other guy with him, he didn't make it. We could trace the gun, but it takes months. We've been missing a janitor that worked here for five days now. Perhaps he has some connection with this incident. We need to find him and maybe we will be able to solve the entire incident. We moved the man who shot your wife to the Administrator segregation, so you don't have to worry anymore."

Nguyen Tam looked warily at the translator, not certain that the imminent danger was over; all he was worried about now was Thuy. "Thuy identified the shooter as the same one who tried to kill her at the island. His face was covered but the eyes gave him up. I have the feeling he was the one."

The translator looked convinced. He spoke to the agents about the facts that Nguyen Tam had just told him. The two agents shook their heads and told him that there wasn't enough evidence to hold up in court. The translator tried to explain to Nguyen Tam, "These two gentlemen just told me that there wasn't enough evidence to hold him in court. He could change the look of his face after the bandages are off. Another thing is that all of his killings were in international waters…"

Nguyen Tam impatiently cut off the translator before he finished his sentence, "So…."

The translator continued, "So, no witness, no evidence. Until we come up with evidence that shows that he destroyed government property, he can get away free."

"So the threat is still on? I just hope that she is doing okay when we are process out of here. By the way, her brother is here now. He just went to the headquarters to do some paperwork to get us out of this hospital. Is there anything that you can do to help us?"

The surprised translator said, "He's here? Wow, that's unbelievable. If everything is all right, you should be out of here in no time. How he get here so fast?"

"I don't know. I didn't have much of a chance to talk to him. You say if everything is all right… is there a problem?" Nguyen Tam questioned the translator.

"Yes, may be just a small problem between you and the suspect. You'll still be a part of the investigation by the Department of Navy." Then he turned to confirm it with the two agents. They both shook their heads to agree with the translator. The translator placed his hand on Nguyen Tam's shoulder and softly spoke to him, "But don't worry, we will speed up the process. You will not have to stay any longer than what is necessary. I believe once the suspect gets better, we will have other victims to identify him. I know somebody is bound to recognize him. Once we have the lead, we will find out who he was and what he was doing on the island. We will let you stay in the same room with her. Is that all right with you?"

Nguyen Tam stood up, and bowed his head to show his appreciate for what the translator has done for them, "Thank you, sir. We will never forget your help. I hope this man is going to leave us alone."

"I think the reason he tried to kill you was because you were known to be key witnesses. But he is now under heavy guard. Still, you have to watch out for anything strange."

"Well, we will. Thank you very much."

Nguyen Tam couldn't believe that his luck was so bad. Every minute that he remained in the hospital he was exposed. They got to him easily and almost killed him. It was obvious that the pirate would stop at nothing to kill Nguyen Tam. Nguyen Tam was left with only two options, kill the pirate now, or run with the worry that he might see the pirate again. The best thing to do now was to let Thuy recover and see if Le Son can get them out of there.

Le Son returned from headquarters and stood beside his sister's bed watching over her. Nguyen Tam turned his head, surprised to see Le Son there, "You're back? You're so quiet I didn't even hear you come in. So many things are on my mind. I don't know what to do."

Le Son raised his brows and asked Nguyen Tam in a serious tone, "What is bothering you? Did something else happen? Tell me what is on your mind."

Nguyen Tam hesitated for a moment then said, "Well, after you left, the agents came and warned me that the pirate may attempt to strike again. I'm thinking about trying to eliminate the main problem once and for all."

Le Son had to agree with Nguyen Tam, and he knew Nguyen Tam better than anybody. He said, "Alright, I see what you're saying. But I doubt he is going to do anything now. They told me that he is heavily guarded. I need to go back to the American embassy to get them to start processing the paper work. It may take longer than we think, but there is a possibility that the United States will take you because you were a soldier and I am the one who will sponsor you. You'll just have to stay low and keep your eyes open until I come back. Don't risk your chance to leave with me by killing him now. You may forfeit your status to immigrate to America. Besides, under the Thai Government, he still is a citizen until they prove him guilty. He is not worth it. Well, I will return here in a couple of days to check things out. Now that the security is beefed up after this incident, you and Thuy should be okay, so look out for her."

Nguyen Tam shook Le Son's hand and answered, "You know I will. She is the most important. If it wasn't for her, I wouldn't be standing here talking to you now."

Looking straight in Nguyen Tam's eye, again Le Son repeated, "Remember what I just told you. Don't do anything you know is wrong. We are so close to being home free. Hang tight, a better day will come." He waved to Nguyen Tam before he disappeared into the hall way.

PART 9

Nguyen Tam waved back to Le Son, sat in his chair, and returned to his thoughts. He still considered killing his enemy. He thought to himself, *it's hard to fight with the invisible enemy without knowing his might*. Nguyen Tam wanted peace for his troubled mind. He had to consider the safety of Thuy and himself. It had been bothering him since the first attack by his enemy. Watching as Thuy's life barely remained within her body, his anger increased. This was the same man who murdered thousands of innocent people. He clinched his fists and made a sudden decision.

Mai Lan and Xuan stayed up late to prepare for the opening of their new business. Xuan was so excited. She couldn't believe that her dream was coming true. She held Mai Lan's hand and said in a sincere voice, "Thank you, sister. If it were not for you, I wouldn't have a business today. I couldn't ask for anything more than this."

Mai Lan patted on Xuan's little shoulder and told her, "That's all that you wanted when you came here? You will have more if you get out of here."

Xuan thought for a moment then answered, "I know that. But for now, this is the best thing in my life. That's what I mean."

Mai Lan rubbed her hand on top Xuan's head, sharing in her happiness, "I am really happy for you, but don't count on this business too much. We have to be ready when the interview comes. Okay?"

"Okay!" Xuan said smiling. She sat down to sort out the utensils for the opening of the business. Mai Lan also sat down to help arrange them. She began to accept the fact that Xuan was right about the business; the busier you stay the better things will be. Perhaps someday, things will change for the better. At least there is no pirate to be frightened of. *This would be their first opportunity to invest in the free world,* Mai Lan thought.

The agents were waiting for Sami to wake up. They had been very patient and wanted to start the interrogation. A custodian has been missing for a few days and the family had filed a missing report to the hospital. Since he disappeared right before the incident, the authorities suspected there was a link between the missing man and the thug who had been fatally wounded. The maintenance man confirmed that the dead man acted like he was a new custodian the night before.

The Navy security department traced the pistol to try and find the original owner but the weapon wasn't registered. They knew for sure that the injured man had something to do with the shooting, but they couldn't find any motive as to why he wanted to kill the Vietnamese refugee.

The nurse came to the agents and said, "He's up but he doesn't want to eat or speak to anyone. Maybe you can make him talk."

One agent winked at the nurse and said, "Oh, yes! We will make him talk. If he can shoot a gun, I imagine he can open his mouth. I don't think he's hurt that bad.

The two agents stepped inside the small white cell. Inside the room they found Sami in a small bed with his face turned toward the wall, pretending he didn't know anyone was there.

One of the agents came to his bed and kicked it, then yelled, "Good morning, mister. We are bringing you some good news."

Sami mumbled, "Why don't you people leave me alone. I'm sick and I don't feel like talking right now. I told you everything I know."

One of the agents pointed his finger at Sami and said, "Look man, we know what you're up to. We found your fingerprints on the trigger and we know that the nurse was an imposter. We want to know who he is. People saw him in your room a day earlier. We will give you a chance to tell the truth, otherwise…" the agent stopped for a moment to see Sami's reaction.

The pirate leader arrogantly asked, "Otherwise…what?

The agent felt like choking the man to death but he held back his anger, "You know we have plenty of evidence on you, man. If we have to, we will put you in a line-up. Somebody is bound to recognize you and your thugs."

Sami resorted to denial, "You know you have nothing on me. If you did, I'd already be dead. That's all I have to tell you. I'm tired and if you don't mind, I need to get some sleep."

The agent began to get frustrated. He came closer to the pirate and said in a commanding voice, "The nurse told us that you have had enough rest. Keep messing around with us and I'm going to kill you myself."

The pirate shrugged his shoulders, pretending like he really cared less about the threatening words from the agent. The other agent came forward to hold back his partner. He paused for a moment then tried a different angle, "Hey, calm down partner. We still have his business partner. He probably can tell us a little more about this guy."

Sami began losing his cool and he asked the agent, "What business partner? I don't have a business partner."

The agent triumphantly smiled then continued, "I got your attention, do I? We have the guy you were supposed to deliver the girls to. I bet he will recognize you. Sooner or later, we will find out the truth. Would you rather tell us everything now? It may lighten your sentence a little bit."

Sami started sweating when he heard the agent mention his long time business associate. Yes, he took the money in advance but never did deliver the goods because all the mishaps. Sami said, "I don't know what your people are talking about. You are supposed to provide more security so nobody can come in here and wheel me out of here anytime they want. Why don't your people leave me alone until I heal, then we will talk?" Sami turned to face the wall pretending that he had no knowledge of the presence of the two agents.

One of the agents knew that it was not the right time for them to get tough with this injured thug, so the agents backed up and said, "Yes, you're right. We will double the security. You will never get out of this room, I can promise you that. We will see you soon, so don't think that you're off the hook." Sami remained silent and ignored the threat. The agents slammed the door and locked the room.

Mai Lan and Xuan both got up early to prepare for the grand opening of their coffee shop. They hired one of the boys who lived in the building with them to help them care for the stuff. Water was so scarce in the camp; they had to purchase more from those who used very little.

The first brew wasn't perfect and Xuan looked disappointed. Mai Lan tasted the coffee and said, "Hey, that's not bad, not bad at all. If you can do it all the time, we're in business."

Xuan shrugged her shoulders and suggested, "You call this good? I could do better, a lot better. I don't know, maybe the coffee isn't as good as what we used to make."

"Yes, but this is the beginning. I know you can do better." Mai Lan was more satisfied with the coffee than Xuan, she continued, "Well, I think we can sell the coffee. I don't think people will have as high expectations as they do in Viet Nam.

Xuan tried another brew and it came out better this time. She bragged, "Well, it's getting better now. I told you I could make it better. I haven't done it for a while."

Mai Lan tasted the new brew and shook her head to agree, "Yes, you're right. This tastes better. I think we're going to do all right. You know we have to bring some coffee to the warden?"

Xuan waved her hand and told Mai Lan, "We have to bring some to the guard who gave us the chairs and the cups, too. I hope we have enough coffee to sell to people."

Mai Lan tasted another sip of coffee and said, "Yes, you make good coffee. They will ask for more and we will go bankrupt if we just give it to them free. Well, let's go."

They both heading out of the door and hurried to the small hut on the corner of the meeting center where many older people sat around playing Chinese chess and gossiping. When they arrived to the coffee stand, the boy was finished setting up the place and Xuan started to brew more coffee. Before long the aroma from the fresh brew filled up the atmosphere which made a couple old men stop playing chess and poke their noses up in the air to smell it. It also grabbed the attention of the people walking by. Soon the first brew was finished.

The first customer arrived to buy some of the coffee. Xuan looked up at the customer. She was a little shy when she realized that her first customer was a guard, the one who offered the cups and chairs. Now everyone's' eyes were mysteriously pointing at her which didn't help her much. Her face became red and her hands were trembling when she tried to pour some coffee into the cup. The guard noticed the curiosity from the crowd and Xuan's shyness. He waved his hand to tell her never mind and winked at her at the same time. Xuan already handed him the coffee, he paid her with Thai money then left without giving Xuan a chance to return change. He was the first customer and he brought good luck to her business. As soon as he left, people started to come for the coffee. This was the first coffee shop in the camp and with its affordable price everybody could enjoy the fresh brewed coffee. Before long, a line of people were waiting for the coffee. Only Xuan and the young boy were taking care of the business, so they could only take care of certain people. Xuan was sweating because she had a hundred things to do. The equipment wasn't working sufficiently and it took more time to brew the coffee. Some customers lost patience and left. Xuan got a little frustrated when the coffee wasn't brewed fast enough for the customer and she yelled, "My God, these coffee filters got clogged up. That's why it gets so slow. How I'm going to run a business with the clogged up filters?"

Mai Lan brought fresh coffee to the warden. She was stopped by the guard in front of his office, so she tried to explain to the guard that she was taking the coffee to the warden. Because she only can speak in her native language with a little Thai dialect, the guard couldn't understand what she really wanted. An authoritative voice came from the office which authorized Mai Lan to enter. The guard then guided Mai Lan inside without asking anymore questions.

The first time Mai Lan entered the warden's office she remembered the time he gave the order to whip the young guy. She just wanted to get out of the office as soon as possible. A Vietnamese translator came to take Mai Lan to meet the warden. The warden himself looked young compared with the old and grumpy warden who she had in mind. She stood there motionless until the translator opened the conversation, "Miss, you have something for the warden?"

Now, Mai Lan mumbled some Vietnamese to the translator; avoiding meeting the warden's tiger eyes which could rip her body apart, "We want to offer the warden the fresh coffee we just made, just to say thanks." Mai Lan placed the coffee on the table, bowed her head to the warden then moved back a little further. The warden took a drink of the coffee, slightly nodded his head to show his approval, and then spoke to the translator. The translator told Mai Lan as he guided her back outside, "The warden likes the coffee, he seems to like you a lot, too. I will stop to buy some coffee later."

Mai Lan's face turned red when the translator mentioned that the warden seemed to like her. When she got to the coffee hut, a crowd was waiting for their coffee. Xuan was sweating and she screamed at Mai Lan when she saw her, "Sister, we're in trouble. The filter isn't working right. We need some new ones fast!"

"Okay but not right at this moment." Then Mai Lan has an idea, "I think I can make the filters flow better. Boy, go find me a needle fast!"

The boy ran to his building for moment and brought back a sewing needle. He gave it to Mai Lan bragging, "I had to steal it from my neighbor."

Mai Lan felt badly because the boy had to steal it from someone. She hesitated for a moment then gave it back to the boy, "You have to bring it back. You don't have to steal it, just ask for it."

"Ask for it? Who would let other people borrow their own needle? Go ahead and use it and I will return it later," the boy replied.

Mai Lan didn't like the idea of using somebody belongings without their permission, but in this case, she didn't have time to argue. Mai Lan used the needle to unclog the holes. She showed it to Xuan vowing, "You see these, it will speed up the flow of the coffee, you'll see."

Xuan, shrugged her shoulder and said, "I hope you're right, sister. A lot of people are leaving already." Then she grabbed one filter then looked at it toward the sunlight. She shook her head with contentment and started to pour the coffee ground into the filter. Waving her hands to the customers, "Hey, hey, don't go. I have coffee ready for you, please…" She pretended like she was going to cry and made the customers feel bad so they stayed to wait for the coffee.

Even Mai Lan thought that Xuan got upset, she patted Xuan's back, "Hey…, you don't have to cry, that's okay more will come if you make good coffee."

Xuan secretly winked to Mai Lan, signaling to her that she had just faked out the customers. Mai Lan smiled and shook her head. She couldn't believe Xuan was really putting her on a show. She whispered to Xuan, "You're real good at that. You got me to believe that you were really upset. I will not feel sorry for you next time."

Xuan gave a big smile and said, "Ha, ha, you know sometimes you have to do anything to keep the customers,. right? My mom always told me that. The coffee filters are working now, I'm glad. We're doing well today. Some people didn't wait for their coffee, but we are still doing okay. We will probably need more condensed milk for the coffee. You think the guy will bring some more stuff anytime soon?"

"How should I know? He promised that he would. He will be here. I don't think he will lie to us. Sometime he's a little late, but I think he'll be here."

Then Xuan remembered something, she asked Mai Lan, "Hey, did you meet the warden? How does he like the coffee?"

Mai Lan, quiet for a moment answered, "I don't know, he told the translator that the coffee was okay. He looked at me with a weird look. I felt creepy in front of him."

Xuan looked straight in Mai Lan's eyes, joking, "He looked at you kind of weird?" Really, I think he likes you."

Mai Lan, embarrassed, hit Xuan on the shoulder and said, "No, nothing like that. I don't mean that he likes me. I just don't like the way that he looked at me. Plus, I remember the time that he ordered the guards to beat the deaf kid. I don't want to stay around him long."

Xuan clinched her teeth and said, "Yea, I know that he was ruthless toward our people, but maybe that was his way to maintain discipline in the camp."

Mai Lan knew that the warden has to do his job, but he didn't have to treat the people in the camp like they were criminals. They were just normal people looking for freedom and now they have to be locked up in here.

Le Son went to the U.S Consular the next day to find out what he needed to take his sister out of the hospital. Le Son worried about her condition and that of Nguyen Tam. He hoped that he would not do anything stupid to get himself in trouble. The U.S. Consulate's response to his request for immediate relocation his family to U.S. was temporarily denied because both parties were keys witnesses for the investigation. The Thai authority never did conclude who was actually the owner of the lethal vessel, but they promised to get the girl out soon as possible. All they could tell him was to sit tight and wait. If his sister gained consciousness then she will have to pass the interview to qualify for a visa to America.

After he left the U.S. Consular, Le Son felt so desperate and frustrate. The outcome of the plan has been changed drastically and he soon has to return to the U.S. To leave them here by themselves wasn't the original plan. He may have to return here a few more times. It was unpredictable because of all the mishaps. He thought it was better off to let his sister stay in the country. But his sister always insisted that she wanted to start a new life with more opportunity and the most important thing was to reunite with him. Thinking of his sister's condition, a roll of tears silently drifted down his cheek. He didn't have power to change anything. He will just have to wait.

Tomorrow he has to tell Nguyen Tam the truth about their status. Hoping that Nguyen Tam wasn't upset, another thing that he worried about was to leave them there for a long period of time. That could cause a security risk for their lives.

The two agents from the Royal Navy headquarters came to see the captain of the other vessel to investigate the business conducted between him and the pirates. Upon seeing their arrival, the captain shook his head, said out loud, "Bad news, you people don't have anything better to do other than mess with me."

One of the agents waved his hand to order the captain to be quiet, "Be quiet, old man. Your business buddy just shot a young girl. You better help us to nail this bastard. Otherwise, you're just guilty as much as him. I bet you have probably killed innocent girls before."

The old captain was quiet for a moment then looked up at the agents, "Your people better get this straight. First of all, I didn't kill any girls. Secondly, I have only done business with him a couple of times. What he is doing on his own time, that's his business."

The agent looked straight into his eyes and found that he didn't tell the truth. He pointed his finger at him and threatened, "You can deny everything if you want. The fact is that you are involved with this man and he destroyed the Government's properties. That's enough to put you behind bar the rest of your life."

The man nodded his head and said, "No I didn't destroy no Government property, I just deal the girls that is all. Don't you try to throw all that junk on me. It's getting old, man."

"No you shot at the Government troops and the fishing boat which are owned by the Government. You have no business shooting at the Government." the agent responded.

The old captain still argued, "How should I know that was a Government boat. Besides, there was no Government flag on it, so there. You need to release me; I'm just a business man."

The agent didn't give up on the challenge. He used another angle to attack the old crack head, "You know that you are too old to see the flag. I bet you can see the Government uniform, didn't you? Besides we found a lot of drugs in your boat, that's enough to put you away."

"That's so! I'm not so sure that it was mine. What do your people want from me?" The old captain was getting a little softer than a moment ago.

The agent demanded the cooperation from the old captain, "We want you to tell us everything you know about your business partner. If you withhold any information, we will make sure that you're going down with him. You must know something about this man."

The old captain raised his hands up in the air, retorted, "Why do your people never leave me alone. Not until I take a look at this man, how do I know who he is."

The agent nodded his head and told the old man, "No, let's say if he was the leader, you can tell us something about him. If you are cooperating with us, we could probably arrange some kind of a deal for you."

The old captain hesitantly spoke, "All right, all I know about this guy is that he has a mother who ran a whore house in Bangkok. She is a mean motherf...er."

"He has a mother?" The agent said with a mocking sound.

The old man shrugged his shoulders and asked, "So you all are going to leave me alone, right?"

"Well! Let us find out if you're telling the truth, then we will talk."

The old man retreated back to his wooden bunk with a careless gesture, knowing that his days of freedom were far to come.

The agents wrote up a report that stated that the suspect possibly has an existing mother, and she could be traced in a matter time.

Le Son came back the hospital the very next day to tell Nguyen Tam about the bad news. When he arrived to the room, Nguyen Tam was already up sitting next to Thuy.

Le Son walked by him and placed his hands on Nguyen Tam's shoulder and said, "How is it going? Are you okay? You don't look alright. Did you get any sleep at all?"

Nguyen Tam looked at Le Son and said, "Hi, you're back. I stayed awake late and I am a little tired but I'm doing okay now. I didn't expect you to return so soon. So, how are thing going?"

Le Son shook his head and said, "Tam, things happened beyond my capability. We have to wait for the Thai government to clear out your case. I didn't plan all these mishaps. I will send you and Thuy enough money to hang on for awhile. You should be pretty comfortable here. You can call me anytime if you ever need anything. In the mean time, I will get ready for the both of you once they dismiss your case. I have to return to America to finish my work. I will come back once the job is completed. You don't have to worry because I'm always on your side. Now, that you don't have to worry about money, just take it easy and taking care of yourself."

Nguyen Tam looked at Le Son and let out a long sigh, "It means that we will be stuck here for a long while, I guess. I am not for sure that we can get out of here alive. They know that we are potential witnesses. You think?"

Le Son said, "I think their security is better since the last incident. Besides, an investigation is going on. Before long they will bust the whole gang. You just have to stay cool and watch out for them. I was told by the chief security officer that the area which they kept the pirate has been sealed off. He is not allowed to have any visitors."

Nguyen Tam rubbed his forehead and said, "I don't remember anymore other survivors, he was the last one who survived. We thought that he was dead because the fire was very intense. I could have killed him the last time, but I chose to save Thuy's life. God must spare his life."

Le Son shook his head and agreed, "Yes, This guy has nine lives. May be God kept him alive for him to pay back all of his wrongdoings. Now that he lost his leg, I think that he lives in hell every minute of it."

"Yes, this man owes our people a lot. Only his own life can pay all his debt."

Le Son thought for a moment and then said, "Well, his life almost has no meaning. You can't trade yours for his. Your whole future is ahead of you and her…" Pointing his finger at Thuy he continued, "You have to stay alive to look out for her. She will always need you. Forget about this looser. I strongly believe that he is going to be paid back for everything, real soon."

Nguyen Tam stared into empty space. He tried to memorize his enemy's face but didn't know for sure the next time he would meet this man again and what action he is going to take. Nguyen Tam said, "Yes, I guess so. As long as he doesn't get around me I'm fine. If I really wanted to kill him, I would. Don't worry, we have survived all this time and we're almost there. I'm not stupid enough to get myself in trouble, unless…" He stopped for moment, then left out a sigh, "Unless, he comes here to try to kill us again."

Le Son snapped his finger and said, "Hey! If he's stupid enough to come here again, you can do anything to protect yourself right? What I mean is, don't go out and do it on your own. I just want you to come to America as soon as possible. There you will have a chance to start your life all over again.

Nguyen Tam said, "You know, so many things have happened. We have escaped death so many times that I just wish we would be left alone."

Le Son walked up to Nguyen Tam and rubbed his shoulder encouraging him, "Tam, your dream is still waiting for you. Now all you have to do is to lay low and wait for Thuy to get better. When they clear your case, you're home free."

Nguyen Tam nodded his head, pretending to agree with Le Son. In the back of his mind, he knew the nature of this man more than anybody. He doesn't give up until he dies. Nguyen Tam silently worked out a plan to defend from a future attack by the pirate. Nguyen Tam still has doubts about the security in this hospital. He didn't want to worry Le Son, so he just sat quietly and thought about the next confrontation.

Le Son said, "Tam, I feel that you are still bothered by the assailants. That's okay I will do my best to get both of you out of here. I will pray to God to protect you both."

Le Son reached for his sister's hand and lightly squeezed to find any small spark of life in her. Even a small movement would be enough to assure him that she will be well soon. Feeling no response from his sister, Le Son shook his head with disappointment and he bent down to kiss her forehead. A tear silently fell on her face. Everything was quiet except the weak beeping sound from the monitor.

Nguyen Tam swore to himself that if Thuy didn't make it through, he is going to make the pirate pay. This time he will make sure that the insurgent will vanish forever.

Le Son turned to Nguyen Tam and said, "You thought this man

was dead and he came back and tried to kill you. Did he remember your face at all?"

Scratching his head, Nguyen Tam tried to remember the whole killing's business, "He might have seen me from a distance. I don't know how he remembered my face. I think the guy who came with him found me. I thought the whole crew was dead, I don't really know where this guy came from. I checked on everybody's condition before this guy shot me. I think he has somebody out here to support him, that's the main reason I'm worried about our lives'. Now you know why I have to be ready to confront everyone, it's not that easy."

Le Son patted on Nguyen Tam's shoulder and diverted the subject to a different direction, "Well at least you have a great view of the ocean. There is a beautiful garden below, if you have a chance…" Le Son stopped realizing that he shouldn't talk about the beautiful scenery outside which is not practical for Nguyen Tam right now. Nguyen Tam approached the window and looked down at the garden and sighed, "Yes… before she got shot, we planned to go down there for a while. Perhaps if we had made it there, things probably would have happened differently."

Le Son shook his head and said, "Well if they want you bad enough, they will come looking for you later. Anyway, I'm glad that you got one of them."

Nguyen Tam was more skeptical about the bandits, "As long as he is still alive, there will be more to come. He has someone out there looking out for him. If Thuy wasn't struck by the bullet, I would have had enough time to kill him."

Le Son agreed, "Yea, I think you did real damage to him and his crew. Now he lives in his sorrow, that's more than killing him, I think."

Nguyen Tam directed his vision toward the blue ocean which somehow soothed his anger, "I wish he would leave everybody alone, maybe then he would find some peace in his life.

Le Son shook his head, he didn't know much about this aggressive person, "Yes I agree. He should let it go. But, you know what? I do think that he could do much about anything now."

Nguyen Tam grinned, "I like to think that he won't do anything. I thought that he couldn't do anything before, not until he popped up from nowhere and... and shoot at us. I was told that he was crippled incapable of doing anything, but he could squeeze off some bullets at us. Life is so unpredictable, that's why I take it day by day and have learned to expect the unexpected. You knew me during the war, that's why we're still alive now. But now I'm not as sharp as I used to be."

Le Son placed his hand on Nguyen Tam's shoulder and implemented his thoughts, "Well, I see you are still sharp. You saved Thuy's life didn't you?"

Nguyen Tam said, "No, she saved my life. I was frozen for a second when I saw him draw the gun. Thuy was a lot faster. She didn't mind any danger. I have never seen anybody as brave as her. She is my hero." Nguyen Tam bent his head down, buried his face in his hands, hiding the tears that kept falling down his face, "She is my hero...she is my hero. God...!" Nguyen Tam found himself drowning in a deep painful sorrow; wishing that all these horrible things would have never happened to her. He would exchange anything in this world, including his own life, for her.

Everything seemed to stand still. Both Le Son and Nguyen Tam heard a small murmur from Thuy. Nguyen Tam got up and quickly grabbed Thuy's hand to feel her pulse. Le Son ran to her bed, calling his sister's name. Thuy's eyes blinked for a short moment. Then a line of tears rolled down her cheeks. Nguyen Tam quickly ran down the hallway, screaming for the nurse. A moment later, the nurses were racing down the hall to Thuy's room.

Nguyen Tam was so happy to see a thread of life start to return to Thuy's body. He knelt down beside her bed and silently prayed to God to spare her life. Lately, instead of blaming, he often prayed to God to bail them out this horrible situation.

Mai Lan was busy at the building trying to set up everything for tomorrows early morning business. They did quite well during their grand opening and Xuan was happier than anybody in the camp. She kept counting and recounting the money and making sure that all the money was there. They will need more supplies for the next couple days and they expected the young man to show up with more stuff. Mai Lan was sorting out the filters when she heard some noises from the front porch. She stopped for moment and looked out and there was the translator who came looking for her. Mai Lan walked outside to greet the translator, "Hi Sir, how are you doing? Is there anything I can help you with?"

The translator, the most respected man in the camp, returned his greetings to Mai Lan and forwarded an invitation from the warden, "The warden is inviting you over for dinner tomorrow evening. Just dress normal, the warden understands you don't have a lot of clothes. Please don't be late."

Mai Lan was caught up in the surprise. She didn't want to come to the warden's dinner. The translator asked her, "Miss, are you all right? You know that the warden will wait for you. You are the first one who has been invited by him. This is an honor for you. Okay, I will see you tomorrow."

Mai Lan answered, "Yes Sir, I will be there for sure. I'm just surprised that the warden spared some time for me."

Before long, the translator came to escort Mai Lan to the dinner. He greeted her from a distance with respect. People stood around the front door staring at Mai Lan. She felt like she was being singled out from the rest of the refugees. Mai Lan quietly followed the translator feeling like a convict who was going to face a real strict judge.

Upon their arrival, the warden already stood on the front porch and greeted her with a big smile to show his hospitality. Mai Lan also bowed her head and returned the greeting with great respect. The warden showed Mai Lan the way to the dining area. He gently pulled out the chair for her and guided her to sit down.

Mai Lan felt a little more comfortable with the warden upon his good hospitality. The arrogance of an authority figure was now replaced by the gentleness of an ordinary man. She tasted the first piece of fried pork cooked by the best Thai chef in the area. It has been months since Mai Lan tasted a real good meal. However, the feeling of being a prisoner was like a barrier that separated her from the real world. She couldn't really indulge in the food in front of the warden because of her family's tradition. Mai Lan was raised in a high class family in Viet Nam with a conservative background. The warden waited patiently for her to get acquainted with the atmosphere, besides, he wasn't in a hurry anyway. Mai Lan remained quiet but her mind was rattled, how is she supposed to act, and what is going to happen next?

Mai Lan was surprised by the warden's very gentle attitude. It somehow created a more comfortable feeling between the two of them. Suddenly another guest came in, it was reverend Si. Mai Lan stood up and bowed her head to greet reverend Si. She was surprised by his presence but also felt more comfortable to have someone there she knew. The warden stood up and greeted the reverend. He shook his hand and invited him to sit next to Mai Lan. He politely pulled out the chair for him with a big smile, "Hi reverend, I'm glad that you came. Some wine?"

The reverend sat down and handed his glass to the warden, and smiled to Mai Lan, "Hi Lady, your business has started up strong, I heard. How do you feel?" The reverend pointed his finger at her belly, asking with care overlooking her sensitivity about her pregnancy.

Mai Lan, with the redness rising in her face, reluctantly answered, "I'm doing… okay sir. Some days I feel so tired that I don't feel like to do anything else. But now with the business, I have to get up early in the morning to get ready and the sickness seems to pass. I appreciate very much the help of you two gentlemen."

The warden and the reverend both looked at Mai Lan smiling. Then the warden spoke to the reverend and wanted him to translate back to Mai Lan. The reverend recognized uneasiness in Mai Lan and knew that she was a little embarrassed about her pregnancy, "The warden is concerned about your condition. He wants to help you with whatever you need. He said you make very good coffee and that everybody here likes it."

Mai Lan turned her grateful eyes toward the warden, and bowed her head to him then spoke softly, "Please tell the warden that we bear so much favor from him, and we don't know how to repay…"

"Don't worry, the warden wants to ask you to do him a favor." All eyes were turned toward the warden. Mai Lan herself was very surprised and curious about what favor he is going to ask of her.

The warden took a moment then spoke slowly, "I want the lady to assist me in trading gold. We want to purchase the gold from the refugees for a good price. Since your coffee business is going well and you're acquainted with a lot of people, that's why I wanted to ask you to work with us. So what do you think?"

While reverend Si translated the message, the warden quietly observed Mai Lan's expression and waited for her reaction.

Mai Lan never expected that the warden would ask her to work for him. Especially being his business partner. The question came so suddenly that it caught her by surprise. Mai Lan reluctantly bowed her head and said, "Yes." She looked at the reverend for help. Reverend Si understood Mai Lan's eyes and spoke to the warden about the difficulty that the woman might face because of her pregnancy.

The warden looked at Mai Lan for a brief moment and assumed that she was worried about working for him. He expected Mai Lan to be happy once he offered her an opportunity to make some real good and easy money. Then the warden, with a kindly smile said, "You are not obligate to do anything and you don't have to do it right away. Just tell people that you can help them to sell their gold for a good price. You will get paid based on the amount of gold that you sell. I think you can use the money for your future. Another thing, when you have your baby I will be a sponsor for him or her, I promise." The warden looked at Mai Lan truly meaning his words. To Mai Lan, he is now a different man than the man she knew before. Mai Lan respectfully bowed her head to the warden. Mai Lan couldn't understand the real motivation of the warden. To make such a commitment, this being only the second time that she met him; and yet, he treated her like he had known her for years.

The dinner was going smooth, contrary to Mai Lan's original thoughts. It turned out that he is one of the nicest men she had ever met.

Nguyen Tam had the feeling that Thuy was trying to get out of her coma. He held onto her hands tightly to convey his love for her. He kept calling her name repeatedly trying to get a reaction. Then with his fingers weaving hers, he collapsed next to her and entered another state of mind in which he found Thuy still alive and well. Thuy's is like an angel with her beautiful shining and relaxing figure. She smiled at him without saying anything. Then she took his hand and guided him to the beautiful beach which they had planned to go just minutes before she had been gunned down. The beach was glowing under the sun with its pure white sand like a million of sparkling diamonds. A thousand colorful butterflies hovered over the red rose garden. Nguyen Tam looked at the perfect clear blue sky and wondered if he was in heaven. The peaceful soothing sounds of the waves washed away all of his worries. Nguyen Tam silently walked side by side with Thuy. He wanted to talk to her but somehow, he was speechless. Then they came to a big tree with full of leaves and white flowers. Thuy reached out for Nguyen Tam's hand and guided him to sit down next to her. They sat under the tree and together they watched the small silvery waves from the blue ocean rolling on the beach, then she spoke to him softly and said in a dreamy voice, "I wish we can stay here forever."

Then she looked at him in a vision of a love. Nguyen Tam caressed her hand and placed a passionate kiss on it then nodded his head and responded, "Yes, we can stay here forever; as long as I have you on my side. We can build a small house...."

Before he could finish his sentence, a sound tore up the calmness of the beach site and he horribly watched Thuy's body began to fade along with the smile on her shining face meaning good bye. Nguyen Tam woke up out of his beautiful dream to find the long steady beeping sound from the monitor alarm warning that the heart had stopped. He felt coldness draping Thuy's body and realized what was happening to his lover. He let out a long and loud scream from the bottom of his heart. He started to pump on her chest to bring back her pulse. The nurses, upon hearing the alarm, rushed toward Thuy's room to save her. They tried to bring Thuy back but only found that her spirit was gone. One of the nurses helped Nguyen Tam to sit in the chair. In a state of shock he said, "No, she can't be… I just talked to her. Help her! She is still alive. Please!" Blood started soaking through his shoulder wound. Nguyen Tam didn't feel the pain. He just sat there stiff, mumbling to Thuy as if she were still alive. Then the doctor arrived, the same one who conducted the emergency surgery. After he thoroughly checked her pulse; he finally shook his head and sadly announced her death then pulled the white sheet over her face. When Nguyen Tam saw the doctor placing the white sheet over Thuy's face he realized that Thuy was really gone. He screamed out in pain then got up and ran toward her covered body to pull the sheet off her face. The nurses were trying to explain to him that Thuy was gone. Nguyen Tam still embraced her face in his chest, hoping somehow, to retrieve her life. The nurses surrounded Nguyen Tam but no one could pull him away from Thuy. They all wiped their tears and left him alone with her in their last minutes together.

The agents came to see Sami in the morning and they notified him that the young woman didn't make it. They walked into Sami's segregation cell and found him awake. "Boy, it's lucky that we found you in the good mood. The girl who you shot didn't make it. I guess it doesn't matter much to you anyway. You probably killed more people than that. Someday, we will find out the truth about you, man. Oh and another thing, your mother is here to visit you, she told us everything. The thug whom you claimed that you didn't know anything about, he worked for your mother."

Sami pretended like he didn't hear what the agent said, instead, he made a comment, "Hi gents, you came to see me kind of early, you know. If your people think that I'm guilty, why don't you go ahead and prosecute me. Do you think I like to live like this? Free me, please."

One agent pointed his finger at Sami's face and said, "You watch out boy, things will catch up with you soon enough. If you're smart you will confess your crimes, and the Government may concede to let you live. As you know, we do have enough evidence to convict you for using a firearm to commit murder. Sooner or later, you will have to talk to us…or… you know what."

Sami remained cool and all he had to do now was to maintain his story. It will take a long time before anybody will find out the truth about the Government speedboat. Beside his team mates, nobody else would know anything, so Sami just had to stay cool. The agents also knew that, but they planned on keeping the man under arrest until he broke down and one day he will talk.

Before the agents left, one of them pointed his finger at Sami and said, "You know that you are going to be here for the rest of your life. Wait until your bandages comes off and we will have the witnesses identify your sorry face. Then we deal with you…"

The other agent added, "Yes, you're better off telling us what happened, this is your last chance boy. When we nail you, we will nail you good."

Sami turned his face to the wall and ignored the threat from the agents. He didn't have anything to lose so he's willing to play hard ball with the law. The two agents figured out the connection between the old woman, Sami's mother, and the suspect. She didn't know much about the speedboat, but she has to know the killings of the custodian and the Vietnamese girl. They also knew that the suspect has nothing to lose. He virtually lost everything already and besides the law, nobody would want him, not even his mother.

Sami rolled off the bed and pulled the bed sheet with him. The sheer pain from the amputated leg caused him to let out a loud grunt. He lay on the floor for a moment to ease the pain, then he torn the sheet in a half and weaved it to a solid white rope and tied it into a loop. Looking around the room for a high and solid overhang, Sami was disappointed when he couldn't find anything that could possibly hold onto his weight. Then he looked out the window and imagined if he was to plunge out of it, and soon it will be over. Throughout his whole life, he never felt as low as he did now.

When he thought of this, the decision to end his life became clear. He took his wooden crutch and tied the white sheet to it. He opened the window and looked out at the scenario for a moment. "This is it."; he said. He placed the rope made out of white bed sheet around his neck, took a deep breath and closed his eyes. By using the remaining strength of his forearms he plunged out the window. His body fell out in the air like a free bird, and his weight quickly fastened the loop which stopped the blood flow to his brain. The atrocities he has done in his life were flashing in front of him during the last moment of his life.

People were screaming in terror when they saw the body hanging on the ledge of the window. Suddenly the bed sheet tore in half because of Sami's weight and his body dropped on the ground like a ripe mango. He was pronounced dead when security found him. Nobody knew the where about of the dead man except the agents who were working on his case. They removed the bandages from his face, and had others try to identify him.

Nguyen Tam finally let go of Thuy's body, the shear pain just torn his heart apart. He felt so empty and so hopeless without her.

Only death would reunite them now, Nguyen Tam miserably thought to himself. Thuy's death has taken away their dream to grow old together in America. The blood was seeping out of Nguyen Tam's white bandage without him knowing it. The mental pain was much greater than the physical pain and both pains were tearing him apart. He finally collapsed on top of Thuy while embracing her body.

When Mai Lan returned to her building, Xuan was still awake. Xuan was anxious to find out about the dinner with the warden. Mai Lan didn't have time to sit down before Xuan grabbed Mai Lan's hands and started to ask a lot of questions, "Hi sister. So everything is all right? Did he flirt with you? Was he nice to you? What did he say about us…or…our business…?"

Mai Lan couldn't believe Xuan's anxiety about the dinner. She stopped for a moment and took in a long breath and said, "Oh my…, listen to you girl. Let me take a seat, will you. Everything is all right. He said that the coffee is very good, another thing…"Mai Lan stopped for a moment, and looked around to see if anyone was listening to their conversation. Then she pulled Xuan to sit down on their bamboo-weaved mat and she spoke with a low tone of voice, "The warden asked me, if we would like to work for him, I did say yes. But I don't know what it's going to be. So, what do you think?"

Xuan was shocked when she heard Mai Lan's story. Nevertheless, after a moment, Xuan regained her cleverness. She hugged Mai Lan and said, "Yes you're right. Opportunity never knocks twice. I will handle the contact with people for you. I know a lot of people in this camp. I will hook you up, don't worry."

Mai Lan actually didn't want to have anything to do with the authority. But it was hard for her to say no to the warden. Since Xuan knew a lot of people in the camp were why she accepted the warden's request. Just to return the favor, Mai Lan thought that they would do it free for the warden. She made sure Xuan understood her plan, "Well, I think that… we ought to do it for the warden as a favor. You agree."

Xuan, with her usual smiling face, agreed with Mai Lan, "Yes, it's up to you. I will talk to people about the gold business, as long as he helps out our business. So when will they start to buy gold?"

Mai Lan, quiet for a moment, slowly responded, "He didn't tell me exactly, but it will be soon."

Xuan said, "Hey, I know exactly who is going to need the money. I will go to see them now."

Mai Lan pulled Xuan's hand to sit back on the bed and said, "Who are you going to see now? Just don't tell them anything yet, wait until we hear from the warden. Okay?"

Xuan patted on Mai Lan's shoulder and said, "I will just go to talk to a few people, I just want to see if they really need money. I'm not going tell them anything. I will let you know later about what I know. Trust me. I'll be back in a few."

Mai Lan reminded Xuan that the coffee shop had to open early in the morning, "Don't stay out too late, we have to get the coffee ready in the morning." Giving another big smile, Xuan waved to Mai Lan and disappeared behind the tin walls.

Nguyen Tam got up to find him alone in the emergency room.

A feeling of a desolate sadness brought back the memory of his yesteryears. He remembered when he sat motionless in front of his family's coffins in the burial grounds in which his heart broke into thousand pieces. Now, the feeling of a man with no country, no relative and no loved one returned to haunt him once more. Then Thuy's innocent figure came back to him and he wanted to get up to find her. The last thing he remembered was Thuy's cold body in his arms…he screamed name desperately. Within seconds after screaming, the nurses and the security agents and translator rushed in to see Nguyen Tam. After the nurse checked on his condition and confirmed that Nguyen Tam was stabile enough to speak to the agents, the translator came to his bed and shook his hand then shared with him the news, "How are you? I have the good news and the bad news."

When he heard the translator mention bad news, Nguyen Tam had the feeling that he will lose Thuy forever. Tears just wouldn't stop rolling down his face. He asked the translator, "She's gone, isn't she? She doesn't deserve to die. God, why…her?"

The translator held Nguyen Tam's hand and said, "They tried to save her, but… she had lost a lot of blood. We contacted her brother in Bangkok and he is going to be here soon. Do you have any idea where you want to bury her?"

Nguyen Tam remembered Thuy's quest to stay in the rose garden forever. He looked at the translator and said, "She wished to stay in the rose garden forever. I thought she was just saying that, but it turned out to be her destiny. I want to ask you to do me a great favor."

The translator slightly patted on Nguyen Tam's shoulder, and promised that he was going to do whatever he could for her, "I will forward for you your request. You mentioned something about the rose garden, that's the place you want to bury her."

Nguyen Tam nodded his head adding, "I think that is the place which she wished to stay and I saw her in my dream right before she passed away. My only regret is that I couldn't be with her for eternity, but I know she will wait for me. Could you forward my request to the commander of the hospital? I would like to work for the hospital and take care of the rose gardens for the rest of my life. I only need a small and simple place to live. There is something else that you want to tell me?"

The translator said something to the two agents and then turned around to speak to Nguyen Tam, "The man who shot your wife took his own life just a few minutes ago. We want you, if you can, to go with us to identify this man."

Nguyen Tam, quite stunned by the good news, never thought that the toughest human being gave up his life so easy; he wanted to confirm that the statement was true, "He killed himself, after all of this, are you sure it is him?"

The translator shook his head and threw his hands up in the air and said, "Well, he's dead all right. That's why we want you to look at him to see if you can identify this guy. It is hard to recognize who is who when their face was completely burned and wrapped up with bandages. We want to find out about this guy. The Thai's Navy Dep. was hoping that he will talk about the speed boat incident, but now he's gone; so the department wants to wrap up the case. If this man is identified as the leader of the bandits, we can conclude that he had something to do with the sunken speed boat."

Nguyen Tam added, "Yes, you're right about that. I did hear some explosions from a distance which is similar to the L.A.W, and gunfire from the pirates. But we thought that it was thunder. Yes, I can make it over there to see what this guy is really made of."

The translator waved his hand to disagree about the pirate, "No, I think he's just a coward who sucked on people's blood. I would have liked to kill him myself. So, we will wheel you down to the morgue now, are you ready? We know you have a lot of things on your mind. It doesn't take long to get down there."

Nguyen Tam nodded his head. He wanted to go see this monster for the last time and make sure this time he is really dead.

Back at the hotel, Le Son was packing his stuff to get ready for the return to the U.S. He got the message from the hospital to convey their sympathy for his sister, and to let him know to prepare for her burial. Le Son felt so sad for his sister's short life, and if not for his crazy idea; she would be still alive. He dropped everything and hurried back to the hospital, hoping to get there before dark.

The translator pushed Nguyen Tam's wheelchair to the emergency room where the staff placed Sami's body temporarily. Nguyen Tam was the first witness to identify Sami, so he got up close to the corpse to take a good look at the bandit's face. He placed his finger on his neck to feel the pulse, if any. Nguyen Tam wanted to make sure that the pirate was really dead this time. This monster has caused him, his girl, and a whole lot of people a great deal of pain and his death alone wouldn't be enough for all his atrocities. Nguyen Tam only saw him from distance, and right before he got shot in the shoulder, he only remembered those angry eyes filled with vengeance. The last time he saw those eyes was right before the pirate pointed the gun at him to take his life.

As Nguyen Tam placed his fingers on the pirate's neck, he felt a slight pulse. Nguyen Tam waved his hand to the translator and tried to alarm him that the pirate might be still alive. He leaned over the chest to listen the heartbeats, but before Nguyen Tam could say anything, the pirate opened his eyes wide starring at Nguyen Tam. Both enemies were close to each other, and both were speechless. Perhaps, both were ready to kill each other. Before Nguyen Tam could alert the translator or the agents, the pirate reached out and grabbed a hold of Nguyen Tam throat and gripped it with all of his might. Nguyen Tam gasping for air felt so defenselessly. The injured shoulder bled again, this time it was more severe. In the most critical moment of his life, he was just about to give up, when he saw a bright light in front of his eyes. The bright light began to form into Thuy's figure. She reached her hands out to touch Nguyen Tam to wake him out of his near death situation. Using his last reserve of air in his lungs, he used his thumbs to press hard into the pirate's eyes, and popped his eyes out of its sockets. The pirate let out a loud scream in agony and quickly withdrew his hands back to cover his eyes cursing the man who took everything from him. When Nguyen Tam was freed from the pirate's grips, he was almost pasted out. Pushing himself away from the pirate he coughed his lungs out clear. The agents and the translator stood outside and overheard the loud screaming from the pirate. They rushed inside to check it out. They found the pirate holding his bloody eyes with his whole body jerking in convulsions; the man went insane.

One of the agents came close to the pirate to check on his condition, shaking his head in disbelief. No one would think the pirate was alive and attacking people. He mocked the inmate, "I told you bastard, you will pay one day. Now, tell me the truth or I'm going to leave you here to bleed to death. Did you sink the patrol boat..?.Yes or No...?"

The pirate ignored them first and then he grunted to the agent with hatred, "Yes, I killed all of you whenever I can. That's right. They tried to take us in and left us no choice."

The agent was angry upon the quick confession from the pirate and felt insulted by his belligerent attitude. He pointed his finger at him and cursed, "You're sorry piece of you f... murderer, I ought to put a bullet in your thick head right now, you bastard!"

The pirate spat at the agent to make him loose his cool. The agent fell into the pirate's trick, rushed toward him and grabbed a hold of his neck and clamped as hard as he could. He then jerked his neck from side to side and was just about to break it. He screamed, "I kill you, bastard. You're dead."

The pirate didn't let out one word and permitted the agent to blow off some steam, and then he reached to his hand gun and drew it out. It was too late for the agent to react, right before he realized what was going on; the pirate already got hold of his gun and fired two shots at the agent at close range. The impact of the bullets pushed the agents backward to the floor. Then he pointed the muzzle toward the general area where Nguyen Tam was at and fired two more shots. Although he wasn't able to see clearly because of his damage vision, he was still very dangerous. Nguyen Tam woke up when he heard the gunshots and the bullets flying toward his direction. He bolted toward the pirate with lightning speed and despite the painfully wound, wrestled with the pirate to save his life. The pirate sensed the upcoming attack from his enemy and squeezed two more rounds toward Nguyen Tam's direction. Nguyen Tam dodged the line of fire and quickly grabbed the revolver, then used all of his strength to turn the pistol on the pirate and forced him to self terminate. The other agent and the translator, upon hearing the shots, raced to the immediate area to find his fellow agent lying on the floor in a pool of blood. Right about that time, another gunshot blasted through the quiet space of the emergency recovery room and this time, the bullet pierced the pirate's throat and exited through his skull and blasted his brains all over the floor.

Nguyen Tam finally collapsed next to the dead pirate. The agent picked up his partner's weapon in disbelief of what had just happened. The translator rushed outside to call the nurses to help the casualties. The agent knelt down next to his partner and quickly removed some of his restrictive clothing and hurried to apply the emergency C.P.R. A few minutes later, nurses and security officers were there. They rushed the wounded agent to the emergency room right after his partner found a slight pulse; "he might have a chance to live." they said, with hope.

The nurse helped Nguyen Tam to recover from his shoulder wound. Nguyen Tam woke from a long rest and found Le Son standing next to his bed with the sadness of someone who had just lost his best and most precious thing in the whole wide world. Le Son held Nguyen Tam's hand, sharing his friend's burden, and said, "Tam, are you okay? We all hurt for Thuy, I never had the chance to talk to her. I just couldn't forgive myself for letting her go on the dangerous trip."

Nguyen Tam also understood the sorrow of his friend. Both men missed their lady. He said to Le Son, "Her last wish was to stay here forever. I couldn't understand then, but now I know why. That was her destiny. She still saved my life even after she's already gone."

Le Son asked, "So what are you going to do now that the pirate is dead? Are you free to go anywhere? I will speed up the process to sponsor you, and probably in a few months, you will…"

Nguyen Tam shook his head, with no intentions of leaving the hospital, at least for now, he said, "You know, we've been together for a long time sharing our hardship. I mean, she is all that I got at this moment. I just want to stay here with her. I appreciate for your concern, but here or America, it's all the same. As long as you're happy where ever you're at, that's Okay"

Le Son said, "Yes, I see what you are coming from. When you change your mind, you let me know. So, do you have a place for her yet?"

Nguyen Tam responded, "I asked for permission from the commander for a designated burial site. I hope that he will grant my request. I applied for a gardener position so I can always take care of her resting place.

Le Son didn't know much about what was going on between these two; he thought that he must loved her very much. Le Son felt very bad for his sister misfortune, and for those who perished.

The translator the agent showed up at the door with another gentleman dressed in a Thai's Navy uniform. By the multiple decorations on his uniform, Nguyen Tam guessed that he must be a high ranking officer. The translator first approached Nguyen Tam to shake his hand, then introduced the gentleman, "Hi, are you all right? This is the deputy director of the hospital. He wanted to meet you and on behalf of your bravery, grant your request. You can choose the area which you want to bury her. By the way, the cafeteria workers got together and donated to cover some of the expenses for your wife's burial ceremony. Your request to be a permanent resident of Thailand is being considered by the Thai Government. However, the authorities have granted you a temporary permanent resident for now. And of course you can have the job of a gardener. The hospital's commandant has given you a small room next to the utility shed; you can stay there long as you want. You can have your peace now, we are really sorry for you and your wife, may Buddha redeem good thing to you. If you need anything later, you can always talk to me about. Because of your bravery, our partner is still alive."

Nguyen Tam squeezed the translator's hand with and said, "I haven't had enough time to consider the danger, that was a reaction, I guess. But I'm glad that this whole mess is over with. I appreciate you very much for your help. I would very much like to stay here, to take care…my girl.

The translator shook his hand and then left the room with the gentleman. When everybody left, Le Son asked Nguyen Tam again about the staying, "Are you sure that you are going to stay here for good. You still have the chance to start all over again, we all love Thuy, but you have to start a new life."

Nguyen Tam walked up to the window, looking at the bluish water of the gulf of Siam and responded with his sight afar to the end of the horizon, "Le Son, this is my new life. Thuy gave it all to me, including her life. I can feel freedom here as much as anywhere else. Besides, Thuy will always be here. This landmark is my paradise."

Le Son couldn't really understand the connection between the two lovers. The solid decision from Nguyen Tam showed him that nothing will change his mind; at least for now. Le Son walked up next to Nguyen Tam and shared his vision of the beautiful and peacefully scene of the ocean.

Nguyen Tam pointed his finger to the ocean and said, "You see… every time I look at the ocean, I see Thuy in it. How can I ever leave this place? I've fought with destiny all these years, up and down, mostly down more than up. There was a time that I lost everything, and I think that I will find peace here. I will keep in contact with you all the time. Okay?"

Nguyen Tam placed his hand on Le Son's shoulder and said, "Okay, but promise that you will come to America to visit me sometime. Well, I have to set up the funeral for Thuy, you stay here and rest. I will return in a few hours."

Nguyen Tam said, "I will go with you, I'll be all right. This is the only time that I can do anything for her. I will have plenty time to rest later."

Both men headed to the small Buddhist temple where the staff had placed Thuy's body.

The young man came to visit Mai Lan the next day. He brought with him enough supplies for a week. He told Mai Lan the news about the death of the pirate leader. She couldn't believe the fact that he had raised up and tried to kill someone. She was glad that the nightmare is over.

The young man sat close to Mai Lan on the front porch of the guest house. Lately the mutual love and respect from both people have grown excitingly fast. This time, the young man held Mai Lan's hand, and slightly massaged each of her fingers, "How is your pregnancy? Your tummy is getting big, you shouldn't work too much. Did you hear anything about how long your stay here will be? They will process a little quicker since you are pregnant, wouldn't they?"

Mai Lan shook her head and said, "I don't really know much about when I will get to interview. The rumor is that the Thai authorities will close all the camps and send all the refugees back to their homeland. I am really worried about being sent back to Viet

Nam with my baby to be born. My child wouldn't have any future if we have to return..."

Mai Lan couldn't hold back her tears when she mentioned about the future of her baby. Suddenly, she broke down crying. The young man found himself in an awkward position. This was the first time he faced Mai Lan with her deep feelings revealed out of her secretive life. Mai Lan silently wiped off her tears. The young man is the only person whom she ever shared her burden, and lately he became closer to her than ever. The young man, right at that moment, was the only one who could understand some of the hardships that Mai Lan had buried in her thoughts.

Sitting close to him, she felt a warm sensation from his flesh. A small temptation of desire sparked in her heart and in a brief moment, she permitted herself to venture into the new edge of romance which was a forgotten luxury that had been buried deep in her mind since she found out about her pregnancy. The young man also felt the same way. He was so busy working to start a new life on his own. He still has his heart set on Mai Lan.

He felt a deep resistance in Mai Lan and truly wanted to conquer all the obstacles which prevented him from winning her heart. He held her hand and then looked straight into her eyes. He wanted to know for sure what would hold her back from loving him. With a soft voice, he asked, "Something has been troubling you, would you like to tell me... the truth."

Mai Lan shook her head and said, "I... really... don't have anything to tell you about. I just don't want... for us to start something which we are not sure of; something that can hurt the both of us. I think the best thing right now is to maintain our friendship. If I come up with the interview and I have to leave here, what does that leave you? That's why I don't want to start up something which we can't finish. Plus I have to go to America to work and help out my family. The communist government has confiscated all my family assets. My dad had to sell our house to have the money for my escape route, and they're now virtually homeless. Now you know that I have to push myself everyday to survive in this camp and all my hopes, as you already know, can be diminished in just a matter of time. I'm sorry that I'm not fully responsive to your request, but I'm telling you what my full intentions are. Hopefully, you will understand and still consider being my great friend. That way we all feel comfortable with each other. Do you agree?" Then she leaned her head against his shoulder with a friendship gesture, and she brought back a smile on his face.

Le Son stood silently beside Nguyen Tam with his tears rolling down on his cheeks. He watched the dirt pile up on top of his sister's coffin. He never could forgive himself for letting his sister end up under the ground like this. Her fragile life was so compatible to her nature. He hasn't had a chance to say hi to his sister, and never will. The sweet memories of the two of them from their childhood constantly rolled in his head.

Nguyen Tam kneeled down next to her coffin to place a red rose on top. He felt the ground which will bury his most precious love forever. He felt numb, only the tears ran down from his cheeks to the coffin. His whole body shook savagely caused by the emotion. The same feeling of despair and hopelessness from the day he buried his wife and child were instantly replaying in his head. The extreme sadness caused Nguyen Tam to start choking and the pain from his shoulder's wound overwhelmed him until he finally collapsed on top of her coffin. Le Son quickly bent down and grabbed a hold of Nguyen Tam and slowly guided him over to the grass.

The nurses who attended the funeral, surrounded Nguyen Tam to check on his condition. They suggested that he should return to his room to rest. But Nguyen Tam didn't want to leave her now. Once they filled up the dirt he will never again feel her presence. Le Son carefully guided Nguyen Tam back to his wheelchair and said, "You have to take care of yourself. It will take time to heal. But we do need to live to remember her, and to cherish her great courage."

Nguyen Tam, with his head down, couldn't stop the tears from pouring. He didn't have any idea that the impact from her was so strong. He still blamed himself for her death.

Mai Lan was in the middle of serving a customer when Reverend Si approached her coffee booth with a piece of paper in his hand, "Child, you have permission to interview for the Australian Government, here is your paper. Well, good luck to you. God be with you."

Mai Lan, who stunned for a moment then broke out in tears. She kneeled down and bowed her head to the reverend and said, "Sir, thank you very much for your help. Both my baby and I will never forget you."

Reverend Si bent down to guide Mai Lan up, sharing in her joy and then softly spoke to her, "God has awarded good things for you and your baby. You deserve it because of your good heart. I wish you all good luck."

Mai Lan felt very fortunate now that all her worries about being sent back to her country were over. The reverend understood her feeling and patted her shoulder to let her know that he is leaving.

Mai Lan got out of her state of shock and bowed her head to the priest until he was gone. Reverend Si was the most respectful religious figure to Mai Lan. He is always there for her and helped her in every way.

A whole new horizon of hope has widened her view. She wanted to scream to show her happiness to everybody but was overwhelmed by the emotion that flooded her throat. All she could do was throw her hands up in the air, triumphantly.

Xuan saw the reverend handed the piece paper to Mai Lan, and figured out what the piece of paper was for. Still, she hesitatingly asked Mai Lan, "Is that… the paper for your… interview… That's mean…!"She couldn't finish her sentence and she didn't know how to act. She was happy for Mai Lan but also felt like she was being left behind. She finally spoke with tears in her eyes, "Sister, I have been with you all this time… now you are ready to leave me…"Then she burst out crying.

Mai Lan embraced Xuan in her arms and cheered her up the best way that she could, "My little sister, I would never forget you. Even though I am not around you, I will always remember you. And, even better, I can get you anything that you want. I will try to get you out of the camp as soon as possible, if you are not out already. Okay my little sister."

Xuan wiped off the tears on her face, and nodded her head. In her heart she really wanted to be with Mai Lan, perhaps forever. A moment later, Xuan sat beside Mai Lan and whispered, "Sister, after you leave, I may…" then she stopped for moment, wiping off her tears, and hesitantly continued, "I may… get married"

Mai Lan was a little shocked when Xuan mentioned marriage. She squeezed Xuan's hand for a moment and asked her, "Married? Are you sure? You marry the guard?"

Xuan nodded her head and perhaps she wasn't so sure about her future either; but to her right now this was the best answer. Xuan added, "I've thought about that, he is a nice guy. If they do close the camp down, I will have somewhere to go. Thailand is a good country, as long as you are willing to work hard. I think he does love me."

Mai Lan had no clue what her life is going to be like. She only knew the continent through her high school geography class, and now she's actually going to rebuild her life there. She didn't know what to say to Xuan. What would make her feel more secure than just to get married and stay in Thailand. Mai Lan said, "If you would like to stay here, it's fine. But you're still young, and it would be waste if somehow you were to come up with an interview to America... There are more opportunities there for you... I don't know... it just my way to look at things. Beside, you didn't know him very well, yet. Just don't rush into something that would make you regret later.

Xuan wiped the tears off on her cheeks as she turned and looked at Mai Lan with appreciation, "Sister... You always have a good judgment. You're right. But if the Government closed the camp down, I think that's the only choice. I will miss you a lot, sister. Please don't forget to write me."

Mai Lan glided her hand through Xuan's hair and promised that she will always write to her, "You know that I always see you as my little sister. Of course I will let you know where I am all the time. I don't really know what is going to happen in the future, but if I'm doing well I will take care of you. That's my promise."

Xuan leaned her head on Mai Lan's shoulder watching the white clouds slowly float to the west. A pair of white herons spread their wings toward that direction and she wished, "You see how lucky that is, those birds; I wish to be like them. I can fly where ever I like."

Mai Lan patted on Xuan's hand, comforting her by sharing her thought, "You know, every evening when I saw the birds fly by, I always wish that I had a pair of wings to fly out of here."

Xuan still gazing until the birds disappeared into the clear blue horizon, worried that her future was slipping away. Mai Lan woke Xuan out of her short dream, and cheered her up, "Hey wake up, now you can run the coffee shop by yourself. Do you think you can handle it?"

Xuan nodded her head. She knew that she could run the little coffee shop herself. Without the young man's supply though, how long will she last? She asked for Mai Lan to help her to maintain the business, in any possible way, "You know, without his help I don't think I can run the coffee shop myself. And without you sister…I don't know, men just like to stare at you."

Mai Lan pinched Xuan's arm and laughed, "You're a little devil! Who would like to stare at me, a pregnant woman?"

Xuan turned around and looked straight at Mai Lan, and tried to prove her statement, "I'm telling you, you have a hidden beauty which men like. Even me, I like to look at you all the time… if I even had a little of your beauty…"

Mai Lan blushed and said, "All right… all right. I will talk to him about helping you out. I don't know how to tell him about my interview, yet. I do hope that he will understand… someday I will leave this place, one way or another."

Xuan, imitating the would be broken hearted young man, teased Mai Lan, "Oh my God! Oh my God! What would I do in the lonely days…?" But when she saw the sadness in Mai Lan's eyes, she stopped teasing and reached out her arms to hug Mai Lan, "I'm sorry, sister. I don't mean to hurt you. Please don't be so sad."

Mai Lan sighed, "I just don't want to look at him when I tell him the news. I don't know how he is going to react when I tell him. It's just not an easy thing to say to someone so special. I owe him a lot."

Xuan suggested, "I think he would understand your situation. As long as you will keep in touch with him, it would make both of you feel better about each other."

Mai Lan responded, "I plan on keeping in touch with him, but I still have someone waiting for me at home. I don't want him to wait for me, and then one day, I will tell him I have somebody else. I think I should tell him the truth… now."

Xuan told Mai Lan, "Well then you have to find a way to tell him without killing him. The way I saw him look at you, I know that you are the only one he ever loved. So…"

Xuan hadn't finished her sentence before the messenger boy showed up at the building yelling for Mai Lan. Mai Lan already knew who was coming so she slowly stood up. She couldn't believe that the young man is here already. Xuan said, "He will understand. Just be truthful. It is better to tell him now then to let him wait forever. Sister, you can do it."

Mai Lan nodded her head and then left the building.

It has been a month since Thuy's burial. Nguyen Tams' shoulder wound was healing and he could trim up the rose garden. He spent hours on Thuy's grave cleaning up the weeds. He grew the red roses which Thuy loved so much right next to her. Nguyen Tam felt that Thuy's soul was in the red blooming roses and that they were so beautiful. One evening he finished trimming the garden and sat down next to Thuy's grave. He enjoyed the rose's fragrance which was delivered to him by the fresh ocean breeze. He was proud of his garden. The Commandant often came to visit the garden and praised Nguyen Tam for his good work. The kitchen staff sometimes brought him food. He always divided the meal with Thuy and sat there eating right beside her grave just like the day Thuy shared her food with him. He never could forget the first time she brought the special meal from the kitchen. She was so happy to share it with him. Every time Nguyen Tam thought about these precious moments, tears silently rolled down his face. He leaned on the tomb stone caressing the roses like he used to caress Thuy's cheeks. Within the mist of the beautiful evening, Nguyen Tam saw Thuy approaching him from a white cloud waving to him. He was so happy to greet her with his wide open arms, screaming with joy and ran to her. He only found Thuy standing there looking at him silently with a smile. She was so bright and transparent, and seemed so far away. Nguyen Tam wanted to reach out and touch her. He wanted to embrace her so tight and never would let go again.

Then, Thuy began to fade away, still with a gloriously smile then placing her fingers on her beautiful full lips to send him a kiss. Then she disappeared through the mist of the late evening. Nguyen Tam tried to follow her but a crash of thunder woke him out of his dream and drops of rain started beating on his face. Nguyen Tam lay still on the ground and let the rain water shower relentlessly on his body; still hoping to find Thuy again. The tropical shower finally stopped, revealing the starry sky which reminded him of the stars which he and Thuy tried to remember when they both were on the boat. Nguyen Tam suddenly found a small bright star that sparkled in its own way and seemed to communicate with him.

He really thought it was Thuy's spirit who wanted to reach him. He felt warmth in his heart when he knew that he could find Thuy in the different dimension whenever the stars were showing. Listening to the sound of the tide mixed with the sound of the breeze fanning the coconut trees along the beach and the rose fragrance which filled the atmosphere, Nguyen Tam felt like he was lost in some kind of paradise; in there, he found peace and Thuy all together.

Mai Lan was on the way to meet the young man and she was nervous to see him this time. As usual, the young man stood up and gave her a big smile but this time, he noticed something changed in her eyes. Mai Lan did try to hide the impression of, perhaps, may be the last time they will see each other. She approached him and he said, "Hi, how are you? What's wrong?"

The young man stood there speechless trying to find out more about the situation. He felt something was definitely wrong. His voice trembled, "I think...you are fixing to leave this place."

Mai Lan came close to him and held his hand guiding him to sit down next to her and calmly explained, "Yes, the Australian Government selected me a couple of days ago for an interview. Hopefully, I can get out of here before my baby is born. I hate for...him or her...to be here in this camp. I hope that you would understand...no matter where I'm at, I never will forget you."

The young man held her hand up and kissed it. He adored her like nothing in this world. He responded, "I have been waiting for this moment. I am sad but I am happy for you, no matter where you are at, I will always remember you as a part of my family."

Mai Lan took his hand and placed it on her cheeks to convey the warmth from her flesh to his. Although they have been close to each other before, Mai Lan still trembled every time he touched her. The silent love which he offered her seemed to last for an eternity. Every time he was close to her, that same love ignited in his heart. He nervously pulled Mai Lan closer and passionately placed a kiss on her full lips. With no signs of rejection from Mai Lan, he began to embrace her body between his muscular arms and then explored the taste of her flesh with his tongue.

Mai Lan, trembling, felt the sensation penetrate deep inside her body. The young man was shaking also. He stood up next to her and guided Mai Lan up with him. He held her tight and looked deep in her eyes once again. He placed a last kiss on her forehead, turned and walked away.

Three weeks later, Mai Lan was on her way to Australia. Looking out from the tiny window from above, the landmark began fading away with the memories. Mai Lan only bore the thought of the young man and her adopted sister. Mai Lan closed her eyes and bowed her head towards the heavens. She thanked God for protecting her and prayed for her brother. Then she caressed her tummy and planned the future for her baby…